The
Billionaires'
Club

A NOVEL

The Billionaires' Club

A NOVEL

JEFF NESBIT

Bancroft Press

bancroft
press
books that enlighten

THE BILLIONAIRES' CLUB

Cover design by Christine Van Bree
Interior Design: cyber-bytz.com

978-1-61088-598-0(HC)
978-1-61088-599-7 (PB)
978-1-61088-600-0 (Ebook)
978-1-61088-601-7 (PDF)

Published by Bancroft Press
"Books that Enlighten"
410-627-0608
4527 Glenwood Ave.
La Crescenta, CA 91214
www.bancroftpress.com

Printed in the U.S.A.

CHAPTER 1

"Just check it out. That's all I'm asking."

I already knew what I'd find, but I didn't feel like arguing with someone half my age. I'd long ago resigned myself to the fact that my editors and bosses were all younger than me, figured they knew more than I did, and could dismiss anything I brought to the table. Experience didn't matter anymore in the digital age.

"Sure," I told him.

The national editor wasn't a bad guy. He was just...young. He hadn't seen much of anything. His version of what happened to change the world was tightly wrapped inside the fungible content of the dozen digital news sites he scanned each morning on his ride into the paper.

"It's a story. Trust me. You'll see," he insisted.

"One I have to write?"

My editor smiled. "Only if your enormous ego allows it."

"And I have to take pictures?"

"A few. That's all I'm asking."

I closed my eyes briefly, resigned to my fate. "Fine. I'll go."

"And make sure you get approvals for the pictures."

"Gee, I'd almost forgotten about that," I deadpanned. "Maybe right after I ask them their names because I need to quote them? Something like that?"

He bobbed his head once, as if checking an internal box, then moved on to whatever was next in his day.

The story was ridiculous. I knew it. My editor likely knew it. But it was precisely the sort of story that attracted traffic—just not any I wanted to spend time on.

There was a coffee shop across the street from the Eisenhower building at the northwest corner of the White House complex.

Not the typical coffee place where young kids took their laptops and camped out all day. No, it was where K Street lobbyists cooled their heels with clients before heading over to the White House.

One of the many digital media sites my editor consumed voraciously had posted a breathless piece about how important people gathered at this particular shop to talk in hushed tones about the great work of national political theater. Washington was, above all else, a government town where significant debates were supposed to take place daily. And, my editor surmised, those moments incubated in this coffee shop before moving across the street into the light of day at White House meetings.

Except it wasn't true. Yes, lobbyists gathered there, sometimes conspiring with White House aides before important meetings. But the lobbyists were paid well for their access to the White House, and the aides who occasionally visited were only a few years removed from the last presidential campaign. Neither came to brainstorm theories or hatch programs for political change. The shop was simply the easiest place to kill time until they had to stand in line for clearance into the White House.

I'd met people there on a number of occasions. Nothing of substance was discussed. The risk of being overheard was too great. You talked about the Nationals, the Caps, NFL football, the latest stupid thing a celebrity said or did, or whatever topic was trending on social media. You sipped your coffee and then walked across the street.

But the facts didn't matter. The appearance of power was alluring, especially in Washington. What my editor wanted was a story about who was in the shop, where they were going across the street, and what they might be talking about there. With luck, I'd run into at least one interesting tidbit not already beaten to death by Politico, Axios, or Punchbowl. It would be forgotten almost the moment its electrons passed through cyberspace but would attract eyeballs and a twentieth of the advertising a similar story once attracted when it graced the printed page of a paper.

But I'd do as I was told. I'd go there, take a couple of pictures, ask a few questions, and then do my best to write something that didn't take yet another piece of my soul with it into the digital abyss.

My cell phone buzzed. A text from an unknown mobile number with a 202 area code read, "Go here first. Get your head out of the cloud, make like Clark Kent, and fly by."

The attached picture of a townhouse looked vaguely familiar. I glanced at the address and then typed it into Google Maps. It was a smallish brown townhouse at the end of Jackson Place, across the street from the White House and a half block from some of the bigger corporate trade groups like the U.S. Chamber of Commerce. The buildings on that unusual street were mainly used by various federal government arms for White House councils that sprang into being or as transitional offices between administrations. One had been a naval museum.

No sign on the front of the townhouse identified it. Google couldn't place the building...or the mobile phone number, which apparently had never been used. But the text had to be from my editor, I figured. He was the only one who knew where I was going and why. He also teased me mercilessly for my Luddite tendency to dislike tech.

I almost texted him back to ask but decided against it. "Screw it," I muttered. What was one more detour? My day was already shot. Might as well stop by the Jackson Place townhouse before heading around the corner to the coffee shop.

I searched the history of the townhouse address a bit more on the cab ride, but there wasn't much. After belonging to a very wealthy family, it had been sold to a historical society and then to some quasi-government entity with connections to the private sector. Nothing of any importance had happened in the townhouse. Dignitaries had stayed there, but it had no real footprint.

The cab let me out on H Street, near a street grate. I could see some of the White House façade through the trees a block away. Hot air gusted up from the subway system. A homeless man had created a semi-permanent encampment on top of the grate. It was a good place to stay warm.

Our eyes met. He thrust a sign in my direction. "The world is ending," the sign read, "so give me a dollar now. It won't be worth anything soon."

It was a decent pitch—better than the usual. The guy could

have worked for the Fed, which was obsessed with hyper-inflation. I dropped a dollar into his bucket.

I walked the few feet to the townhouse. A guardhouse directly across it kept unauthorized cars from coming and going, but there was no security for pedestrians. The guards weren't paying attention, so I approached the door of the townhouse. It was unlocked. I didn't need to be buzzed in or to check in with security like most office buildings in the city. I opened the door and stepped inside.

The place had clearly been a residence once. Now there was simply a foyer and a desk. A nicely dressed middle-aged woman sat behind the desk, which was bare except for a laptop.

She stood to greet me. "Mr. Thomas?" With quick steps, she met me in the center of the foyer and extended a hand. I glanced down at her other hand and saw no wedding band.

I scanned my surroundings. It was a habit, more than anything. I wasn't all that curious. I'd seen dozens of buildings in Washington over the years. They were generally the same, though this one seemed a bit spare as a place where the powerful worked.

"Yes, Seth Thomas," I answered. "I'm with—"

"The Washington Post," she said with a pleasant smile. "I know. I read you all the time."

I shook her hand. "So look, I'm not sure why I'm here. My boss sent me a text. He said to stop by here first."

She nodded. "I understand. I'm not quite sure why you're here, either. Today is my first day."

"Your first day?" I squinted in her direction.

"Yes, the agency said it was a temporary job, but they'd reevaluate after I'd been here for a time."

"Agency?"

"A federal jobs center at the corner of 20th and L Street. I've been looking for a while now, since my husband passed away. They told me to expect you this morning at some point."

Now I was thoroughly confused. "And what am I expected to do?"

"I don't know, honestly." She glanced over her shoulder at a door and the desk. "They asked me to show you into the office. I figured you'd know what to do."

4

"So, who am I meeting with? What is this place? Which branch of the federal government is using it right now?"

She tilted her head and frowned. "I don't know that, either. Like I said—"

"Yeah, this is your first day. And they really sent you here without explaining what you'd be doing once you got here?"

She leaned forward. "I admit I was curious. But the agency contacted me shortly after I sent my résumé, interviewed me, and then told me my new job was here, starting today."

"No other instructions?"

"No. But it's right across the street from the White House, so I figured it was for something important. I didn't ask questions."

I gazed at the door to the closed office. "So, someone else is in there?"

"No, there's just a desk and two chairs."

I moved toward the office and she followed. Opening the door, I peered in. As she'd said, there was only a non-descript desk at the back of the room, with one chair behind it and a second positioned to one side.

"And you really have no idea who I'm supposed to be meeting here, or what this place is?"

"No, Mr. Thomas, I don't," she said, clearly embarrassed. "I assumed it would be clear when I'd arrived."

"Well, not your fault." I was annoyed at being sent on a wild goose chase but tried to keep that sense from seeping into my voice. "I guess I'll wait a bit and see who shows up."

She gestured toward one of the chairs. "You could wait here if you'd like."

"I suppose." I draped my satchel over the side of the chair. "You'll let me know when someone arrives, and who it is?"

"Of course." She left the office and closed the door behind her.

I scanned the room again. The empty walls had been freshly painted—I could see no shadows from former pictures. The wood floor, sans a single nick or scuff, was newly buffed.

I checked emails on my cell for a few minutes, then texted the 202 number to ask my boss about this truly bizarre meeting he'd sent me to without explanation. There was no return text, though my text did show as delivered.

After 10 minutes, I moved to the other side of the desk and sat in the chair. I stared at the door, half-expecting it to whip open with security in tow. But the door didn't open. The silence bothered me. Glancing at the sole drawer in front of me, I pulled it open.

Only one item was inside—a black leather cover that appeared to house a checkbook. I picked it up and flipped it open. It seemed to be a new checking account with Chase Bank. A fresh batch of checks started with number 101. I opened the account ledger at the front. No entries.

Closing the checkbook, I placed it back in the drawer and shut it. Moving to the other side of the desk, I checked my cell again. Still no return text. Ten minutes later, I'd had enough. Whoever or whatever this place was, I wasn't going to wait around any longer.

I stopped at the receptionist's desk on my way out and noticed, for the first time, that there was no phone. She looked up from her laptop. I wondered what wireless internet she connected to here.

"Still no one?" I asked, not expecting much of an answer.

"I'm so sorry," she said. "I didn't mean to waste your valuable time."

"Not your fault. But I'm going to read the riot act to my editor for not filling me in."

"Will you be back today?" Her expression revealed she was as confused as I was.

"Don't know," I said. "Depends on what my editor says."

"Well, I'll be here when you return."

"I see. Okay, then."

I left. I thought I'd seen and heard every power move in this city. But this was a first.

CHAPTER 2

"You did *what*?" my editor asked after I'd dutifully gone by the coffee shop, asked a few patrons some leading questions, taken a few pictures with my iPhone, and returned to the *Post* offices.

As I was writing the idiotic coffee shop piece, he stopped by my cubicle to check on my progress. When I explained I'd been delayed by the wild goose chase to the Jackson Place townhouse, he leaned against my desk with a bemused look.

"Why'd you wait 30 minutes if no one was there?"

"Because you *sent* me there," I said, exasperated. "I figured it had to be important."

"Let me see the number." He stretched out one hand.

I located the text and gave him my cell.

"This one? The 202 number?" he asked.

I nodded.

He stared at it for a moment and then handed the phone back. "Not mine. I know we're all Clark Kent wannabes in the newsroom, but that isn't me."

"Really? I got it literally two minutes after you stopped by my desk and sent me to that coffee shop. You were the only one who knew where I was going, so I figured it was you."

My editor shook his head. "Well, wasn't me."

"Maybe someone else in the office?"

"Nope. I didn't talk about your story with anyone."

I leaned back in my chair. I was getting that feeling, the one I always got when I'd latched onto something I knew would take me down an interesting, productive road. "That's pretty damned curious," I muttered.

"So, who's the number belong to?" my editor asked. "You know, search it—"

"I did. Nothing. Doesn't come up—not once."

"Weird. No way to track it?"

"Not that I can think of, since it's a number that's never been used. There's no history to it that would show up in a search."

My editor pushed off the desk. "Pretty funny, though." He chuckled. "Looks like someone pulled one over on the mighty Seth Thomas."

"Maybe," I shot back. "We'll see."

"So, you gonna have the piece done…"

"You'll have it COB today," I said. "Quit worrying."

"With pictures we can use?"

"Yes, plenty of pictures. It'll get lots of eyeballs."

"Good." He gave a satisfied nod and left.

He'd probably already forgotten about my wayward visit to the townhouse. But I hadn't. It was firmly on my mind.

CHAPTER 3

I had to return to the townhouse on Jackson Place at least one more time. I knew this thing would eat at me until I found the bottom of the well. I *needed* to know who had sent me that text.

But, first, I stopped by the Chamber of Commerce across the street. An old colleague and drinking buddy, Tom Kyle, had left his White House beat at the Associated Press to run the media shop for the Chamber. He was earning more money than he knew what to do with now that he'd sold his soul to the dark side. But he was a good guy. He and I went way back.

"You've never seen anyone coming in and out of the place?" I asked him.

We were standing at his window on the third floor of the Chamber building. He had one of the most spectacular, coveted office views in Washington, overlooking Lafayette Park at the White House.

"Never," Tom said. "But I haven't paid all that much attention." He peered down at the street. "Let me show you something. It might help. Follow me."

He strode out of his office. I trailed behind. We entered the stairwell and climbed three levels. After unlocking a door at the top, we stepped out onto the roof. A covered tent with a permanent television bay inside opened toward the White House.

"For remotes?" I asked.

Tom nodded. "Best shot in the city."

"Better than the front lawn of the West Wing?"

"Yeah, look for yourself. This is a much better view, especially at night when the lights are on across the street. If you really want to frame the shot, it doesn't get any better than right here. You only get the front doors at eye level from the lawn."

I smiled. "You know, I've seen this shot before on some of the network coverage. I'd never thought about it before. But let me guess…"

"Yeah, I let the networks up here all the time. They do a stand up from here and get the entire front of the White House behind them. They love this shot."

"And you do a little whispering in their ear along the way," I added. "Make sure they get the Chamber's big business view."

"It's why they pay me the big bucks, dude."

"Disgustingly simple, but kind of genius," I said.

"Look." Tom spread his arms wide to take in the entire panorama below. From this vantage point, even the Washington Monument was framed in the shot, directly behind the White House. "We all gotta earn a living."

"And I can see you're earning your keep." I glanced at his nicely tailored suit. It likely cost more than everything combined inside my own clothes closet.

Tom tilted his head. "You know—"

I'd heard the pitch a hundred times. "Not happening. Money isn't everything. It can't buy happiness."

"But it sure can buy a helluva lot of toys." Tom laughed. "Box seats at the Nationals, the Caps, the Wizards."

He was right. But toys held no fascination for me. They never had.

"Look, why am I here?"

Tom directed my gaze out over the park. "See those snipers on the roof over at the West Wing?"

I followed his gaze and started to point.

He pulled my arm down. "Don't. It'll make them nervous."

"Wait. They can see me from way over there?"

"They can see *everything*." Tom very slowly reached a hand up and waved it in the direction of the White House. I thought I could see a slight nod back from one of the snipers. But it also could have been my imagination.

"They're always there, stationed like that?" I asked.

"24/7. It's been that way ever since I've been here. Mostly they look over the West Wing grounds. But I've also seen snipers on the roofs at the Jackson Place townhouses, especially when heads of state visit. They meet at those offices all the time."

"Including the one I went to yesterday?" I asked.

"No. Never this close to our building. Actually, I can't remember seeing anyone ever come and go from that place."

"Which means it might not be part of the White House complex?"

He shrugged. "Who knows? I've always assumed everything on that street belonged to the executive branch. But maybe not."

We watched cars go through the Jackson Place guard gate for a few moments. But none of them stopped outside the townhouse I'd visited.

"So weird," I said finally.

"Yeah, it is. What're you gonna do?"

"Visit the place again. Something's going on there I don't understand."

"Pretty much every important CEO in the country stops by our offices at one point or another. Let me know if I can help in any way," he offered.

"I might take you up on that."

"And if your roads lead you to the White House, remember that I know the president's chief of staff, Admiral Symons, really well. He was always helpful to me on background when I was there. Whatever you find, I can connect you if you need it."

"Good to know."

"And if you ever want to cash in your chips and join the dark side, I can hook you up. I hear about great gigs all the time now."

"Not happening, Tom. We both know it. I'll die a hack." I cast a sidelong glance at him. "Why'd you bring me up here, really?"

"To brag." He chuckled. "You can't beat the view."

***

I didn't knock as I entered the townhouse. I didn't have a game plan. Mostly, I was curious. I had a few more questions. I figured I'd take it from there.

The well-mannered receptionist was seated at the desk in the foyer almost precisely as she had been the day before. She looked up from her laptop and smiled.

"You're back," she said. "I was afraid I wouldn't see you again."

I stood in front of her desk. "Tell me again what the agency told you when they sent you here?"

"They said I should expect you to arrive shortly."

"And then?"

She blinked furiously. "They said you would know what to do, that it would be clear."

"Nothing about what the job is, who the employer is, what I'd be doing once I arrived?"

"No. Only that I was here to help you any way I could. Those were their exact words."

That was interesting. "They said to help *me*? Not to help your new boss when you got here?"

She nodded.

I glanced at her desk. "When you got here and set up your laptop, no phone? Nothing else here?"

"Nothing."

"And that didn't seem strange to you?"

"Yes, it seemed exceedingly strange." She lowered her voice. "But like I said, it's a reputable agency. They place people in important temp jobs all over the city. I have several friends who landed great jobs through it."

"So you didn't ask questions."

"That's right. I didn't. I've always been able to sort through things on my own. I can handle just about anything. I figured I could do that here."

I smiled. "What have you figured out, now that you're on your second day of the job?"

"That it's going to be a lonely place if my boss doesn't show up soon to tell me what I'm doing here."

"Who is your boss, do you think? Where are we, exactly?"

When she didn't look around the building but continued to gaze at me, I knew she'd put in a great deal of time thinking through that very question the past 24 hours. "I have a thought about that. It will sound crazy, though."

"Try me."

She walked from her desk into the office behind her. I followed.

Swiveling to face me, she said, "When I got here yesterday, there were no instructions. Nothing about phones, wireless internet, or even the name of the building. The door was unlocked. No one greeted me. So I just waited for you. After you left, I tried all the Wi-Fi possibilities that came up on my laptop. I couldn't get any to work. They're all locked, and I had no way to guess at the passwords."

I nodded. "There are all sorts of secure offices in the area."

She leaned against the desk. "But one I kept coming back to throughout the day had four bars—a strong, steady Wi-Fi signal. I decided to look for a router, to see if it might have instructions."

"And did you find one?"

"I did. There's a second story to this townhouse. There was a router in the closet, but nothing else. All the rooms upstairs are empty."

"Anything on the router?"

She folded her arms. I knew from many years of reading body language during interviews that this is an especially human tell for caution.

"It has four letters in all caps on the bottom: SCTE. It matches the strong Wi-Fi signal I found—SCT Enterprises. So I searched for SCT Enterprises via my cell. Nothing came up, at least not anywhere in the Washington area. I began to wonder…"

"I'm assuming you figured it out? The password for the Wi-Fi signal?"

"I did," she said fiercely. "They gave me only one name at the agency. Yours. So I started searching references for you. I found some of your earlier stories…"

In one extraordinary moment, I realized what she'd discovered the day before. "You found my old byline, with my middle initial."

"Yes. Seth C. Thomas."

"I used my middle initial once, years ago. My middle name is Charles."

She went on. "Then I started looking for other information: your bio, places you've lived, things like that. It was your birth date that eventually worked. I tried those eight numbers—the month, day, and year. It's the wireless internet password for this place."

We looked at each other.

"So SCT Enterprises…?" I said.

"It's you, I think. Seth C. Thomas Enterprises. This place is somehow meant to be yours. I believe you're my new boss."

CHAPTER 4

"You realize that's insane, right?"

The receptionist, who now believed she worked for me, didn't answer right away. She moved to the other side of the desk and opened the drawer. Removing the checkbook, she placed it on the table. "There's one way to find out."

"Come on." I sighed. "That's crazy, too."

"Why?"

I glanced at the checkbook. "What would you do?"

"Something simple, like buy office furniture, a couple of phones, a painting or two for the reception area. Maybe some throw rugs."

I laughed out loud. "And you'll sign your name at the bottom, on behalf of SCT Enterprises?"

"Sure, why not? Or you can sign it."

I threw my hands out in front of me, like I was warding off an evil spell. "No chance. I'm not getting dragged into this thing."

She picked up the checkbook. "But you'd let me try it? As an experiment?"

"I can't stop you."

"But what if you're my boss?"

"I'm not."

"What if you *are?* Don't you want to know?"

"Actually, no, I don't. I'm a journalist. I ask people questions for a living, and then I write down what they tell me. I don't start businesses with money from some benefactor who's a helluva lot more likely to be a Russian oligarch, or some weird, new venture fund from the CIA, or some pipe-dream fetish of a super PAC in Washington."

"So, I can buy those things, as a test? Just to see what happens?" she persisted.

"It's your life. But look, I don't even know your name or any-thing about you. And you for damn sure don't know anything about me."

"It's Dorothy Rungren," she said with an easy smile. "All my friends call me Dotty."

"Well, Dotty, you do what you feel you need to do. This is your job, your place of employment. The agency sent you here, so may-be…"

"I went there first thing this morning. Asked them everything I could think of. Pressed them pretty hard."

Her blue eyes narrowed in an intense way that surprised me. It was typical in Washington for people to look right past assistants. It was a mistake, one I didn't usually make, and I vowed not to make it again here. For the first time, I noted that she'd allowed her hair to turn gray, which I knew was always a big decision for someone her age re-entering the workplace. She was dressed casually in a button-down shirt, loosely fitting blue sweater, and nicely pressed gray slacks.

"And they didn't tell you a thing, right?" I asked.

"Not a thing. It made me mad. I demanded to see the personnel file on me. They wouldn't show it to me right away. But I insisted."

"Good for you." I laughed. "What did it contain?"

"My résumé and the instructions to help you yesterday."

"That's it? Nothing else? It didn't have the name of this place? SCT Enterprises?"

She shook her head. "And when I asked them to search their computer records for the employer's name, it came up as 'Anon-ymous.' Both my salary and the agency cut were paid from a Fi-delity Investments account—an anonymous, donor-advised fund. They're apparently all the rage these days."

"Was there a name?"

"Not that I could see. Just a Fidelity check."

"Probably authorized by an investment banker there," I mused. "They do that all the time. Places like Fidelity Investments are au-thorized to send checks from anonymous donors who don't want their names public. They work for their donors, not the people who receive their checks."

"I don't know anything about that. All I know is, I'm here for a month. And my boss, as near as I can tell, is you. So it's all right if I buy those things? You won't mind?"

"I'm not your boss, so knock yourself out. Try to buy whatever you'd like. I can't stop you. The check will bounce, more than likely."

"And if it doesn't? What if it clears after I've paid an office supply store to deliver things and turn this place into a real office? Will you come back?"

"I'm not promising a damn thing. I don't know what's going on here. This whole thing reeks of a front group for someone."

"Will you at least try to find out more about it—about what might be going on here?" she pressed. "Can you at least do that?"

I grimaced. "I can ask a few more questions. That's as far as I'll go."

"But you'll come back?" Dotty's eyes were fixed on mine. She didn't look frightened by the uncertainty of this weird situation. She looked…determined.

"I'll come back," I said. "But on one condition. That you get to the bottom of that Chase checking account. Find out how much is in it, who can sign for it, who set it up, that kind of thing. Tell them you at least need to know what your limits are for the account. They have to tell you that much."

Dotty nodded. "Gladly."

"And it will be an office." I smiled. "If the check doesn't bounce."

"SCT Enterprises will be open for business."

"Whatever that is. Do your thing. Ask questions. Send a check to the office supply store if you want. Just don't sign my name to anything. This is your job. This is your place. It's not mine."

"If you say so," Dotty said. "But I give you my word: Next time you come here, I'll have answers. You'll see."

CHAPTER 5

Who does something this crazy? I thought as I made my way back to the newsroom. Who sets a thing like this in motion, for no discernible motive at all? Was I being set up so I'd have no choice but to walk away from my chosen profession in the midst of a crazy tax dodge I'd allowed myself to get tangled up in?

Sure, I'd made plenty of enemies. In fact, I'd managed to keep the *Post's* outside law firm gainfully employed. But lately I'd grown weary … even bored with the constant pursuit of corruption, malfeasance, and chicanery. Nothing ever seemed to change. Crooks and con artists who'd taken gullible suckers for a ride went to jail but were replaced by seven times as many crooks and con artists. It had been years since my last big investigative takedown. This wasn't the first time I'd questioned the impact of what I did.

The American public, if anything, had grown dumber and more easily conned than it was when I became a journalist. Trust in the media—in people like me, who were scrupulous in ascertaining the closest approximation of truth around a given story—was at an historic low. No one cared any more about science, evidence, or facts.

The biggest social media sites with the largest numbers of people liking, sharing, following, and circulating their favorite "news stories" were dominated by heavily slanted advocacy groups on both the right and the left, with far more on the right than on the left. Those sites kept pushing further to the fringes of what once passed for the center of the political spectrum. Fake news sites that covered the same general topic as mainstream news sites but tilted toward one belief system or another were often three to four times the size of "real" news sites that tightly adhered to what was left of the journalistic code. In the brave new world, propaganda was now more valuable and marketable than real news.

It's been said that a well-told lie travels around the world much faster than the truth. Now a lie is also much more valuable financially, because so many people pass the propaganda along, generating online traffic that attracts even more advertisers to those propagating the fake news.

I was mentally exhausted constantly fighting the good fight. Who cared whether you got it right any longer? I did. But hardly anyone else in America seemed to. So what was the point?

As I settled at my desk at the newspaper, I started to go through a mental checklist of some of the wealthier people I'd angered over the years. A few had the means. A few more had the motive. But this was an infinitely bizarre way to try to ruin a career. Those with wealth didn't go to such lengths. Direct routes to control, discredit, or shut down reporters and the media had been used for years. There was no need to play cute games or set up elaborate scams.

Billionaires had bought most of the national media in recent years and turned them in one political direction or another. Others had financed lawsuits against journalists and news organizations they loathed, putting some out of business. One very wealthy individual, who had financed big chunks of the cornerstones of the Internet, had made suing news organizations into oblivion the central focus of his "philanthropic" efforts.

Given all that, I concluded, there was no reason to come at me indirectly. What possible purpose would it serve? I had lost my juice as an investigative reporter. I wasn't a real threat to anyone now. One more buyout, one more newsroom purge, and I'd be gone anyway. I was a dinosaur, and a species-ending meteor had long ago hit the journalistic land in which I dwelt. There was no need to take me out; I'd all but taken myself out already. A fickle American public that no longer cared about objective truth, added to a viciously amoral financial and digital world where no one valued the sort of work I'd dedicated my life to, would finish me off.

Now I had nothing to lose. In this weird state of freedom, I could pursue this crazy, surreal venture without any fear of consequences. *Someone* had targeted me, but I had no idea *why*. It seemed more like a game than an orchestrated scheme by a corporate or government intelligence agency to trap me, so I vowed to see it through. As long as I didn't break any laws, or do something un-toward, then, if it all went south, I could easily suffer the conse-quences. If I had to resign my job, so be it. I was almost out the door anyway.

At least this was a real story—one I knew I'd pursue to what-ever logical conclusion it reached. I wasn't sure about the morality of it all, but I'd cross that bridge later. For now, I'd take one step at a time.

The first step was to find out where the original text had come from. I called one of my longtime sources at the CIA.

CHAPTER 6

"You know I'll have to log this on the books, right?"

My friend at the CIA had agreed to meet me at a Starbucks on Chain Bridge Road, about a mile from the CIA's headquarters in Langley, Virginia. It was an ordinary coffee shop, surrounded by a suburban shopping complex. It was hardly cloak-and-dagger stuff.

Silas had a mundane job at the agency. He was an analyst on the Russia desk, with a narrow focus on how money moved in, through, and around a country that used finances to direct traffic in their geostrategic interest. You could find a bio of him if you looked closely enough through various research documents around the web.

Mostly, the agency analyzed an enormous amount of publicly available information to find trends, patterns, and likely outcomes. Silas had an interesting job, if you didn't mind staring at a screen all day, sorting through an endless sea of financial dealings from groups with indirect ties to the oligarchs orbiting Russia's enigmatic leader.

"Show me the phone number," Silas said.

I scrolled until I found the text, then handed my phone across the small circular table. The table wobbled as I leaned on it. When he didn't look up right away, I folded a napkin I'd grabbed from the counter and stuffed it under one of the legs to stabilize the table. It was an old habit. I couldn't stand wobbly tables in public spaces like this.

"So? What do you make of it?" I asked.

I could see he was troubled when his eyes met mine. Silas had been a colleague for years. We played poker regularly at a friendly game that rotated homes. The stakes were relatively low. You could lose a couple hundred dollars, but you had to work hard to make or lose a lot of money. Still, the stakes were high enough that people took the games seriously.

From years of sitting across tables from him, I knew Silas was a good poker player. He had studied its intricacies enough not to make fatal mistakes. He didn't have any obvious tells…at least, none an amateur like me could find. He bluffed just enough to make people question his true intent. He laughed and talked casually at the table to make sure others never really knew why he was in one hand to the next. He never went on tilt and didn't show emotion.

But right now he was having trouble keeping any semblance of a poker face. Something about the number, text, or circumstances was giving him considerable pause. He wasn't trying to hide it.

"You're not thinking about pursuing this, are you?" His voice was quiet. I could see he wanted to wave me off this particular story, something he'd done for me on more than a dozen occasions over the years.

"I am."

Silas leaned back in his chair. "You can't. Or, I should say, you shouldn't. You can pursue it if you like. You always have that pre-rogative. But my strong advice is that it's not wise. Don't pursue it."

Silas knew me well enough that telling me *not* to pursue a story was like throwing an old, bloody sock in front of a bloodhound. He likely knew my next question.

"Not good enough," I answered. "I need more to go on. I need a few more answers before I let this thing go. Come on. You're clearly seeing something here. Tell me. What is it?"

Dotty was likely sitting in the townhouse at Jackson Place, wrestling with the same unanswered questions. I'd known her for all of two conversations, but I could feel myself getting sucked in. I wanted answers for her as well.

Silas leaned forward again. He placed his chin in his hands and stared at me. Clearly, he was weighing how much he could tell me without going too far. It was an old game for veterans like Silas. He rarely did this with me, however, so I knew something serious was behind his demeanor.

"Let me ask you a few questions," he said finally.

"Good. I can live with that."

"The Panama Papers…you know the basic gist? The origin? Why they matter?"

"Of course. Some of us *care* about those kinds of things and spend a considerable part of our lives chasing rabbits down the holes and trails that you find littered in documents like—"

Silas held up a hand. "Stop. I know that you, of all people, understand why the Panama Papers should matter. That's not why I asked. I want you to tell me what they signify to you, and why you think it set certain forces in motion."

The Panama Papers were more than 11 million documents deliberately leaked to expose roughly 200,000 offshore bank accounts and financial transactions. They revealed how leaders in various countries had looted tens of billions of dollars and funneled them offshore. They also exposed the underbelly of state-supported organized crime, along with the many ways business interests pushed the envelope on tax evasion and transparency from one country to the next.

Dozens of journalists had analyzed the documents for up to two years and written as many stories as they could possibly run to ground. But the reality of what the Panama Papers exposed was lost in the rush of other events and largely forgotten by the public.

Several prominent world leaders had been embarrassed and affected by the big document leak. Dozens of business interests, large and small, had similarly been forced out into the open. Curiously, very few Americans had been drawn into the Panama Papers' web, and none had ever been linked to the way in which global business interests were interwoven with state actors. The focus of both the massive leak and the subsequent media coverage was almost entirely on foreign adversaries of the United States. That fact had not been lost on me.

No one had ever credibly taken credit for the leak, though it had been widely reported that one anonymous leaker was responsible. But it was impossible to know, for sure, who actually was behind it. There were lots of theories. I had one, but I'd never been pressed to validate it. I wasn't part of any of the investigative journalism teams that had gone through the cache of documents, now available in a database for those who cared to chase leads.

"The papers dented a few prows," I said, mulling it over. "None in the United States."

"Yes, there's that," Silas interjected.

"And it exposed some unfortunate...coincidences in countries and places and bank accounts that analysts like you could examine and start connecting dots."

"Coincidences that forced more than one interest to shift from one country to another," he added.

"I can only imagine, though I doubt these leaders or interests care all that much."

"No, they don't. No one can touch them. But that's not the point, or what I'm asking."

I took a deep breath. "You're asking me what they mean?"

"Yes."

"OK, then." I liked this game, where questions were answered with more questions. It was like a Russian doll. Unscrew one layer, and the layer underneath was revealed, and so on. "Well, in the broadest sense, they represent one form of power attacking another. People often hide money they've made illegally. The Panama Papers brought a great deal of that out into the open. I can imagine some people weren't pleased."

"They weren't."

"But it's not like they're going to be taxed on the ill-gotten gains in their own countries, even if investigators or journalists pinned them down," I argued.

"That's right. They're not."

"I mean, just to name one person who *wasn't* in those papers but is now pretty well-established...Yemen's leader looted billions from his treasury, but no one cared in the slightest. He stashed billions all over the world in offshore accounts, and no one lifted a finger."

"So, who *was* in the papers?" Silas prompted.

"Your crowd of Russian oligarchs featured prominently, as well as their many enterprises all over the world. Some legal. Most not. Am I getting warmer?"

Silas's poker face was back.

I pressed on. "I'm guessing you've seen some downstream actions and consequences. Retaliation for the release of the Panama Papers?"

Silas nodded. "One of the immutable laws of physics. For every action, there's a nearly opposite action."

"So, someone, or something, didn't take kindly to the Panama Papers," I reasoned. "They're covering their tracks. More importantly, they're exacting revenge. Likely where it hurts, and in ways that inflict the most damage."

"What might those efforts look like?"

"Money spigots turned off," I mused. "Or turned on. Put out bread crumbs, see who picks them up, and follow the trail."

Silas pushed his chair back from the table. I'd gotten what I'd come for, but he offered two last thoughts.

"I'd look at Iceland if I were you."

"Because?"

"Just look at Iceland," Silas repeated. "One other question you need to answer: Who's the richest man in the world?"

"Come on, we all know—"

"I'm serious," Silas said. "It isn't who you, or anyone else, thinks. Trust me."

CHAPTER 7

The first part of Silas's puzzle, to look at Iceland, was relatively easy to solve. What wasn't patently obvious—from news reports, the Panama Papers, lawsuits, a handful of financial analyst reports from staid banking organizations, and a congressional oversight committee report that investigated whether any prominent Americans had been swept up in the carnage—was lurking just offstage.

Iceland had become a convenient piggy bank for Russia's leaders, who looted every state-owned business and industry meant to feed, house, power, and move millions of citizens of the former Soviet Union. It was possibly the biggest, most brazen, most ruthless transfer of wealth and power in human history.

Iceland was living proof of what the vaunted, feared Russian oligarchs could accomplish when they set their minds to it. And they were supported in every endeavor by the head of state, who almost certainly profited from the financial web that now encircled every nook and cranny of the Kremlin.

Once, when the former Soviet Union was a world-straddling power with a confederation of Communist nation-states in its grasp, satellite countries like Iceland managed to stand apart without much trouble. While the Cold War raged between the Soviets and the Americans, countries like Iceland couldn't contribute much in a military or national security way but could go about their business with little interference.

Iceland was safely tucked halfway between the two warring superpowers, in the middle of the ocean and away from any of the real action. Greenland separated it from the United States. Sweden, Norway, and Finland physically separated it from Russia. When it did pay attention to that part of the world, the United States preferred to study Greenland to determine whether its gigantic ice sheet would someday slide into the ocean.

Moscow was more concerned with the progressive politics of its immediate neighbors to the west. For decades, Iceland was a wonderful place for world leaders to visit for conferences and meetings. It wasn't, however, a place of strategic importance. Reykjavik was marvelous to fly into, and then leave.

That all changed as the Cold War began to melt, and the Soviet Union started to break apart. As a variety of Soviet leaders desperately tried to keep that from happening, others in positions of authority in the intelligence arms of the USSR's largest country—Russia—planned their jailbreak and subsequent rise to power. In this new world, financial power was the only thing that mattered. The smarter, faster, more ruthless officials who could see what was happening moved swiftly.

They formed alliances with those inside and outside the government and moved hundreds of billions of dollars from state-owned businesses and industries in Russia into the ready and willing hands of the private sector. The financial machinations and movements were complicated. They required willing accomplices outside the state-owned businesses that had served as the backbone of the Russian state.

Iceland, it appeared, had been at the center of much of that movement. It had taken a bit of time and patience, but I was eventually able to piece together what Silas meant for me to find. The Iceland "story" was as old as it was sad.

As the Soviet Union faded away and its vast state-owned enterprises changed hands, it was replaced by Russian oligarchs who wielded enormous financial power with the absolute authority of the Kremlin, because the Russian president empowered them at every important fulcrum point in the global financial system.

But even Russian oligarchs needed a place to wash their newfound financial wealth. They couldn't risk leaving all that new wealth inside any of the former countries of the Soviet Union. It wasn't safe to park it inside Russia. Europe, even to the east, was out of the question. South America was an option, of course, but governments changed hands far too quickly in that part of the world to offer a truly safe haven.

Iceland had become their best option. The country was small enough that the Russians could wield extraordinary control over its small network of banks. Yet it was connected enough to the rest of the world that wealth could easily move in and out of those banks, with rubles turning seamlessly into dollars. It was a marriage made in heaven. A few of those small banks became mind-numbingly wealthy almost overnight as money exited Russian state-owned industries straight into the hands of a few Russian oligarchs.

It was the perfect solution on multiple levels. At the height of the gold rush, Russian oligarchs regularly jetted in and out of Reykjavik. But it was inevitable that, amid the frenzy of so much easy money—far more than the small island nation had ever seen—the system would tumble at the first signs of turbulence. Three of Iceland's largest banks had extended themselves so much that outstanding financing and assets represented ten times the country's annual GDP.

Toward the end of the first decade of the 21st century, Iceland's economy imploded. Bank officials, politicians, and others were caught up in the collapse. Offshore banking accounts for Iceland's prime minister were tagged in the Panama Papers. People went to jail for financial and political corruption. A dogged police investigator and his sidekick, now a member of the European Parliament in Brussels, ran a tireless campaign to expose the banks' financial mismanagement.

But when all the big banks collapsed, it was the few hundred thousand Icelanders who suffered the most. Some bank officials were convicted of tax and accounting fraud, and some went to prison. But the Russian oligarchs merely moved their money away from Iceland to another part of the world. No one knew where that money went, or even how much of it had truly washed through Iceland's banking community.

I tried to understand where all the Russian money might have gone after Iceland's economy collapsed and the banks it controlled had disappeared. But I couldn't, beyond a few educated guesses. I wondered if Silas, or anyone else for that matter, knew where all that new wealth had gone. Where was it now that the Iceland option had vanished, and the Panama Papers had exposed thousands of offshore banking accounts tucked away across the world?

All that remained of the economic collapse in Iceland were the legends of the financial raiders. "The Vikings" is what Icelanders called the risk-taking, hard-charging financiers who'd seized control of their main banks and subsequently reduced their country's economy to rubble. It wasn't lost on anyone that the privatization of Iceland's banks so closely mirrored the privatization of so much of Russia, or that so many uber-wealthy Russian billionaires had been a near-constant presence in Reykjavik at the height of the daring transfer of wealth.

In its heyday, Iceland's interlocking banking system had been into everything, from boring industries like insurance or shipping to higher-profile sectors like gambling and liquor businesses. Nothing had been off-limits for the Iceland banks, provided there was money to be made through highly leveraged acquisitions, loans, or joint ventures.

Even now, no one knew the extent to which "The Vikings" had managed to move such vast sums from extraordinarily complicated global acquisitions through the banks they controlled. No one could possibly unwind that many interlocking business partnerships—well into the hundreds and then the thousands. There were also hundreds of reckless loans, made with god-knows-what ulterior motives. The Panama Papers had listed all of them on a spreadsheet. One thread alone, for one particularly notorious Russian oligarch, ran out to 600 or 700 different business arrangements.

Only a place with vast, deep investigative resources, like the financial crimes division of the Treasury Department or the Internal Revenue Service, had any hope of following the threads. But they were unlikely to do so in Iceland's case because, until recently, no prominent American business interests had been implicated in the years-earlier collapse of Iceland's economy and banking interests.

What had changed—and now offered me a slim chance to investigate this particular path if I decided to keep pursuing it—was that there was, in fact, a top official in the current presidential administration with at least one clear, direct tie to the Iceland banks. That official was Vice President Howard Phelps. The American vice president had become wealthy—not a billionaire, but quite well off according to the limited public disclosure forms he'd been required to file with the U.S. Senate—by parlaying his iconic status as the CEO of a well-known national cable television network into both public fame and private wealth. The American public admired Phelps' handsome good looks and carefully crafted persona as both a truth-teller and a rugged outdoorsman.

While Phelps' media presence gave him public acclaim, his actual wealth had been built through speculative land development in countries ranging from Indonesia to Brazil. One of those deals, involving a railway construction project in the Amazon, had been partially financed by an Iceland bank. His name had shown up once in the Panama Papers.

But Phelps had never released his tax returns, and no one had ever pursued the Iceland financing angle. He clearly aspired to be a member of the Billionaires' Club, was often seen in their company at high-dollar fundraising events in the Hamptons, Hollywood, or Silicon Valley, and would likely achieve that status once he left office.

After briefly flirting with a run at the presidency himself, Phelps eventually agreed to join the ticket of a progressive, female Democratic senator who won the party's nomination after a brutal primary season. She desperately needed the backing of both the elite media and the Billionaires' Club. The ticket—the progressive populist trying to become the country's first female president, paired with the more moderate, card-carrying gatekeeper to both the elite media and the Billionaires' Club—had proved irresistible to voters. They won the presidency easily and were poised to coast to an easy re-election if one believed the latest polling.

The media never made much of the fact that the vice president had obtained partial financing for at least one land-development deal from an Iceland bank with obvious ties to Russian oligarchs because such financing had pre-dated Phelps' political career. But likely there was more to the story. I could pursue it through Iceland if I wanted, simply by hanging a trip or two on that fact alone.

I didn't really care whether the vice president had taken money from Russian oligarchs. I assumed he had. I'd investigated so many politicians and business interests that intersected with those politics over the years that the topic no longer intrigued me.

However, I knew my editors would care about such connections, and I now had an excuse to go to Reykjavik. Phelps had apparently leaned on wealth looted from Russia's public entities for at least one land deal. But no one had ever tried to link his holdings to what was publicly available in the Panama Papers.

It was the answer to Silas's second question—about the richest man in the world—that gave me pause. I'd heard rumblings of it in odd places but never had any occasion to look at it closely. National magazines like *Forbes* and *Fortune* and financial newspapers like the *Wall Street Journal* regularly jockeyed for position by naming the lists of all the world's billionaires. These news organizations invested considerable effort in piercing the veil of financial secrecy that shrouded the lives of the billionaires on the list, to accurately assess who was number one in the world and who might be merely the 200th billionaire on it.

Most people had heard of the most prominent people near the top of the annual Billionaires' Club lists—names like Elon Musk, Bill Gates, Jeff Bezos, Warren Buffett, Charles Koch, Mark Zuckerberg, Carlos Slim, Michael Bloomberg, and various members of the Walton family. Others, such as Amancio Ortega or Larry Ellison, weren't as well known. And virtually no one knew much about the billionaires in the middle of the pack. There were about 2,700 known billionaires on the planet. The average billionaire was worth almost $7 billion. Most of the "ordinary" billionaires couldn't crack the top 400.

To crack the top ten, you had to be *really* wealthy. If you weren't worth at least $50 billion, you weren't likely to make the top ten. Like the other seven billion people on the planet, I had no idea what it meant to be so wealthy that you could buy entire countries with your checkbook. The world's wealthiest—especially those near the top of the list—were so rich they'd probably forgotten what it was like to be human. They had no real cares or worries. They could take private jets anywhere every single day. They could own a home in every country. They could see and do anything their heart desired.

All that remained of their humanity was likely a drive to pass their bounty on to their progeny and to improve the human condition somehow. But who knew? The world had never seen the amalgamation of such vast wealth in the clutches of a few hundred who could each singly shape the destinies of nation-states and peoples through sheer force of financial will.

At the top of that list was a name that didn't appear anywhere, I'd discovered with only a bit of work. No one—not *Forbes, Fortune,* the *Financial Times, The Economist,* the *Wall Street Journal,* or any other news organization that tracked such things—had ever placed this person on the list. Yet it seemed obvious to me he belonged there and was at the top, by a wide country mile.

Russia's long-standing president was now likely the richest man on Earth. By some unofficial estimates, he controlled financial assets of more than $200 billion. Every effort to move public assets into the private sector certainly benefited Russia's leader, who ruled the country with an iron fist. When oil and gas interests were privatized, which meant hundreds of billions of U.S. dollars in assets moved from one ledger to the next, some portion of that wealth must have attached itself to the Russian leader. After all, he'd plotted his path to absolute political power through financial power from his earliest days as the deputy mayor of St. Petersburg.

Everyone who'd done business with him came away with essentially the same story. To do business in Russia, you also had to do business with Russia's president and a small, elite circle of financial advisors who'd grown wealthy beyond reason from their proximity to that power center.

That explained why the Panama Papers had been akin to setting off a nuclear weapon in Russian financial circles. They had exposed the thousands upon thousands of offshore banking entities with links back to the center of Russia's oligarch and political system. It exposed Russia's president in the only way that likely mattered to him—to investigative, financial, and regulatory authorities who could seize assets or fence them in. Most likely, he'd vowed some measure of revenge even as he rushed to shield those financial connections and assets from further exposure.

Russia's decision to aggressively interfere in America's 2016 presidential election seemed a direct response to the frontal attacks the leak of the Panama Papers represented. My strong suspicion was that Russia's leaders, believing the United States had deliberately leaked the Panama Papers, responded by foisting raw propaganda on American citizens in a crude attempt to interfere in American elections.

That's what Silas was warning me about. He could see the patterns relating to Russia's organized crime, financial, and political circles and was troubled that I might walk into something well beyond my ability to deal with.

I could see it now. But I also wasn't convinced that the Russians were behind the mysterious text. I didn't know who had sent it to me. But I'd never been afraid of anything in my life, and I wasn't going to walk away from this challenge. If anything, Silas's questions had made me more curious. I was now determined to ask questions in Reykjavik. But, first, I decided to send Dotty out on an interesting and potentially helpful fishing expedition.

CHAPTER 8

"So, you're in?"

Dotty was beside herself. I hadn't known her for very long, but I still knew. She was pleased with this new path.

"I'm not in," I countered.

"But you're letting me pull money from the account and invest it?"

"It's your decision. Money is sitting there. No reason it can't be put to work. If it's something you'd like to do, I'll give you a list of public companies with interesting connections. You can buy shares in each and start to receive communications from them."

"But that's—"

I held up a hand. I was still uneasy about the Jackson Place office. Nothing about it made sense. I knew with every fiber of my being that it was a front for something. But it was also a siren song nearly impossible to stop listening to after I'd heard the first few strains.

We were standing in the office foyer on a rug that had the crisp smell of newness. Paintings hung on the wall. Dotty had placed fresh accoutrements on her desk. My glimpse through to the inner office noted additional furniture. The place now had the look of a real business.

"Let's take a walk," I suggested.

Dotty took her sweater from her new chair and slipped it on. We walked out the front door and stood on the steps. The White House was one block away, to our right. I noticed a tiny, discreet *SCT Enterprises* nameplate now to the side of the door. I winced but didn't say anything.

"Where to, Boss?" she asked.

"I'm not your boss," I said half-heartedly. Glancing across the street at the sentry box to the White House, I instinctively moved in the opposite direction.

"Whatever you say."

Dotty trailed behind as I strode to the corner of the private, guarded street along Jackson Place. I didn't hesitate at the crosswalk or wait for the light. Instead, I hurried across the street.

"We can sit and talk at the Hay Adams," I told her on the other side of the street. "Plenty of places there to talk privately."

Dotty moved to my side. "You don't need to worry," she said as we neared the entrance to the hotel.

"About?"

"About the office, your office. About its privacy...whether conversations are being taped or not."

I nodded at the Hay Adams' doorman and stepped inside. I'd had dozens of meetings there over the years I'd been in the city. I was comfortable here. This was my home turf. The office at Jackson Place was *not* such a place.

"How do you know that?" I asked, choosing to ignore her reference to ownership of the office.

"I had it swept," she replied. "By a firm I've used in the past. One of the best in the city. They did a thorough job. The place was clean. Nothing whatsoever, they said. At least not in the way of electronic equipment."

I looked at Dotty. "You know about that sort of thing?"

She laughed. Her blue eyes sparkled. "You really are clueless, aren't you?"

"At times. Both my ex-wives have said as much."

I moved into an open booth and gestured at one of the two open chairs. Dotty sat down and waited.

"So there was no electronic equipment...," I began.

"Right. Not even old outlets for it. Everything was new."

"But there was something else?"

"Yes." Her eyes locked on mine. "They found reinforced walls, completely soundproof, in the entire building. The place is essentially sealed. No chance any sound from inside can be picked up from the outside."

I squinted in her direction. "Every wall?"

"Every single wall. Throughout the entire office complex."

"So, a truck on the street..."

"Couldn't pick up anything, not even through the windows. They're bulletproof, by the way, as well as soundproof."

I sat back in my chair. "That must have cost a lot."

"Obviously. It was new work, the guys said. Whoever set the office up wanted to make sure SCT Enterprises could operate precisely as it saw fit, with no prying eyes or ears."

I laughed. "Yeah, and right across the street from the White House."

"The guys said the location afforded an extra layer of security. With so much going on in and around Jackson Place, our office is one of the most secure places you'll find anywhere on the planet. Other than monitoring who comes and goes, there's no way to track what happens inside the walls."

I nodded. "Honestly, between satellites and the millions of cameras everywhere these days, it's impossible for anyone to come and go unnoticed anymore. Especially in a city like Washington. Everything out on the street is essentially public."

Dotty leaned forward in her chair. "Which means, now that you're in, you need to think about who you invite to our office. Assume everything and everyone who comes through those doors is recorded somehow, somewhere."

"I'm not in," I interjected.

"I know. I heard you the first time," Dotty said. "Still, you need to think of this like a choreographed play. Consider who, or what, walks in and out. I'll help you make those decisions for now, while you're still pretending. So, when I start to buy shares in these publicly traded companies, is there anything special you want me to look for when I get the shareholder material?"

"You'll start to get calls from investment officers from some of these companies. Maybe from all of them. Who knows? They'll want to meet. Accept some of the invitations. I'll give you a set of initial questions to ask. We'll add to the list as you go through these meetings."

"Myself?"

"Yeah, by yourself. You've promoted yourself to business manager."

"Of SCT Enterprises?"

"Of whatever you'd like," I answered. "Do whatever makes the most sense to you."

Dotty nodded. "Got it. I'll have business cards printed."

"No need for a website. They'll find you from the address and phone number you list on the investment docs."

"Right. Now that we're doing this, I'm assuming you'd like everything to be in my name? No reference to you?"

I shook my head, chuckling. Even though I'd made the decision to set out on this path, I could already see I would come to regret it. No way would this end well. The best I could hope for was that I wouldn't go to prison for something I didn't yet fully grasp or understand.

Then again, I'd never had a plan in life. I had no stomach for planning and foresight. That character flaw had ultimately sabotaged both my marriages. I did everything on instinct. I never saved money. I never wanted kids, mortgages, retirement accounts, or anything that would attach itself to me. I couldn't even make myself take a vacation. All I'd ever wanted was the freedom to pursue the next great adventure, the next big story. Well, since this was likely the end of my career, I might as well go out spectacularly, for the best of all possible reasons—in pursuit of the story of all stories.

"Yeah, in your name," I replied. "When you tell them you're the business manager for SCTE, they'll ask for more. Don't provide it."

"Got it. Do you need money for travel, or anything else?"

"No. The paper authorized my trip to Reykjavik. I'm leaving in the morning." I paused. "But I meant to ask before. Clearly, there's money in the checking account to pay for office supplies. But how much, exactly, is in that account?"

Dotty smiled broadly. "It's unusual...to say the least."

"Why am I not surprised?"

"You'll be surprised at this," she replied.

"So, what's the answer?"

"That there's enough in it," Dotty answered.

"For what?"

"For whatever you'd like."

"What does that mean, exactly?" I said, confused.

"When I called Chase on the account, they put me through right away to someone. They'd already assigned a personal investment and banking advisor. He picked up and said I could call him, night or day, with any question or request. He's in New York. We've made plans to meet. He gave me the name of an accountant, who's making sure we set up the LLC properly in Delaware."

"So, you're an important client…"

"Not just an important client. His only client."

I stared at her. "But that means?"

"That there's a lot of money in the account? Yes, that's what it means."

"But how much is in it?" I persisted.

"'Enough for anything. Whatever you'd like.' That's what he said."

"So it's an open credit line, with no upper limit?"

"It's not a credit line," she answered. "These aren't loans or lines of credit. He said it's an open-ended account, with no upper limit he's aware of from his own boss. There are assurances that any amount will be covered, anonymously."

I sat very still in my chair. "Are you trying to tell me that you could write a check to me for a million dollars, right now, and that they'd cash it?"

"Yes, that's precisely what I'm saying."

"Or for…ten million?"

"Presumably. He said there was no upper limit."

I tried to imagine such a thing. I couldn't. This made no sense. "But, surely, there must be an actual limit. If you tried to write a check for some obscene amount, surely it wouldn't go through?"

Dotty smiled. "I guess we'll see, won't we?"

Chapter 9

Now I knew why Russian oligarchs and world leaders liked Reykjavik so much. It was an adorable city.

Reykjavik wanted to be a destination city for tourists, a place that visitors marveled at for its warmth and friendliness. Its small, clean airport itself reflected that DNA. The shops displayed precisely this message, enticing visitors with "Delicious Iceland" or "Sweet, Sweet Iceland" fare. Restaurants touted "tax free" food.

Keflavik International Airport brought new money and new thinking to the island nation otherwise isolated in the physical shadow of Greenland in the north Atlantic. The flights that came in and out were, almost by their very nature, "international" to some degree. People were either returning home from a destination outside the country or arriving for meetings.

But the airport also understood its role as a tourist hub. Signs actively discouraged backpackers from arriving and settling in wherever they felt like it while sightseeing. "Sleeping, camping, and cooking are prohibited in the building and on the grounds" stated one prominent sign greeting every passenger who headed to the luggage carousel.

So, I wondered, if they didn't want you camping *at* the airport, did that mean you were free to do so throughout the rest of the country? It wasn't like I'd ever test the proposition. I wasn't exactly a camping and backpacking guy. A clean hotel bed in a room where you could get a decent Wi-Fi signal and the ability to get a morning cup of coffee without working overly hard for it was all I cared about.

I'd learned over the years that the quickest, easiest way to fly in and out of cities was to put your bag up at the cheapest, halfway decent hotel near an airport and travel where you needed to from there. Because of people like me, who don't want to sort through hotel options in places they'll never visit again, there are a lot of hotels in or near airports all over the world. Sure, some people read every comment on Yelp, every review on every travel site they can find before setting foot in a new city. I sure as hell wasn't one of those people. If there was a hotel shuttle from an airport that I could find on my own without too much distraction, and the rooms at the booking site at least pretended to be spacious, clean, and inviting, I booked my travel, then forgot about it.

While in Iceland, I had no interest in seeing any sites now…or ever. I didn't plan a walking tour of the coastline or a visit to any of the tourist traps sprinkled throughout the city. I only cared about one thing—the person I was flying to Reykjavik to meet. He was the story.

People, to me, were a means to the narrative I was pursuing and never an end unto themselves. That's why both my ex-wives had told me I was emotionally stunted, incapable of empathy, obsessively focused on things of the mind and never of the heart, obtuse about nearly anything that might pass for romance, and incapable of listening or hearing things from partners or friends if it didn't serve some greater narrative. They were both right. I'd never bought flowers for either of my wives. They had given up, and so had I.

I know caring only about the story makes me a lousy human being. But I'm not changing of my own volition, and I've never met anyone who could make me change that approach. If I die alone, with no friends, colleagues, or family to mourn my passing, I accept that.

I spent the 40-mile cab ride from the airport trying to understand my cell phone's international plan. I deliberately ignored the driver's overly eager efforts to strike up a conversation, though I admired the fixed price we'd negotiated beforehand as I watched the meter tick off the miles. He'd clearly negotiated the better deal. Not that I cared. The paper was covering my costs, so good for him for taking advantage of this ignorant first-time traveler to Reykjavik.

I glanced out the left side of the cab at the ocean, immediately to the north and west. It was a nice view but not much different from any other shoreline in the world. There's a lot of water, seemingly going on forever, with only a few white wisps in the distance. Most people assume it's the massive mountain glaciers that ring Greenland. But you can't see Greenland from Iceland, no matter how clear the day.

When we got to Reykjavik, I had to admit it *was* cute, colorful, and inviting. Funky arches over some smaller streets, a curious gate with an old bicycle welded onto it blocking a side street, and a church that looked like a giant...oh, never mind. People seemed to enjoy walking along the streets downtown, unlike cities like New York, where every trip along a sidewalk was like pedestrian demolition derby. There were no blaring car horns, and the air seemed clean, as if no pollution had ever hovered over the city.

I had made one concession on this trip. I'd allowed Dotty to talk me into staying at the Grand Hotel a few minutes from downtown, rather than at my usual generic airport hotel with no view. As I exited the cab and looked around, I grunted to myself. Dotty was right. The views of the city, and the mountains beyond, were spectacular. For a fleeting moment, I wanted to snap a picture and text it back to her with a note of thanks, then thought better of the impulse. I'd never taken casual or tourist pictures in my life. Why would I start now, even if this particular view was unique, picturesque, and memorable? The mental image was fine. I didn't need a permanent digital image to remind me.

I had a couple of hours to kill before my meeting with the bank inspector I'd exchanged emails with over the past day or so. We were meeting in his new place of business, a private investigations outfit that worked closely with the government on financial crimes but made its real money on corporate espionage. I didn't probe too much over email. I figured we could get into all that when we met.

I left my bags in the hotel and grabbed the two small recorders, notebook, and extra batteries I always took with me to interviews. I liked using recorders when I interviewed people—one for the record and the second for backup in case the first balked or stopped. I could take notes quickly, but the recorders allowed me to pay close attention to the person I was talking to.

Over the years, I'd found that there were two kinds of people in meetings—those who spent all their time taking notes, and those who engaged in conversations that moved things in different, unexpected directions. I liked the latter. You could tell a lot about a person by looking at their mannerisms and by paying attention to even the smallest details.

For instance, if someone hesitates before answering a question, they might be deciding how much to lie or evade, they might be embarrassed, or they might be angry you've stumbled upon a secret they'd rather not see the light of day. You miss all that nuance and meaning if your eyes are glued to your notebook.

I shifted my backpack onto one shoulder and set off for downtown Reykjavik. As I made my way down the gently sloping streets, the white snowcaps against the gray mountaintops were so clear I felt I could reach out and touch them.

I wanted to visit at least two of the three banks at the center of the country's financial meltdown a decade earlier. The banks had morphed into something else after the collapse but had managed, according to a few news accounts, to remain in the business of moving people's money from one place to another. I had no idea how that was possible, so I wanted to see it for myself.

I was disappointed when I arrived at the first bank. Not only had it disappeared, but people in the lobby and one of the offices off the atrium told me it had gone away for good a few years earlier. Once its reputation was destroyed and some of its leaders went to prison, people were reluctant to invest their money there.

The bank had tried to become a home mortgage company but had failed spectacularly. The new company still existed with a small handful of employees, but they'd relocated to another part of the city. It was a tiny operation now, with no reach or importance. The bank's huge office complex was filled by a half dozen other companies.

The second bank, though no longer a bank, still handled a lot of money for someone. I tried to talk to people in the outer office but got mostly cool stares and clipped answers about what they did. After 20 minutes of meaningless conversations, I retreated. I studied the names of the various divisions of the new financial entity on the building's registry, including a cryptocurrency division called Pozolochennyy Limited, a Russian entity. It seemed as if they did institutional investing under a brand-new name, but I'd have to do more research.

Clearly, though, they were successful. The new company occupied the entire building in downtown Reykjavik. Every office with a window no doubt had a magnificent view of the ocean, city, and mountains.

Jasper Olafsson was waiting for me in his firm's lobby as I arrived. He greeted me warmly nearly the instant I walked through the outer door. I didn't wonder how he'd known it was me. The Internet made it easy to stalk virtually anyone on the planet. Google yields at least a handful of pictures of nearly anyone in a developed country. A search of my name likely yielded dozens of pictures from various events I'd covered over the years.

"Delighted to meet you." Jasper pumped my hand twice, then released it. "I assume you had an uneventful flight here. All set up in your hotel?"

"I did, thank you, and yes."

I studied Jasper. It was nearly impossible to tell from his casual, efficient dress whether he was well off or not. One button of his light blue, pressed shirt was open, and his gray slacks worked with the color of the shirt. His hair was closely cropped in the manner of nearly every policeman or military official. He didn't wear any jewelry, save a slim wedding band.

But his shoes—extra padding on the bottom, the outer edges worn from walking—gave him away. Jasper valued comfort over style and apparently didn't like to purchase new shoes. I liked him instantly.

Jasper leaned in a bit, so only I could hear his words. "I have to ask: Did you fly all this way from the United States just to meet with me?"

I smiled. His directness and lack of guile was a breath of fresh air in my world. I'd have little trouble getting whatever answers he might have at his disposal.

"Yes, I did," I answered. "I like to see things for myself. I prefer doing it in person. There's only so much you can tell about a situation from pictures and emails."

Jasper nodded. "I'm like that as well."

"So, may I ask you something?"

"By all means."

"Why in the world do you make it so difficult to understand people's names in Iceland?"

"Precisely to confound people like you," Jasper said with a broad, toothy grin. "We don't want to make it too easy for you Americans to keep track of us Icelanders."

"I can see that. I assume Olaf was your father?"

"That he was. Or is. He's still alive."

"And your brothers?"

"Proud Olaffsons, like me."

"And your sisters? Their last names…?"

"Just one. Named after Helga, our mother."

I shook my head. "And you do that to confuse the rest of the world?"

"Well, it *does* make each generation special and unique."

I glanced around the atrium for clues about the nature of the company Jasper worked for. "This place…?"

Jasper began to walk toward the stairs. I followed. "It's a private investigations center. Not for people. For corporations. We spy on each other."

"I see," I answered. There were any number of such places in Washington and other large American cities. Corporate espionage was big business. Nearly all the Freedom of Information requests at big regulatory agencies in Washington were from law firms conducting legal corporate espionage on their competitors. Hardly any were from the media or the public.

"It's a good job," he said as we boarded the elevator. "Pays the bills. And I get to spend at least part of my time on work that I really enjoy."

"For the government, on financial crimes?"

"Yes, but more than that."

We got off on the top floor and quickly made our way to a large conference room with a spectacular view of the city and mountains. Jasper sat with his back to the window, and I took a seat at the end of the table where I could talk easily.

"You don't like the view?" I teased as I placed my two recorders and notebook on the table. I didn't turn the recorders on just yet, though. I wanted to talk first. I'd also learned, long ago, that the simple act of turning on an audio recorder changed the dynamics of a conversation. Sometimes you did it for precisely that reason. At other times, like now, there was no need.

"I've seen it," Jasper answered with an easy smile. "Quite often."

"I can only imagine. It must be nice. Living here, I mean."

"It is. It's also a small country," he offered. "We tend to know our neighbors, and who's visiting us."

I decided to jump in the water. "Which is why I'm here, Jasper. I wanted to ask about your investigation of a few years ago. If you don't mind, I'd like to cut through some of the niceties. We don't need to turn the recorder on just yet."

"Ask away."

"Here's the thing. I've reported on an awful lot of corruption—political corruption, corporate and financial corruption. I've put people in jail, as you have. But what I've read about Iceland, which *your* investigation evidently turned up or confirmed, is unlike anything I've heard about or seen. It didn't make sense back then, and it doesn't make sense today. I stopped by two of the banks you put out of business. One is truly out of business. But the second bank? It's still around, as something else. And it might be bigger than it was before your investigation."

"You'd like to know what really happened? What I didn't investigate? What I ultimately concluded was outside the scope of my investigation? What wasn't in the reports or the papers?"

I nodded. "If you don't mind, that's precisely what I'm asking."

Jasper leaned forward. "Fine. But first, Mr. Thomas, may I ask a question of you?"

"Of course. Ask away."

"Is this for a story? Or for your own curiosity?"

I liked this guy. There was certainly more to him than met the eye. "Both, to be honest. Officially, I'm here on assignment for the paper. I fully intend to write something about all this, depending on which direction the investigation takes me."

"But that isn't how you came across this, is it?" Jasper asked.

"Someone brought you into this story, didn't they?"

"Yes, that's true, though—"

"And it's something that didn't quite add up. Looked much bigger than anything you were accustomed to. Led you in directions you hadn't thought about before. Introduced you to something well outside your comfort zone. But, still, you wanted to investigate? Am I close?"

I shook my head in wonder. "Yes, you're close. Uncomfortably so, actually. But how in the hell could you know any of that?"

"I've seen it before, on several occasions. You're not the first."

I sat back in my chair. "What's that mean—*I'm not the first?*"

"I mean this. A great deal of money is sloshing around the global financial markets these days...more so now than when I investigated the banks and the collapse of our country's financial and economic system a decade ago. Since then, I've kept track of the players, and those I suspected of driving our economy to the edge of the abyss. Every so often I hear... interesting stories. One is that someone, or something, is sending unusually inquisitive people after this story. Or, I should say, they come here because it's such an obvious starting point and because I know a great deal about what the Russian oligarchy is up to. Then, for whatever reason, no one hears from them again. They seemingly vanish from the picture."

"Vanish?"

"Not killed, though that certainly happens with players in and around the Russian president and his circle of financial advisors," Jasper explained. "I mean, they stop doing whatever it was they were doing. They go off in another direction or fall off the grid altogether."

"People do change jobs."

"Yeah, they do. I certainly have. But that isn't what I'm talking about here. I mean, *something* suddenly changed in their lives. Something big enough to bump them from one track onto another. They went from asking questions to not asking questions or talking about what they'd come across. Their public personas basically vanished."

I still hadn't turned on the audio recorders. I wasn't sure I would, at this point. "You said I wasn't the first? The first *what?*"

"The first person to start asking questions about where all this money is, who's behind it, where it comes from and where it goes, who has control of it, that sort of thing. In each case, it seemed to be personal…not tied to their job, per se. Like knowing who was pulling strings mattered to them way beyond their own job."

"How do you know this, exactly?"

"Three people have emailed, called, or traveled here with questions like yours in the past 10 years. All wanted to know what I'd learned."

"They came to Reykjavik? To meet with you?"

"One did. Another called. Both asked lots of questions. One said she was a financial analyst with a big firm in New York. The other was a U.S. federal agent. Both were used to getting to the bottom of things."

"And what happened to them?" I asked.

"One of them lied. Her name wasn't real. Her job wasn't real. When I followed up with her, she'd vanished into thin air."

"Let me guess. It was the financial analyst?"

Jasper laughed. "Yeah, that's right. She probably did work for one of the big outfits. She just lied to me about which one. I could probably track her down if I was so inclined. But I'm not. It's not my job and wasn't when I talked to her. Why she lied, and what she's doing now, is none of my business."

"And the other person? The agent?"

"He's gone, too. No longer working, at least not publicly. I know he's real. He at least worked where he said he'd worked. But he hasn't worked there for years. And, as far as I can tell, he hasn't worked anywhere since then. He dropped off the grid."

"And you're sure they haven't disappeared for any malicious reason?"

"Nah," Jasper said. "The second person, the agent, seemed calm about his questions. I talked to him again, right before he dropped off the grid. He said he was leaving his job and no longer pursuing what we'd talked about. He thanked me for my help. He didn't seem all that stressed about things. Just resigned to whatever he was going to do next."

"And the third person?"

"She contacted me by email. She said she was a lawyer doing

research for a client who wanted to establish a private island, Paradise Island, for wealthy patrons who wished to avoid taxes altogether. She said their clients were looking at various options, and they wondered whether I could advise them. They were starting an offshore tax haven island from scratch."

"Why you?"

"Because, in addition to a reputation as an expert on the huge sums of money swirling around the global financial system from Russian oligarchs that had washed ashore here in Iceland, I'm also now an expert on the Panama Papers and offshore tax havens. I know that world quite well. But I never heard from her after that initial email. And, as you know, some people are *intensely* interested in how the Panama Papers ended up in the public sphere."

"So curious," I muttered, more to myself than to Jasper. "Were you able to help the two? Answer their questions?"

"As much as I could. The sad truth is, during my investigation, it became obvious where all that money was coming from. It was *so much* money that it could only have originated from one place."

"From Russia? From privatizing the state system, which created the oligarchs?"

"Yes, exactly. But that wasn't my job—to determine where all the money came from. I only wanted to know how it was deliberately mismanaged and misappropriated once it arrived here, on the island."

"And it was misappropriated?" I guessed.

"At every turn. Imagine what happens when people working at banks are basically handed blank checks and told they can invest anywhere and do anything they want. Inflate the loan amounts as high as they'd like. Make investments so outside the usual risk parameters set by prudent financial institutions that it would shock you. Even when they lost money, they were promised 10 times that amount to replace it." Jasper flung his arms wide. "It was like hitting a gushing oil well, with no bottom to it."

"But the money spigot eventually was turned off?"

Jasper nodded. "It was turned off. By someone or something…I could never tell exactly. But at some point, every one of those bank officials was left holding a massive portfolio of extraordinarily risky loan and investment vehicles. No money was coming in behind them when they failed, and they did fail. Most of them. The whole thing collapsed like a house of cards."

"And you never asked the source of all that money?"

"It wasn't my job," Jasper said. "But I knew. Everyone knew. It was obvious where the money was coming from. But no one seemed to care. It was like free money."

"Nothing is ever free."

"Tell me about it," Jasper agreed. "Everything comes with a price. In this case, an entire country suffered. We still are today, at some level."

"I'm sorry."

"Don't be sorry," Jasper said. "If you want to help, find some answers. And, after you do, don't vanish like the others."

CHAPTER 10

Warning signs were everywhere. All of them told me to stop…
to run away as fast as possible. No way would any of this end well.

The oligarchs were as single-minded in their pursuit of absolute
wealth and power as their political patron, the Russian president,
who was fusing wealth and power in an unprecedented effort to
rebuild the former Soviet empire. It was profoundly foolish of me
to pursue them, or anything remotely connected to them. They'd
learned from the Mafia in America and the Yakuza in Japan. They'd
taken centuries of knowledge of organized crime and merged it
with one of the world's remaining superpowers.

It was a toxic brew not seen since the days of the Roman Empire, when it *meant* something to be both a Roman citizen and
wealthy. When power and wealth were combined, virtually any ex-
cess, whim, or desire was possible. There were no rules—moral,
legal, political, or otherwise.

Russia was now like the Roman Empire of those days. Immea-
surable wealth combined with absolute state authority meant any
geopolitical scheme was possible. Truth held no sway. Propaganda
was infinitely more useful. Only political power and wealth mattered, organized around fiefdoms established by the person at the
center of the new state. There was a very real chance the former
Soviet empire could reincarnate itself around the new paradigm
that had emerged from the rubble.

People tossed around phrases like the "Russian mafia" with no
understanding of what that meant. I knew precisely what it meant.
If you wanted to do business with Russia, with Russian money,
then you played by their rules and their authority, fully knowing you
were then a permanent part of this new system of power.

They were now connected to the American presidency and its

democratic institutions in ways neither I nor anyone else likely understood. I'd investigated enough financial and political corruption cases to understand that even the best—like a special counsel at the FBI pursuing Russia's interference in American politics—never touched more than a few places on the elephant. No one obtained an entire picture. You could only understand the parts you were in contact with at any given moment. Everything else was conjecture.

Jasper Olafsson knew that. He'd done what he could to expose the roots causing the collapse of Iceland's banking industry. But, as he'd made clear in our conversation, he could only speculate about what was beyond the scope of his investigation. He could ask only so many questions before entering areas either beyond his reach or outside the scope of what he could genuinely, reasonably, and safely pursue.

Those facts weighed on my mind. I knew I was a fool to go any further, given the risks and complexities on both sides of the ocean. But there was no turning back now. I would pursue this story as far and as fast as I possibly could. Someone or something had given me a unique opening and was using me for an as-of-yet undetermined reason. I meant to find out why.

I called Dotty from my cell phone the minute I landed at Dulles airport. She picked up on the first ring.

"What did you find out?" she asked without preamble.

"Not over the phone. I'll be in the office shortly. We can talk then. But did you start to set up the meetings?"

"I did, and I've already had some of them. You'd be surprised—"

"Later," I said. "I'll be there in an hour or so."

I decided to do a bit of work during the ride from the airport into the city. I sent a text to my editor at the *Post*, with the outlines of a story I knew would appeal to him. Because Russia's decision to hack the Democratic Party and wage information-warfare against the American election system in 2016 had dominated the news cycle for months afterwards, I pitched him on a story about Iceland and Russian financial influence in the banking system there as a cautionary tale. It wouldn't take much to tie it to the events in the United States and geopolitics and wars in Eastern Europe.

The truth was that what had happened to Iceland's banking system could happen anywhere—even in the United States—if you were willing to look the other way as billions were laundered through your financial systems. It was more difficult to get away with money laundering in the States, but it wasn't impossible... especially if you parked the money offshore and washed it through legitimate ventures. Real-estate deals worked especially well.

My editor responded immediately. He loved the story and asked me for a rough word count. I had enough color to stretch it to a thousand words. I also had pictures, which made it even easier. I started writing in the cab. I'd about finished by the time I pulled up to Jackson Place.

Dotty was standing in front of the office. She opened the door as I walked up the steps.

"You were waiting on me?" I asked.

Dotty closed the door firmly once I was inside and turned to face me. "Seth, I need you to pay attention. I need to make sure you understand what I'm about to tell you."

Though Dotty seemed like a tough, strong woman, I could see the fear in her eyes.

"I understand, and I'm paying attention. So what's happened?"

Dotty took a deep breath. "I had those investor meetings we talked about. Most were entirely normal. We just talked and traded business cards. But one meeting in particular went way beyond anything I anticipated. He offered us a company."

"A *company*? What sort of company?"

"An oil and gas exploration company."

"A wildcatter?" I asked. "Those things are—"

"No, it's a big, legitimate company with revolutionary technology to drill—anywhere on Earth—several miles straight down with a laser, hitting geothermal levels. I've already vetted it with an engineering firm. The company has contracts with American Standard. He showed them to me. They're set to drill in a half-dozen countries for oil and for geothermal energy. They have patents—good ones. Some of the best scientific societies in the world have blessed them, according to our guy at Chase."

American Standard was the largest oil and gas company in the world. They'd once been the largest publicly traded company until the Silicon Valley tech giants eclipsed them. They had their hooks into everything, in virtually every part of the world. They even aggressively tried to take a piece of the expensive Saudi Aramco IPO when it seemed like it would be offered. So, if American Standard had given this company a contract to drill for them, they had something real.

"Then what do they need us for?" I asked.

Dotty frowned. "I don't know. But they're willing to give us a significant position in the company, with preferred stock, through a Series A round."

"Where did they get their initial investment?"

"A private investor. They said we'd meet him if we come in. But there's more," Dotty rushed to say. "The man I met with? It was Ivan Fedorisky. I didn't know who he was until after he left."

"Fedorisky came here…and offered us a significant piece of a company he's invested in?"

"Yes, he did," she said firmly.

Now I knew why she was afraid. Ivan Fedorisky was a quiet legend in Silicon Valley. He'd been a Series A investor in several of the biggest technology, aerospace, and AI companies on the planet, which had made him a very wealthy man. But he was also a naturalized American citizen originally from Russia. And he'd been on the periphery of the FBI special counsel investigation of the 2016 presidential election.

There were constant rumors about the true source of his investments—rumors centered on the darkest corners of the Russian economy. When the Russian election scandal broke, my paper and several others tried to tie him to the money that washed into fake accounts at Facebook and elsewhere. But even after the FBI's special prosecutor announced indictments against more than a dozen Russian nationals for setting up dummy accounts, posing as Americans on social media to peddle propaganda to unsuspecting voters and meddling with the presidential election to sow confusion, none of the laundered money trails ever led to Fedorisky. Everyone still welcomed his investments.

"Damn," I said. "That would be something, investing with Fedorisky."

"The stories I read about him seemed to say that he is, or was, connected to Russian organized crime."

"No one's ever proved it," I said. "Not even the Panama Papers turned up anything on him."

"But what do you think?"

"If I had to bet, I'd say he got his investments from Moscow."

"So we can't possibly do anything with him, then, can we?"

I shrugged. "Probably not. But it's not like we have the sort of money Fedorisky is used to rounding up for a deal like this. He's probably trying to fill out a $25 million round, maybe even larger."

Dotty pursed her lips. "Actually, about that..."

"Oh, come on." I laughed. "Don't tell me..."

"I checked with our guy at Chase. He said we could invest if we wanted—that he could wire the money to Fedorisky."

"Just like that?"

"Just like that," she announced.

"We have *that* kind of money at our disposal?"

"The Chase guy said we could invest in this company, and several others, if we wanted," Dotty said, her voice small. "And that we should never worry about the limits. Whoever our benefactor is has allowed us to manage a considerable sum. He also said we could own stock as part of any deal we make."

"Wait. Then all this could get very real, very fast. It also means we'll have to get official, as a fund that can invest someone's else's money."

Dotty blinked fiercely. "I know. That became obvious after my first couple of meetings. They kept asking when we started the fund and worked the margins trying to learn more about the general partners. I've already started the registration process, so we can legally manage investment funds. I've got a couple of consultants working on the paperwork."

"I should have figured. What'd you say about the general partners?"

"I didn't. I said the fund had grown quickly in recent months, in order to take advantage of some interesting opportunities in the national security space that had opened up with this new administration."

"That's good. And almost true," I said, smiling.

Dotty didn't return the smile. Her face was still a tight mask. "Seth, I'm worried. I wasn't before. It seemed like a game then. It was kind of fun, trying to figure out what was going on. I liked talking to businesses, pretending I might invest in them. But I'm not so sure anymore."

"Yeah, I know. If we own stock in a company like the one Fedorisky is peddling…that changes everything."

"What do we do now?" she asked.

"Honestly, Dotty, I don't know."

***

I couldn't sleep. After several hours of tossing in my bed, checking my social media feed on my iPhone, and watching minutes inch by, I gave up. "Screw it," I muttered and sat up.

I slipped on the same socks I'd thrown to one side before collapsing in bed and then tossed the covers to one side. I didn't bother making the bed. What was the point? I hadn't shared my miserable one-bedroom apartment with anyone for years.

I padded from the bedroom and made myself a cup of coffee. Glancing at the dirty dishes in the sink, I thought briefly about cleaning them properly with soap and water. But this, too, seemed pointless since I'd just re-use the same dishes. So I ran warm water over them, scrubbed off the crusted food, and propped them next to the sink to dry.

As the coffee perked, I peered out the window. It was still dark outside. The sun wouldn't be up for at least another two hours.

I was at an incredibly dangerous crossroads. Dotty's meeting with Fedorisky weighed on me. I'd never met him, but I *knew* he wasn't clean. There was no chance his initial stake in several big tech companies had *not* come from oligarchs in Russia, who were almost certainly laundering that money. Now? Who knew? Fedorisky's wealth these days came from his stock in those companies and legitimate investments in companies like the one he was dangling in front of us. He didn't need to launder Russian money any longer.

The deal he was offering us now wasn't all that different from the one he'd likely made with Russian billionaires in the past. He'd been given the chance to manage someone's money as it was invested and was rewarded with board seats and preferred stock. He'd been incredibly lucky in several Series A rounds that had turned his 20 percent profit shares into hundreds of millions of dollars. Once he owned that stock, the world forgot where the original investment had come from.

The manager at Chase said we had the right to invest in Fedorisky's company, or anyone else's company, with seemingly no conditions or fences. If SCT Enterprises was rewarded with stock for managing the investment in Fedorisky's company, we'd be fine legally, if Dotty's consultants could establish the investment properly in the right places.

But massive questions existed on either end of such a transaction. If the money invested was dirty, we'd be on the hook for it. And if Fedorsky's company wasn't clean—or, worse, a target of the international crimes division at Treasury—we'd find ourselves in that mess, too.

"What the hell do I do?" I said out loud in the stillness of the kitchen.

Even as I let the words echo into the night, I already knew what I was going to do. It was why I hadn't been able to sleep. I was going to meet with Fedorisky…and agree to an investment.

I had no interest in being wealthy. I'd never thought about money. My ex-wives had complained endlessly about this. It was a constant source of friction and anxiety. But I *was* fascinated by wealth and the powerful—and familiar with its trappings after so many investigations over the years.

Now I had a chance to see what it was like inside this club. This was the first uncertain step on what could be the road to that Billionaires' Club. Fedorisky had traveled that path and was part of that club. I had no idea yet why he'd come to us. But I meant to find out, to take that first step.

I could still turn away if it became obvious he was entangling us in something beyond the pale. And Chase would have to be responsible for the source of the money it was allowing us to manage. Ultimately, whoever provided that money and gave us this opportunity was responsible. It was their problem, not ours.

If Fedorisky's company took off, and we owned stock in it, well, that would present its own challenges down the road. But, for now, I wanted to see where it might lead. I was willing to take the risk. I wanted to see the inside of the club for myself.

I'd never have another chance.

CHAPTER 11

I made up yet another excuse for my editor, saying I needed to go to San Francisco to talk to senior executives at one of Silicon Valley's tech companies about their role in the presidential election and plans to use tech to safeguard future elections from Russian hacking, and that it might take a couple of days. He authorized the trip without even asking what I was chasing.

There was some shred of truth in the excuse. Fedorisky was, in fact, on the board of one of the central actors in the 2016 presidential election drama. I intended to ask him about that when we met. I might even find a story somewhere in the conversation.

It had been awhile since I'd visited San Francisco. Unlike most of my colleagues, I didn't like the place that much. Half the journalists I worked with harbored secret fantasies of leaving their jobs, heading out west to found a hot digital media startup that would make them both famous and wealthy. Not me. I didn't particularly like the weather, which was always on the chilly side, and I knew no digital media venture would ever succeed in a meaningful way as long as Google and Facebook were sucking all the oxygen out of the advertising world. A few of my colleagues had tried their hand at such media ventures. Nearly all had ended ignominiously.

Still, it was a pleasant enough place to visit on occasion. The nice strip along Embarcadero had plenty of places to grab coffee or a drink. I booked a room at one of the hotels off that strip, which gave me easy access to Market Street and downtown.

Fedorisky kept an office in San Francisco, not farther south in Palo Alto off Sand Hill Road or in and around the Googleplex like so many other investors in the area. Most of the successful tech companies had big office footprints in San Francisco, which is why there was such a massive affordable housing crunch in the city. The vast majority of workers had to commute from more affordable places across the bay in order to work in the city.

My cross-country flight landed at midday at San Francisco International Airport, when rush hour was allegedly over. But rush hour is never truly over in San Francisco. I didn't feel like risking the hideous traffic on U.S. 101, so I took the BART train into the city. BART may be ridiculously slow, but at least it's consistent. It drops you off anywhere you need to go along Market Street.

Three different people hit me up for money as I exited the BART station. The large homeless population was one of the least endearing qualities of the city. I hardly acknowledged their requests as I made my way above ground to the street and the short walk to Fedorisky's office. I was capable of ignoring beggars in Washington or San Francisco, but I did notice the beggars here were particularly aggressive. They didn't take "no" all that easily. Perhaps it was because the police didn't harass them here as much as they did in other cities.

I'd decided to see Fedorisky first and check into the hotel later. That meant I had to lug my backpack with me, but I didn't care. I never paid much attention to my appearance. Today was no different. Fedorisky knew who I was, and where I worked. What I couldn't tell, until I was in the room with him, was what he might think of my new sideline career in investment.

It was laughable. I had no legitimate reason to go to this meeting. I was an investigative reporter. I asked important people difficult questions for a living and sometimes wrote about their answers. I wasn't one of the important people on the other end of those questions.

Yet, here I was, walking along Market Street in the middle of a sunny day in downtown San Francisco to meet with one of the most well-known early supporters of what were now the biggest, most profitable companies in the history of the world. And I wasn't here to interview him. I was here to talk to him about an investment in a company that most of the world had not yet heard about. It was all so...very odd.

Fedorisky's office was on the third floor of one of the office buildings at a pier along Embarcadero. I showed my driver's license at the front desk and waited for several minutes in the lobby for one of his assistants to fetch me and escort me upstairs. But Fedorisky came to get me himself.

"Seth Thomas!" he called out loudly from the stairwell as he made his way into the lobby and across the open area with long, purposeful strides.

I stood to greet him and shook his hand firmly. "Mr. Fedorisky, thanks for agreeing to see me on such short notice."

"It's Ivan. And of course I'm going to make time for you. We're going to be partners, you and I." He still had a thick Russian accent, though he'd been in the States for close to two decades. "Please, we'll talk." He directed me toward the stairwell. We walked up the two flights to his office at a brisk pace.

He ushered me into a conference room on the north side of the building. As I'd expected, we had a spectacular view of the Golden Gate Bridge and the bay. I moved over to the window and stared out at Alcatraz. It was so close from here that I felt as if I could see inside its walls.

"You know," I said, still staring out at the bay, "I've never been to Alcatraz."

"You should go. It's quite a place. Interesting. You can almost feel the ghosts of the characters forced to spend their days there."

"I know, but it takes up so much of your day to buy the tickets, wait in line, and then sail over to it on the ferry."

"It doesn't have to be like that." Fedorisky laughed. "Private tours are much easier."

"Yeah, if you have that sort of money to burn."

Fedorisky stared at me, clearly weighing something. Then he made the decision. I could see it in his narrowed eyes. With a slight nod, he turned and leaned out of the open door. "Maya," he called down the hall, "come here for a moment."

I could hear a chair scrape back from a desk. Heels clicked loudly and quickly. A young woman walked in and looked up at Fedorisky. "Sir?" she asked.

"The helicopter? It's on the roof?"

"It is, sir. Would you like to go somewhere?"

Fedorisky nodded. "I would. We're going to pay a visit to Alcatraz."

I watched in awe as his assistant managed to keep her composure. "Right now?"

"Yes, Maya. I assume you'll take care of the details so we may land and pay a visit."

"Yes, sir, I'll take care of it," she said evenly.

"Radio me the details when we're in the air."

Maya nodded, then glanced over at me. "You are Seth Thomas, yes?"

"Yes, that's me."

"Very well," she said, turned, and left the room as briskly as she'd entered it.

Fedorisky turned back to me. "So? You will see Alcatraz today."

"You're serious?"

"Quite serious."

"But...how, exactly?"

Fedorisky chuckled. "All things are possible when you have... what was the phrase you used...*money to burn.*"

Reaching behind the door, he grabbed two windbreakers from a hook and tossed one in my direction. I caught it before it fell to the floor. "You might want to put it on. It can get windy on Alcatraz." He turned and left the conference room. I followed.

I could hear Maya talking to someone on the phone in an insistent monotone as we made our way down the hallway to the stairwell. I had no idea how you could arrange such a private visit at the last minute.

Fedorisky took the stairs two at a time. I hurried to keep pace. He burst through the door to the rooftop and strode across it to a small, two-seat helicopter on a helipad. Opening the door on the left, he gestured for me to sit in the passenger side. I buckled in.

Fedorisky had us up in the air in less than a minute. I didn't ask how he knew to pilot it. He took one long arc toward the ocean, pulling up high as we neared the Golden Gate Bridge so I could get a good view from above. Then he made his way back across the water toward Alcatraz.

As we approached, he called his assistant on his cell phone. "All set?" He listened intently for her answer, nodded once, and then hung up.

"We're good?"

"All good," Fedorisky said with a broad smile.

"How in the world did your assistant manage this?"

"Maya is quite good at her job." Fedorisky glanced down at Alcatraz. Someone in an orange jumpsuit sprinted out onto the empty parking lot at what had once been one of the most notorious supermax prisons in America. With two lights in either hand, he guided us down onto the parking lot. We landed an instant later.

"I know they have helicopter tours of this place for the public. But do they let helicopters land like this on Alcatraz?" I asked as he killed the engine.

"Not as a rule, no." Fedorisky smiled. "But I'm on several of the mayor's various boards. I donate quite a lot to the city. It means we are granted certain...allowances."

I shook my head as we stepped down from the helicopter. Fedorisky had clearly wanted to make a point, for my benefit. He'd made it. I was impressed.

The man in the orange jumpsuit gestured to follow him toward a long path that led to the famous prison. The guard's tower, on the other side of the island, looked out over the prison complex.

"I assume you'd like to see where they kept Al Capone?" Fedorisky asked.

I shrugged. "Sure, why not?"

I generally knew Capone's story. One of the first imprisoned in Alcatraz, he'd been sent there from a federal penitentiary in Atlanta, where he'd run the place even as a prisoner. But he hadn't been able to crack Alcatraz.

We made our way up to the second floor, stopping outside the cell where Capone had been locked up for nearly five years before they transferred him to a medical prison in southern California to deal with his syphilis. The cell was non-descript. Clearly, despite his notoriety, "Public Enemy Number One" had been just another prisoner here. He'd played in a prison band. He wrote letters to his son. He played games in the yard with the other prisoners.

It was hard to separate myths from facts when it came to Al Capone. He'd lived in a different era in America, when gangsters could run cops and City Hall with impunity. It was more difficult for organized crime to run politicians now. Not impossible, but considerably harder and more intricate. The days where you could buy half the police force and keep running prostitutes, gambling, and drugs in the streets in the open were gone.

As I stared at the small cell where Capone had spent most of his last days on Earth, I wondered how he'd fare in today's world. Most likely, he'd have succeeded as he had in his day. Ruthlessness has a way of finding its way in the world, no matter the obstacles. And Al Capone had been ruthless…not unlike the folks atop the syndicate represented by the man standing beside me.

"It's something, isn't it?" Fedorisky said. "The guy was responsible for hundreds of murders, the St. Valentine's Day massacre. He ran circles around City Hall in Chicago. The White House ordered the FBI to lock the guy up. And it was his taxes that got him in the end."

I looked at Fedorisky. It was just the two of us standing here, together, outside Al Capone's cell. The guy in the orange jumpsuit had led us in, showed us the way to Capone's cell, and disappeared. We were alone in the heart of Alcatraz.

"So, you're making a point with all of this?" I asked.

"Am I?"

"Yeah, you are," I answered. "I get it. You have money to burn, and you also can make things happen. Like this."

"Precisely," he said, nodding.

"Why me?" I asked, genuinely curious. "Why try to impress me? You can find anyone in the world to invest in your Series A round. You don't need the money I can bring to the table. I'm sure you could make all kinds of folks fabulously wealthy with a significant stake in a company that's about to strike gold…people who might be interesting partners. I mean, just look at Google's Series A investors. You want that list. Not me."

Fedorisky tilted his head. "But I want you specifically. I'd like *you* to invest. No one else."

I shook my head. "But, really, I'm serious. Why me?"

"Because you are…a curiosity. I don't understand the game you're playing. My colleagues don't understand it, either. We've tried, but we can't. You have immense authority from somewhere. That much is obvious. And I…we…would like to partner with you in this."

I recalled the conversation I'd had with Jasper in Iceland, about the others he'd spoken to. I remembered Silas' warning. I thought about Russia's intense interest in the Panama Papers, and who had exposed them. "Have you approached others like me in the past?"

Fedorisky smiled. "I have. It didn't progress as I'd expected. In the end, they weren't suitable partners."

"They didn't invest with you?"

"They chose to take early retirement from the game. We never got a chance to know each other."

I stared at Fedorisky. I'd interviewed some of the best liars and con artists in the world. But I didn't think he was lying. Rather, he was genuinely trying to understand who was staking me. If true, that meant his network in Russia was wondering about me and the checkbook I was carrying. It was perplexing, and not at all what I'd been expecting.

"You'd really like me to invest in your Series A?" I asked.

He nodded once. "I would. Very much."

"And the company?"

"Is about to take off like a rocket. It will be worth quite a lot in a short time."

"And you're fine with me as your partner in this, even though..."

"Yes. There will be time to find out more. For now, your investment is enough. It is all we require. And, trust me, it will be more than worth your time."

I glanced back at Al Capone's cell, letting Fedorisky's words sink in. I closed my eyes and imagined what it must have been like for the most notorious gangster in America's history to find himself locked up here in such a small place. Now I was standing *outside* that cell with someone whose network had clearly learned from Capone's history.

The parallels were obvious. But I didn't care. I'd already made my decision. I was in. The only question left was how far.

"I'll have Dotty talk to Maya," I said. "We'll arrange for the wire transfer. We can talk stock options and details later. But we're in. We'll join your Series A."

CHAPTER 12

Crossing the line had been far easier to rationalize than I'd imagined. I wrestled with it for the better part of the day after leaving Fedorisky. I tried to game it out to several obvious ends. Tried to see the flaws, the weaknesses, and the places I was vulnerable.

Finally, I gave up. The truth was, I had no idea what I was involved in. But I wasn't breaking any laws. I wasn't bribing officials. I wasn't laundering money. There was no law against someone setting up an investment fund to manage money for someone else. I wasn't qualified, but if someone, somewhere, wanted me to invest their money, well, that was their own damn business.

As long as I set up the investment fund properly, I would be on safe ground legally. I'd given Dotty instructions about how to do precisely that, but she'd been way out in front of me. She already had two D.C. law firms on retainer. She'd hired three outside financial investment consultants to serve as an advisory board. All had outstanding résumés; they were experts. She'd also hired an accounting firm with a very long track record. They would become involved the moment SCTE made its first investment with Fedorisky.

The only part still bothering me was the rapidly disappearing fiction that I was pursuing an investigative story for the paper. Yes, I was doing so. But with each passing minute, my role as dispassionate observer faded quickly. I was entering the story as an active participant.

But the "Why me?" question continued to haunt me. I'd been dangling my legs over the edge of the abyss as a journalist for years. I'd lost my will to expose corruption. Doing so didn't change a damn thing. What was once a noble profession had become a hated universe of carnival barkers at one end and embittered hacks at the other. Though I'd never aspired to be anything other than an investigative journalist, I'd learned that, at some point, the system grinds you into despair.

A previous occupant of the Oval Office at the White House was proof that almost nothing the media reported changed anything. The American people had elected a con artist and congenital liar patently unfit for office. Yet even when journalists like me had thrown everything but the kitchen sink at him, he doubled down on every lie, and the populist ranks of his party supported him. I doubted anything would change that equation.

I also believed he was the beginning of what would be much worse to come in national politics. Once the Fourth Estate was removed, replaced by much more effective propaganda machines that took full advantage of the massive technology platforms available for mass information campaigns, truth would matter very little. Journalists like me would be irrelevant.

That's why crossing over the line from observer to participant had been such a small step. I had no family or close friends to ask about it. My utility as truth-teller had disappeared a long time ago. Might as well try the game itself, I figured.

So I took the step.

Once I was on the other side, a curious thing happened: in what was a complete shock, I felt liberated. Here, in the game, there were different rules. I didn't understand them, but I was unexpectedly intent on understanding and mastering them.

I'd have to resign at the paper at some point, perhaps soon. But I could maintain the fiction for at least a while longer, even as I started to embrace the new rules as swiftly as I could manage. I also needed to track down one of the people Jasper had met.

For the first time in a very long time, I was looking forward to what might happen tomorrow. It was a feeling I'd pushed far into the recesses of my mind.

But I liked it—a lot, in fact.

***

When I'd met with Jasper in Reykjavik, he'd said that three others before me had asked about many of the same things I was pursuing. The financial analyst had not only lied about her actual employer but vanished without a trace. The lawyer had never followed up after her initial email. The other person was a federal agent I'd assumed was FBI. But when I called Jasper to follow up, he said that, no, the guy had been a civil servant in the Treasury Department.

He wasn't any civil servant, I knew. He was one of the key members of a task force assembled inside FinCEN—the acronym for the Treasury's vaunted Financial Crimes Enforcement Network—to explicitly look at Russian oligarch connections. Virtually no one in the public knew what it was, or what it did. But it was an extraordinary arm of the U.S. government, with unlimited access to the national security monitoring network to track money-laundering activities.

FinCEN had cracked Silk Road wide open and was largely responsible for freezing billions of dollars tied to Iran's nuclear regime. In all probability, it was somewhat responsible for the Panama Papers leak to an international consortium of investigative journalists.

When the FBI special counsel indicted a dozen Russian intelligence agents for trying to hack into the Democratic Party and change the course of the 2016 presidential election, FinCEN had done most of the heavy lifting about how the money moved, where it went, and how it was spent.

FinCEN worked closely with the IRS as well. This collaboration was one of the reasons Americans had such a difficult job laundering or concealing vast amounts of illegal money. Al Capone would have had his hands full with FinCEN and the IRS. They could even track cash these days. Criminals laundered money through cryptocurrencies, but FinCEN had its arms around even that underground network.

One of the few areas that regularly thwarted FinCEN and the IRS were massively complicated LLC networks that handled real-estate developments—especially real-estate developments all around the globe—and other businesses that used cash and investments for future activities and speculation. Both also had an exceedingly difficult time keeping track of the ways in which the world's largest companies parked cash reserves and profits in offshore accounts to avoid paying U.S. taxes.

The 2017 corporate tax cut had encouraged companies to bring their money back into the United States, but they continued to hedge their bets with a byzantine accounting approach that masked much of their finances. The largest corporations in America used the most complicated accounting systems known to man and made certain FinCEN and the IRS had to devote significant resources if they chose to unravel their business.

Despite the changes in the U.S. tax code, many of the largest American multi-national corporations still kept their headquarters in Dublin, Ireland, and forced both FinCEN and the IRS to jump through hoops to track what they actually owed.

The name of the federal agent at FinCEN, John Andrews, wasn't widely quoted in official papers or agency releases, but it hadn't taken me long to track down the work he'd done for FinCEN. They'd set up a task force in the wake of the Panama Papers release. It was a smart move to deflect suspicion that FinCEN was responsible for a leak that had thoroughly embarrassed and angered Russian political leaders who had circulated so much money outside of Russia. But it also provided the department an excuse to create a public road map for the various places the Russian oligarchs had parked money at the behest of the Russian president and his inner circle.

Andrews, an African-American who had grown up in a large family in one of the poorest neighborhoods in downtown Baltimore, was the first in his family to go to college. He'd attended the University of Maryland on a full academic scholarship. His first job out of college was with the Treasury Department. He'd risen to the highest ranks of the civil service at FinCEN and been a GS 15, Step 10, civil servant.

Strangely, though, he'd never managed to make it into the Senior Executive Service, an exclusive club of roughly 5,000 or so career government officials who ran the U.S. government just below the political appointees who came and went with each new presidential administration.

It was hard to tell from a distance why Andrews had never made SES. Perhaps he liked his job as a federal investigator too much to get embroiled in the bureaucratic fights that consumed most of the SES corps. Perhaps, like me, he'd never had any interest in climbing the ranks to land in a management position, even though it paid more. Or, perhaps, he was such a dogged, relentless investigator that his superiors kept him in place.

I'd heard that very logic from my editors over the years. I was too good an investigative journalist to become an editor. There was some truth to it, but it still grated when I heard it from editors who were paid a lot more than me and coasted off my work.

Until I tracked Andrews down, though, I couldn't truly know what had kept him in place at FinCEN or why he'd chosen to leave the department. His handiwork was obvious on numerous Treasury investigations. He'd been on every major inter-agency task force that looked at foreign government efforts to launder money around the globe through companies and consortiums with American interests. There had been several spin-off reports from the Panama Papers. I was certain Andrews had been the lead investigator.

After several days of research, I located him. It came as a shock that he'd moved to St. Barts two years after retiring. With only a few phone calls to my Treasury sources, I found out Andrews had taken early retirement from the civil service, which afforded a certain level of benefits. But they were by no means enough to pay for living on St. Barts.

Saint Barthélemy had once been a sleepy French colony in the Caribbean. But as it became a wealthy tourist attraction, France began to take an interest…until St. Barts took its destiny in its hands and became independent. Residents don't pay income tax. It's a tiny island. Only about 10,000 people live on it.

But they aren't just any 10,000 people. Rock stars, billionaires, CEOs, and movie stars have second homes on St. Barts. It might cost $5 million for a modest villa on the stunning beaches and coastline, but it's well worth it. The locals don't hassle any of the celebrities. There are no high-rise hotels or casinos. You can't fly direct to St. Barts. You have to stop in St. Maarten and take a twin-engine flight to the small airport on the island.

I had no idea how Andrews could afford a villa on St. Barts on his civil service salary and early retirement benefits. But I had an inkling of what he must have been up to during the two years before he moved there.

I booked a flight to St. Maarten, then a commuter flight from there to St. Barts, plus the cheapest room rental I could find, as well as a car. I decided to pay for it myself, rather than try to convince my editor that I somehow needed to go. The trip would set me back a couple of thousand dollars, but I needed answers. Andrews was the quickest, cheapest route.

Dotty tried to convince me to put it on the credit card account that her Chase contact wanted to establish for SCT Enterprises, but I wasn't ready. Though I'd committed to the Series A investment with Fedorisky, we didn't have any income coming in. I didn't want to start running up debt from the start. I wasn't prepared to bet on an uncertain financial future.

So I paid for the trip from my meager checking account and left on a Friday. I planned to be back at work on Monday, after I'd talked to Andrews in person. I had no idea how I'd make contact once I was there, but I wasn't worried. It was a small place, and I was sure I'd find a way to see him. If all else failed, I'd go knock on his front door.

The moment I set foot outside the plane, I noticed that, while the locals speak French, nearly everyone on the island also speaks English. I was taken aback by Gustaff airport. No lines. No questions about why I was visiting the island. It wasn't difficult to find my rental car, either. In less than an hour after landing, I'd arrived at the villa where I'd booked a room. Along the way, I'd noticed no gated communities, which meant no one worried about crime on the island.

Because I'd converted my dollars to Euros in the U.S., I intended to grab a quick dinner first and then drive to eyeball the villa Andrews had bought on the "wild" coast of St. Barts—the remote, idyllic section known as "La Cote Sauvage." But after chatting up the location with the hotel concierge to make sure I could find it by car, she convinced me to simply drive there and eat at the restaurant of Le Toiny, the five-star luxury hotel nearby. Dining there was something every traveler should experience even if you couldn't afford a room, she said. The meal might set me back 100 Euros, but it was well worth it. She made a reservation for me.

Like so much of St. Barts, the hotel had been severely damaged by Hurricane Irma in 2017. But after more than a year of rebuilding, it was gleaming and bright again. As I drove along the coastline, I looked closely at the immaculate white beaches but couldn't find any hint of the hurricane's devastation. Unlike Puerto Rico, a physical wreck years after the hurricane had hit, St. Barts had returned to its spectacular tourist glory.

Le Toiny's suites looked out over the Bay of Toiny and the blue Caribbean Sea. With the sun setting, the water surrounding the hotel sparkled like a thousand diamonds. The scene was remote, calm, and spectacularly beautiful. I couldn't help but wonder what it must be like to live here in this corner of the world. It seemed genuinely like paradise.

I parked the rental near the front entrance and made my way inside. As I was about to ask for directions to the restaurant, an older black gentleman sitting in a chair to one side of the lobby rose and walked toward me. He was dressed casually, with loose-fitting slacks and a short-sleeved linen shirt that hung on his frame perfectly. Gliding across the floor, he extended a hand.

"Mr. Thomas?" he asked.

I smiled and shook his hand once, firmly. "Mr. Andrews, I presume?"

CHAPTER 13

"You obviously knew I was coming here," I said after we were seated at a private table at one end of a magnificent deck. The view overlooked a tranquil pool spilling downhill and into the nearby bay. It was early evening, and only a few other patrons were in the restaurant. "But how? I hadn't told anyone I was coming. Not even my editors."

Andrews lifted the corners of his mouth into a practiced smile. "There's no magic to it. It's a small island. I've been waiting for someone to show up. I have a standing request with the concierge at every hotel to let me know if anyone asks about me."

"Really? You were expecting me?"

"Not you, per se. But someone like you who wants to ask how I might have arrived on this island with enough wealth to live here so comfortably."

I sat back in my chair. "OK, I'll bite. So how *did* you arrive here?"

"Happy to oblige… in due time. But first, would you mind telling me who you are, exactly, and why you're here? Beyond the obvious—that you're an investigative journalist from Washington. That much I know already."

I gave him the backstory from my perspective as a journalist trying to understand a story I was in the middle of reporting. I told him I'd visited Jasper Olafsson in Reykjavik, who'd shared a bit about him, and that I was trying to understand who'd been behind the financial shenanigans with Iceland's banks.

"You're not buying any of this, are you?" I asked after finishing my little monologue.

"Oh, I'm quite sure the parts about you asking questions as a journalist are real," he replied. "But you didn't come all this way to ask about the work I did at FinCEN, did you?"

I studied him for several seconds. "No, I didn't."

"Why don't you tell me why you're really here, and perhaps I can help get our real conversation started." He paused. "They found you, too...right? You've stumbled across something you don't quite understand."

"Yes, *someone* found me. And you're right. I have no idea what to make of it, or what it means. I have no idea who 'they' might be. None at all. That's why I came here. I'm hoping you know more about this than I do. Did they send you a mysterious text? It's how they pulled me in."

"Not a text," he said. "A computer-generated voice on my office phone from Wayne Construction...a company fairly well known in the area I'd investigated several years back as part of the BCCI investigation. It told me to visit a bank teller, who gave me a key to a box."

"Where was the bank?"

"In a rural town west of Washington—Hamilton, Virginia, in Loudoun County. There was only one bank teller in the building when I got there. I showed him my driver's license, and he didn't ask any questions. Simply handed me the key and left me alone in the back with the box. The box was in my name. I have no idea how they pulled that off."

I leaned forward. "And the box—what was in it?"

"An address to a local office building two blocks down the street."

"Let me guess. The office was empty when you arrived, except for a receptionist who'd just been hired?"

He nodded. "To work for me, yes."

"And that local construction firm...?"

"Never sent the message. Clueless, and baffled about why I called them."

"You eventually found the checkbook?"

"I did."

"Was it connected to an account of some sort at Chase Bank?"

Andrews smiled. "Ah, *there's* a slight difference. My account was with Bank of America, the second largest bank in the U.S. You got Chase, which is the largest. Which means..."

"That they—whoever *they* are—have the ability to set things in motion through the biggest banking institutions in the world."

"Yes, and without a trace. I spent weeks, then months, trying to pin down exactly who had created an account for me at Bank of America."

"And did you get anywhere with it? Any idea who…"

"Not a clue. I never got close."

"But did you act on anything?" I asked.

"Not right away. I was careful. I let the receptionist go that first day. I wanted no part of it."

"Yet you kept asking questions?"

"I did, and they went in lots of different directions."

"And the office in that small town?" I pressed.

"At first, I'd visit it once or twice a month. The electricity bill had been paid a full year in advance. The lights were on. I could have worked out of that office if I'd chosen to."

"But you didn't?"

"Not in the beginning. I bought a separate laptop to keep track of my searches and queries. I used a personal cell phone to make calls. I tried to limit my digital footprint as much as possible."

"What do you mean…*not in the beginning?*"

Andrews hesitated. "I spent the better part of my last two years at FinCEN trying to understand what that bank key meant. I never got a satisfactory answer. I probed as much as I could, short of an actual investigation, to see if the Bank of America account was illegal but was eventually satisfied with its legitimacy. The source was protected, part of an anonymous donor-advised fund. But it wasn't laundered or the subject of any inquiry anywhere, ever, from any branch of the U.S. government. It was real, and somehow I could use it for my own purposes. So I retired from FinCEN and got started."

"Just like that? It's quite a leap of faith."

Andrews sighed. "I'd reached early retirement age by then, so it wasn't as big a leap as you might think. But, remember, I'd done a *massive* amount of legwork before I made that leap. I'd tried to discredit the source with every type of investigation I could conceive. I'd followed every trail. Before I left, I tested my thesis and asked several firms if they could accept investments from it. After talking to the Bank of America, they all said they could."

"So, you started investing after you retired from the government?"

Andrews nodded. "I started slowly at first. I always expected the investment fund would dry up at some point."

"But it didn't?"

"No. I made a dozen investments within the first three months of my retirement. Two of them hit quickly, in a really big way. Not on the scale of the investors in Google's Series A round, where they turned $2 million into $200 million. But it was big, and I owned 15 percent of the profit in stock in both after exiting."

"That was your fee? Fifteen percent from the net profit?"

"Yeah," Andrews said. "I thought about being conservative and charging a two-percent fee in cash to manage it each year as well as profit-carry. But, in the end, I went for an all-stock fee at 15 percent net and held my breath. The Bank of America didn't blink. Whoever was fronting the money didn't balk at the back-end, maybe because it's lower than a typical profit-carry for, say, a VC or a hedge fund."

"But they could have?"

"Sure. Every traditional investor would balk at that sort of arrangement. But this was so unusual from the start that I decided, oh hell, why not? Agents charge 10 or 15 percent for managing careers. Why not charge 15 percent in stock from net profit that only worked if the plan worked?"

"That was a big roll of the dice."

"Yes. But once I'd made the decision and it held, I kept moving forward...until I hit the wall."

"What happened?"

"I thought I was being smart," Andrews said, regret obvious on his face. "I pivoted and took profits from those two and found others to invest in that weren't quite as risky but held promise. Some of those paid off, too. I owned a lot of valuable stock only two years after retiring. So did the originator of the fund with Bank of America. They own some pretty valuable stock now."

"Which is what you imagine this is all about—a highly unusual but perfectly legal investment scheme?"

Andrews shrugged. "There are crazier ways to invest money, but, sure, yes. That's what I finally assumed. But honestly, I never got close to an answer on that question, no matter how much I tried. And I tried a *lot*."

"Do you know how much money was in the account when you got started?"

"At the time, I had no idea. The Bank of America would never tell me. They said, rather obliquely, that there was enough to make investments in ventures I brought to them."

I gave him a curious look. "Didn't you find that odd?"

"Of course. It was exceedingly odd and beyond strange. No one does that. You'd have to have an awful lot of money to set up an investment fund with a seemingly bottomless well. There aren't many people on this planet with access to that sort of wealth. A few hundred, maybe."

"The Russians do," I said quietly. "The Saudis. Others in the Middle East. And any number of billionaires in America. Any ideas on the source of funds?"

"I assumed it was an eccentric billionaire who thought it might be a fun diversion to let someone other than a traditional investment firm try to line up ventures to pursue."

"Like the two percent extraordinarily high-risk funds that university and pension funds set aside for investments that really pay off if they hit?" I asked.

"Something like that. Quirky, different, off the beaten path. I've seen some bizarre investments made by billionaires who have way too much money in their accounts. I know one billionaire from a Middle Eastern company who spent $150 million of his inherited wealth on a dying media property that tanked within a year after the purchase. He bought it because he'd loved the brand when he was a kid. He remained a billionaire after throwing all that money away."

"Yeah, when people have money to burn, they do some strange things," I agreed. "A billionaire I knew gave the Smithsonian a $5 million gift because he wanted them to smuggle in a big, endangered animal he'd killed in Africa for a trophy. So, you figured this fund was from someone who'd grown bored with traditional investment opportunities? Their idea of a unique, high-risk effort?"

"That's what I assumed. But I never got a chance to prove it."

"Why?"

"Because it ended after two years," he said wistfully. "I made a mistake. And when I did, that was it. The experiment—whatever it was—ended."

I leaned back in my chair. "What'd you do—buy a private jet or something?"

Andrews laughed. "I wish, though I'll bet others who've been approached *did* do something like that and got themselves kicked out of the club." He sobered. "After my first two rounds, I thought it would be prudent to take a good chunk of the profits and buy blue chip stocks with a consistent track record of paying dividends."

"That's a smart strategy. Lots of investment firms do precisely that for their clients. It's an easy way to lock in guaranteed, ongoing profits."

"Yeah, well, it isn't what *this* client—whoever he, she, or they are—wanted. The next time I went to make an investment, after shifting almost $200 million in stock out of the portfolio into traditional, well-recognized blue-chip stocks with an established track record of paying regular dividends, my contact at Bank of America said the fund had been closed."

"Just like that?"

He nodded. "Poof, it was gone. Moved somewhere else."

"But you were able to keep the money you'd made…the profit from the stock you'd accumulated from two years of investments?"

"Yes, I was able to keep the stock attached to the $200 million I'd moved over to the blue-chips. I was free to keep it. There just wasn't any more coming."

I whistled. "That's still a nice chunk of change."

"I'm not complaining. I'm sitting on a nest egg that throws off a few million dollars a year, and will for the rest of my life. Not bad for a kid who grew up poor as a church mouse in Baltimore."

I looked out at the tranquil bay of Toiny. "Which explains how you're able to afford a villa here on St. Barts."

"Precisely. It's an awfully nice place to sit on a pile of money. All legal and above board. Just a large retirement account. I can afford to pay cash for a small yacht, sail out to other parts of the

Caribbean whenever I like. No need to do anything ever again if I don't feel like it. But…"

I noted his wan smile. "But you feel like you missed a much bigger opportunity? You didn't realize you'd made a mistake … until you'd made it?"

"Yeah, I'd be lying if I said I didn't have any regrets. I thought I was being so smart, so thorough. I thought I had it figured out— what the true nature of the game was. But I missed the plot entirely."

"It was the blue-chip stocks?"

"I assume so, since the instant I made a conservative, calculated decision, it was over. The opportunity vanished."

"How long do you think it might have lasted if you'd been able to figure out the rules of the game?" I asked.

"Who knows? Years maybe?" He sighed. "Someone gave me a gift, but I feel that, somehow, I squandered it without knowing how or why."

I swept a hand across the white beach, tranquil water, and the interior of the five-star restaurant. "Still, you landed here, with all this. Quite a consolation prize, don't you think?"

"I'm content. I find things to do. But I do grow weary and bored at times. I also wish…"

"That you were still in the game?"

"Yes. I liked the hunt. Liked not knowing what might happen next. I miss it. I'm not sure what to do now. Even though it's too late, I wake sometimes in the night, still wondering who was behind my good fortune. But I guess I'll never know."

I smiled. "Perhaps I can tell you some day."

CHAPTER 14

As strange as it sounds, I could see how John Andrews might grow bored with his life. It was idyllic. Perfect in nearly every way. He had everything you could ever want—a villa on a small, remote island in the Caribbean; enough money to travel anywhere in the world that might strike his fancy; and no financial worries for the rest of his life. But there would be no more grand adventures for him—not like the one he'd briefly experienced. And, for all its beauty, the island was small.

After spending Saturday sitting in my own villa and taking long walks on the pristine beaches, I was more than ready to head back home. On Sunday morning, before heading to the airport, I had nothing better to do than drive around the perimeter of the island in my rental car. It was the same image everywhere I turned—an endless, sparkling, blue expanse as far as the eye could see. I was bored to tears. I longed to walk down the street for a casual meal at a fast-food restaurant or stroll the clean, crisp aisles of a modern supermarket.

I know that sounds crazy. It *is* crazy. But I like chaos, conflict, mystery, and confusion. I have no interest in spending the rest of my days trapped on a tiny luxury island resort. After less than three days, I was ready to bolt. I couldn't imagine what it would be like to live here year-round with no purpose beyond a walk along the beach in the evening. I was glad to head to the airport...so eager, in fact, that I almost missed my shadow.

He looked like every other local—or regular visitor—on the island. He had the casual pants, the free-flowing linen-shirt that rolled up at the sleeves, and the nice sandals that seemed like a custom fit. He was wearing a strange, floppy hat when I first noticed him at the rental car facility. He was still wearing it when I spotted him the second and then the third time in the airport lines. What gave him away, though, was wearing dark sunglasses indoors all three times I spotted him.

After the third time, I stared at him directly from where I sat, at the back of the lounge, while waiting for the small twin-propeller plane to arrive from St. Maarten. A few minutes later, he looked away, stood, then walked toward another part of the airport.

I followed him. He paused at another lounge and took a seat. I took a seat two rows away and stared at him again. After a few more minutes, he got up again and walked away.

I'm not sure what I was thinking. It wasn't the brightest idea to expose a tail, but I wasn't about to be cowed by someone who was clearly following me. Most likely, he'd followed me to St. Barts, and I'd been too wrapped up in my pursuit of John Andrews to notice. I had no idea who he might be, or why he was following me, but there were some obvious possibilities.

At the top of my list was the GRU from Russia. I now believed Ivan Fedorisky had told me the truth—that he wanted to partner with me, essentially because his colleagues were desperate to know the source of the funds I was investing. If he and the Russian oligarchs he represented truly had no idea who was behind the game I was playing—and if they were unable to find a digital paper trail—it made sense to track my movements after agreeing to the investment.

But it also could be someone from inside America's intelligence community. Andrews had told me that, once he retired, he decided the safest, easiest thing was to be transparent. He didn't conceal he was investing money, but he didn't go out of his way to advertise it, either. That meant the intelligence community was likely tracking whatever this game might be.

There was a third possibility—my tail was connected to the source of my funds, who wanted to keep physical tabs on where I went and what I might be up to—but I swiftly dismissed that idea. Nothing I'd seen to date indicated that the person who'd set me up at Jackson Place had any interest in giving himself or herself away like this.

In the end, I decided not to confront my shadow. Most likely, he'd been told to follow me and report back. There was little chance he knew anything. Exposing him would gain nothing and might cause me more trouble than it was worth. So I ended my little charade, walked back to the lounge, and waited for the plane to arrive.

I did note, with some satisfaction, that he didn't board the aircraft with me. That meant he was handing me off to someone else, most likely in St. Maarten. In that case, he was probably GRU.

I studied the passengers on the flight from St. Barts to St. Maarten. No one stood out or paid much attention to me, though the best tails didn't give themselves away easily. But if the guy in St. Barts had been part of a team that was only supposed to track my movements, there was no need to put someone on the plane with me. I wasn't going to parachute over the ocean.

As I exited the plane, I kept careful track of those waiting in the boarding area and those who might be hanging around without any intention of making the return trip to St. Barts. A young Caucasian woman in a mid-length floral dress and sun hat, casually browsing at a kiosk a few yards from the boarding area, stared at the disembarking passengers until she spotted me in line. Then she looked away swiftly.

This time I didn't draw attention to myself. I glanced at this new tail simply to make sure she was following me as I went to my connecting gate. She was.

As we walked along, I narrowed the choices. If she boarded the flight back to the U.S., she was probably part of the U.S. intelligence community. The GRU didn't usually risk exposure, so didn't fly in and out of the U.S. unless absolutely necessary.

The young woman kept a respectful distance behind me. When I got to my gate, I stopped to grab a cup of coffee. The young woman ducked into another retail store and started browsing.

I took a seat in the boarding area where I could keep an eye on the boarding line and the retail store. She stayed in the store as I began to board, then made one quick movement to the entrance to ensure that I was, in fact, headed back to the mainland. Then she glided back inside the store.

So, she's GRU, I thought. The whole thing seemed comical, rather than nefarious, even if I knew enough about the ruthless oligarch network that surrounded Russia's president to genuinely fear what they could do to someone who got sideways with them.

But I was nowhere near sideways with them. They were courting me. At this point, they only wanted information and figured they might be able to pick it up by tracking my movements.

Fine. What they didn't realize was that I was as much in the dark as they were. But I had more than ample incentive to determine who was behind this.

I didn't want to be part of the Russian oligarch system. I didn't want to owe them now or in the future. It was one thing to invest in a legitimate company they also had a stake in. It was quite another to accept investment funds from them directly. I had no desire to make myself a target of the American intelligence community.

But, by meeting with Andrews, I could safely dismiss the probability that the investment money was tied up in some bizarre money-laundering scheme. The money was real, and it belonged to someone who wasn't triggering any tripwires. Andrews' only mistake, it seemed, was being too cautious with his investment strategy.

I now knew what my next move was. I sent a text to Dotty while on the plane. "Wire the money to Fedorisky. Make the investment."

It was time to enter the game. I wouldn't play it safe. I would play to win.

CHAPTER 15

I tried to quit. I really did.

When I walked into the managing editor's office to tell him I would take the buyout on the newsroom table—the fifth or sixth offered by the company—he stared at me. Then he leaned forward, smiling. "I wondered how long it would take you to arrive at this and come to me."

I liked Jacob Shapiro. He'd been in the job almost three years. He'd won a Pulitzer leading an aggressive investigative team at the *Boston Globe*. He was my sort of newspaperman—clear-eyed, no nonsense, not overly partisan, and committed to the core of what journalism was about. Report the facts, give them to the people, and let them decide. Don't skew the reporting of those facts to try to force them toward your predisposed conclusion. The facts had to stand on their own.

"I'm serious," I insisted. "I'm done. I can't take the grind anymore. The pay's lousy. This White House is nearly as bad as the previous one. It learned all of the wrong lessons. It has no shame. They lie without even thinking and play only to their propaganda media outlets that reinforce whatever nonsense they're peddling on any given day. Members of Congress get caught running insider-trading scams from the steps of the Capitol or the White House lawn. CEOs use Washington as a cesspool of inside deals that make them hundreds of millions of dollars. It's one big blur to the public. Nobody cares what we expose anymore."

"I care," he answered, folding his hands on his desk. "The other editors here care. So does every reporter in the newsroom. Everyone in this place knows why they're here, and why their jobs matter."

"So what?" I shot back. "The public doesn't give a damn. A third of the people who vote these fools into office have no clue what's real and what's not. They believe that black presidents are born in Africa and aren't American citizens. They believe that millions of illegal immigrants vote in American elections, or that everyone is coming for their guns in the dead of night. They're constantly hoodwinked into believing the dumbest conspiracy theories about false-flag mass shootings staged at elementary schools, or that politicians are running pedophilia sex trafficking rings out of pizza parlors. They believe that science facts like evolution or climate change are a hoax—that scientists are making it up. They'd believe the moon was made of Swiss cheese if their propaganda networks told them so. A third of the country has lost its ability to separate fact from fiction."

"Which makes our job here even more important," Shapiro said. "You know that. You've always known that."

"Yeah, well, maybe I'm *really tired* of trying so hard to give people facts about things they no longer want to hear about. If they don't care, why should I?"

Shapiro laughed. "It's a fair question. But you know there are plenty who *do* care about what we report on. Democracy is founded…"

"Oh, please. I don't need the democracy lecture. I've heard you give it several times. It's a great talk. But democracy has been co-opted by those with an awful lot of money. The muckrakers like me went out of style a long time ago. We put one set of corrupt billionaires out of business, and a new set takes their place. We break up one awful monopoly, or shut down one con artist CEO, and seven others take their place. Those with money own the rules and every corner of national politics, and there isn't much you or I can do about it."

He tilted his head. "You done ranting?"

"For now."

"Good. I wasn't going to give you the democracy lecture. You don't need it. I know you believe it. You may not think it's working all that well right now, but somewhere in that cold heart of yours is a genuine belief that what we do here is the last check on what corrupts a democracy. So, what would it take to keep you here, on the investigative team? I don't want to lose you."

He was serious. It wasn't about the budget in the newsroom. Yes, he could save money with younger reporters and editors who didn't cost as much as someone with decades of experience. But he couldn't afford to lose too many veterans in each wave of buyouts. He needed leaders in the newsroom, like me, who'd been through the wars. It wasn't only the institutional memory that walked out the door. It was the commitment to the absolute core of what made journalism an actual Fourth Estate and hedge against the corrupting forces of democracy.

But there weren't four estates anymore. There was one estate, managed by those with more concentrated wealth than at any time in human history. A club of considerably wealthy individuals who'd constructed an elaborate game with a unique set of rules only a few understood.

I had no desire to be a master of the universe. But some part of me wanted to test-drive it a bit. I wanted to see what the inside of that game looked like. Not because I wanted anything for myself, or because I wanted to write about it or expose it. I wanted to *know*.

"What would it take?" I asked, repeating Shapiro's question. "There's nothing that would keep me here. No reporting assignment that would make me think it was worth it. I don't want to be an editor. I don't want to take a sabbatical to write a book. I have zero interest in taking a year off in some high-minded fellowship. I want…to quit. Walk away. Go sit on a beach somewhere and drink cheap beer."

Shapiro studied me. "No, I don't think so. That's not you. I don't see beaches and beer in your future. You'd go crazy inside a week. Something else is pulling you out the door. You have a *reason* to quit, I'm guessing."

I almost told him but pulled back. "Not really. Certainly no other job, like an idiotic corporate PR flak job. If I wanted to stay in journalism, it would be here. That's not it. I'm just tired of it all. But you're right about the beaches. I really can't stand them."

"What would you do?"

"Who knows? I might try my hand at being entrepreneurial. But I need to get away and clear my head first."

Shapiro nodded. "Okay, I get it. But I'm gonna make you a deal. An offer I don't think you want to walk away from."

"Which is?"

"That you go off the daily reporting books for a few months. Pick an investigative project of your own choosing—anything. Whatever you want. No check-ins, either. You don't have to report back to me or anyone else. You can work from your miserable apartment for all I care. Keep your paycheck for a while, and your healthcare coverage. I'll give you a modest budget for occasional expenses. Then, at the end of those months, let's talk again about what you came up with."

"And if it's nothing? If I come back empty-handed?"

"Then it's nothing. You gave it your best shot, and it didn't pan out. That's all any of us can do."

I stared at my managing editor. "That's insane. There's no way your own bosses would approve an arrangement like that."

"I've already cleared it with the executive editor. Not that I really needed to. I have that authority over this newsroom. I can deploy folks as I see fit, and I choose to deploy you like that. I have faith in you. I believe you'll come across something no one else would ever have dreamed of pursuing. And then you'll tell the rest of us about it."

"You're serious about this?"

"As serious as I've ever been about anything. I meant what I said. I don't want to lose you. I wanted to know what it would take to keep you on the investigative team. I believe this might do it. For now at least."

"I have no idea what I'll be going after," I offered.

"I'm sure you'll figure something out. You always do."

"I can be a bit entrepreneurial while I'm wandering around in the wilderness on this thing? Like maybe start a business on the side for the hell of it? That wouldn't bother you?"

"Knock yourself out," he said. "Everyone is a bit entrepreneurial these days. No reason you shouldn't be as well. If there are entanglements, reporting on it is another matter. But we can cross that bridge later. Go hunting first."

"You really want me to do this?"

"I do. Don't quit on us, or what this place stands for. Go after something…and don't stop until you catch it."

94

Chapter 16

There are now about 2,700 people whose combined net worth exceeds $9 trillion. That's the number of billionaires—give or take a few dozen like Russia's president or a dictator here and there who have stashed billions off the books and aren't officially listed—who control most of the wealth in the world's financial system.

Bill Gates started something called the Giving Club a few years ago. He pledged to give away half his wealth and then talked 200 others into doing so as well. Gates was worth about $53 billion at the time. After making the pledge, his wealth kept growing. Five years or so after making headlines about how much he was going to give away, his personal wealth had doubled, to nearly $100 billion. So he could give away half his enormous wealth and still end up where he'd begun just a few years earlier.

Every billionaire's net worth grows like this. It's like breathing. Once you have a certain amount of money, almost everything you touch turns to gold. And there are hundreds of financial advisors at your beck and call to add to this wealth.

Nine trillion dollars is an awful lot of money. It takes hundreds and hundreds of billions of dollars just to make one trillion. And a few thousand people own all of it. They aren't only masters of the universe; they control nearly every aspect of the global economy. They can make or break entire industries if it strikes their fancy.

They aren't some vast global conspiracy, like the Illuminati. Each member of this unofficial club has his or her own peculiarities and distinct political, financial, and personal goals. They don't coordinate as a group. They didn't set out to take over the global economy—it just happened. And now the gulf between the very, very, very rich and everyone else on the planet is so wide that it's beyond fixing. Nobody in the club is going to give all their money away to everyone else on Earth.

They could rule the Earth collectively if they wanted. But they don't. They actually keep each other in check. You see it most readily in the American political system. One group of billionaires donates vast sums to the Republican Party. Another small group gives vast amounts to the Democrats. Each side draws up strategies and deploys the money across the board, trying to convince their side that their political philosophy is the best possible strategy to divide up the pie and govern.

There are growing exceptions to this rule. Russia is an obvious example. Russia's president, Alexi Simon, emerged from the bowels of the KGB system to take absolute political and financial control of the state. He fused wealth and power in a way that hasn't been seen since the days of the Roman Empire. Several dozen oligarchs have risen to the pinnacle with him.

China's premier, Zheng Li, has similarly consolidated power in that Communist state. He's now the country's ruler for life. He shares power with only five others, and they run the country with an iron fist more oppressive in its own way than Simon's rule in Russia. And, like Russia, there is a relatively small group of Chinese billionaires who straddle the financial world with the permission of Zheng and the five others who rule China. Westerners who wish to do business in China have no choice but to negotiate with this small ruling party.

But Russia and China are the exception. The vast majority of the Billionaires' Club live and work in parts of the world not under the thumb of oppressive dictators. They work in places where it's perfectly acceptable to let wealth accumulate unchecked. They cross borders with impunity in both their personal and professional capacity. They can live in New Zealand or Switzerland when they like; in the Maldives when it strikes their fancy. They can kill an endangered species in Africa mid-week and dine in Paris at a Michelin three-star restaurant a day later. They can ride the express train from the Upper West Side in New York to the financial district at the southern tip of Manhattan in relative obscurity, and then take a private jet from JFK to a theater opening in London the next day. They can sail from Mallorca, Spain, to the Greek Islands and hop from there to a casino in Macau.

There are no boundaries for the members of this club. They go wherever the action is and wherever money buys unlimited access. They spend billions on building out private tropical islands they can rule. They buy professional sports franchises to play around with or entertainment centers that pull in money from everyone else. In the past few years, some of the best-known club members appear to have given up on Earth. Now they focus their vast sums on settling colonies on Mars; building ecospheres in the reaches of space; or building submarines to go to the bottom of the ocean.

What they *aren't* doing is choosing to devote their wealth to solving basic problems that are easily solvable on the planet, such as making sure millions of children survive past the age of five, or receive a rudimentary public education, or have basic health care, or live in a sustainable, livable community that has clean air, clean water, and renewable energy. For a mere one percent of their net worth, the billionaires could *guarantee* every child has the basics to not only live but potentially be lifted out of poverty.

But they won't do it. Nearly all who make it to the Billionaires' Club do one thing: slam the door shut once they've made it inside. Nearly six million children under the age of five continue to die every year due to no access to a health clinic, no real ability to receive a $1 dose of an anti-malaria medicine that counters a mosquito bite, or some other tiny intervention those in countries like the United States take for granted. As the digital and technology era shifts trillions of dollars from the bottom of the pyramid to the very pinnacle of the super-rich, skilled workers who lose their jobs to robots and artificial intelligence will have nowhere to go.

The situation is bad enough in developed countries, but it's dire in undeveloped countries. Half the world's population now lives in countries that can't grow enough food to feed their native population. Water resources are a problem in dozens of countries. Climate impacts are disrupting natural resources in nearly every corner of the globe.

But the uber-wealthy turn a blind eye. Their corporate entities have refined the art of moving intellectual property and revenue into a dozen countries that serve as offshore tax havens. Only 200 in this club have joined Gates in his giving pledge. The other 2,500 have no interest in ending poverty or distributing their wealth. They simply pursue extravagant luxuries and sequester themselves from the masses.

Such realities made my decision easy. Playing to win in this game of emperors and kings meant making an absurd gamble. The spigot would certainly be shut off the instant I set my plan in motion, just as it had for John Andrews. But I didn't care. I had no desire to retire to St. Barts or to create a careful, strategic investment portfolio that made a million dollars here and there.

I'd thought about tracking down others, like Andrews, who'd been invited into the game. But now I knew what I'd find—people who had made a fatal mistake, either through greed or caution, and been cut off. Finding them would only confirm what I'd already learned. It would not get me closer to the center of the game.

Someone had invited me in. I could spend a lifetime testing the connections one by one to see where the roads might go. Or I could test all of them at once and see what road emerged.

There was only one way to get to the center of the maze. I had to join the club. I needed to become a billionaire as quickly as possible.

CHAPTER 17

"*All* of them?" Dotty asked, incredulous. "You know what that will cost, right?"

"Yes, but it'll be money well spent. It'll give us the road map we need for investing purposes. We have to find the exact, right play connected to those on the list."

We were sitting at a small table in my office at Jackson Place. While I'd been gone, Dotty had bought some tasteful pieces of furniture, a few replicas of famous paintings, a couch, and a large circular rug that took up most of the floor space.

Now she looked a bit stunned. She'd clearly been expecting me to come back with questions about the investment in Fedorisky's Series A round and to look at a handful of other potential investments. In fact, she already had the financial consultants we'd hired pull together discreet investment opportunities. Each one was in a folder, with background info. I'd let her go through each one, in order, before dropping my bombshell.

My idea was relatively simple—and also insane. But it was this or nothing. I was willing to take the risk. Fedorisky's opportunity had sparked the seeds of my plan. Dotty had already made the investment, and now we received confidential information from the company's leadership on a near-daily basis.

Fedorisky himself had called me twice, just to chat. Clearly he'd invited me inside his tent because he wanted to know more about my backer. Engaging with him in the business would tell me an awful lot about him and what he was in to. It had already allowed me to rule him out as the person who'd sent me the text. But investing had brought me into his orbit. I was convinced doing the same in other opportunities would likewise offer clues.

The trick was to make certain they were the right kinds of investments—ones that would attract the personal interest of those, like Fedorisky, at the top of the pyramid. It wasn't about the money that might be made but about the information I could derive from the interaction. What mattered was a personal connection to the members of the club.

I'd asked Dotty to discreetly hire every available opposition research team in Washington and ask each to assemble detailed research on every member of the world's class of billionaires—all 2,700 of them, and some others, like Simon and Zheng, who were billionaires even if the official record didn't reflect it. I wanted to know specifically what each of them cared about in business, where each had a personal interest. From there, we would quietly reach out and invest anywhere from several million to more, if necessary—in as many directions as possible, all at once.

"The opposition research is going to cost a small fortune," she argued. "Fifteen million or more. Maybe double that."

"Yeah, I know. And our benefactor isn't likely to sign off on it."

"The research…it's not an investment?" Dotty asked.

"Right. It's not. But it *will* give us what we need to take the next step. It's necessary for financial planning. And if the Chase guy doesn't sign off, then, well, we close up and go home."

"Just like that?"

"Yeah, just like that," I said, smiling. "It's only the beginning of what we're going to try. If they knew what we had up our sleeve once the reports are in hand…"

"Which is?"

I glanced around the office even though Dotty had assured me no recording devices were found on the premises. Then, in a quieter voice, I said, "We're going to invest $10 billion into companies as closely connected personally to as many of those on this list as we can possibly manage. Every Series A, every angel or seed-round opportunity, every block of private shares, every investment group involved in public companies they care about, and every business development play at an early stage."

"Ten billion dollars?" Dotty's face paled.

"Ten billion dollars," I repeated. "We're going all in. We're not doing what John Andrews did, which was financially sound and perfectly reasonable as part of a diversified investment strategy. We're going to be entirely unreasonable."

"But…"

"It's insane. I know." I jabbed an insistent finger in the air. "But it's not *actually* out of the realm of what's possible. There are people who make big bets like this. The Saudis, for one. The kingdom's rulers will control $2 trillion all on their own in a little more than a decade. Their Public Investment Fund already controls nearly $300 billion. They make $10 billion bets several times a year. And it's usually a decision made by one person, talking it over with a couple of others."

"Really?"

"Yes, really. They bought five percent of Tesla in one fell swoop. That's a $3 billion bet on *one company*. They have to diversify before they run out of water and oil, so they're making enormous bets…in some cases, bets four or five times the size of what I'm proposing here.

"They made one enormous bet of $45 billion on a technology fund run by Japan's SoftBank. They're building a $500 billion city called Neom on the Red Sea. They have a $5 billion project to redevelop the Jeddah waterfront, also on the Red Sea. And they put $20 billion into *one* fund—managed by Blackstone—in the United States for infrastructure projects. The Saudis make enormous bets like this all the time. It's not unreasonable for them at all."

"So, do you think…"

"The Saudis are behind this? No, because it makes no sense for them. They operate in the shadows. A couple of ex-journalists I know jumped ship to work for them. No way would the Saudis be involved in a deal like this. They're hyper-focused on making money to run the kingdom and transition away from oil wealth. Of course, anything is possible…"

"But what you're proposing is a way to test that, isn't it?" Dotty asked.

"Precisely. It'll connect us to the Saudis…and to pretty much anyone else who might be behind this."

Dotty took a deep breath. "We're going to need a small army of advisors and investors to pursue all of those."

"So, hire them or put them on notice. Once we have the road map, we're going to move all at once. Storm every castle in sight."

"And if Chase Bank says no?"

"Then they say no. They could stop us when we hire an army of investment advisors, or when we make our first investments. But they could have stopped us from making the investment with Fedorisky and they didn't. We're going to test how far they'll let us go. My hunch is, they'll let us go after the entire thing. I mean, think about it. It's not like we're squandering money on private jets or yachts. We'll be making investments in companies with real value and the potential to make lots of money."

"But…it's *ten billion* dollars," she protested.

"What's that phrase—a billion here, a billion there, and pretty soon you're talking about real money?" I laughed.

Dotty shook her head, but I could see she was already working the plan through in her mind. "You know, if this works, and we're able to invest all that money, it could also mean you'll have an awfully good shot at the club."

"On paper, perhaps. But only if the investments make money. It's not our money we're putting at risk. It belongs to someone else."

"With shares that have some value."

"Ultimately, but only if the investments are sound and pay off."

"Which they will." Dotty glanced at the folders I'd tossed onto the small table between us. "All these opportunities are good ones. The shares will become valuable in fairly short order. I have to assume that the others we now select will be similar."

"Great. We'll make money. That's the goal."

"But if we make money with such a big bet, then we could make…an *awful* lot of money in a very short time." Her voice trailed off.

"Look, I know this sounds crazy. But right now there are 2,700 people worth hundreds of billions of dollars—trillions of dollars—and have no idea what to do with it. Someone decided, for whatever reason, to play around with the crazy scheme we find ourselves in. So let's play. See how far we can go. The worst that can happen is we make hundreds of investments with one sliver of that very large pie and it doesn't go as well as whoever put us up to this might have hoped."

"Which would be bad."

"Perhaps," I said. "But people who have that kind of money have infinite ways to make lots more. Those at the very top of this food chain add another billion dollars to their net worth over the course of a year just by staying above ground. I don't think this is about money or investments."

"Then what is it about?" she asked.

"I don't know. But if they let us play, we're going to find out."

CHAPTER 18

I noticed the van as I walked back to my apartment from the Dupont Circle subway stop. Under normal circumstances, I rarely noted things like that, but now I looked for signs that I was being monitored.

The white Mercedes-Benz Sprinter van—the type people converted into sleeper vans—was tucked between two other parked cars on the opposite side of the street from my apartment. Its outside was unusually clean, with no dirt or road streaks. With the windows shaded, it was nearly impossible to peer inside, even if I felt like sidling up close to it.

Dotty had hired seven of Washington's best opposition research teams within a matter of days. I wasn't surprised. She and I split up the Billionaires' Club members into buckets of a few hundred each, based on geography, and parceled each bucket out to the seven firms. We offered each a flat fee of $2 million for connect-the-dots reports on their list. It was a no-brainer for them. Their out-of-pocket costs for a few post-docs and analysts to do targeted research from their desks represented a tenth of that fee.

What *had* surprised me, though, was how swiftly our guy at Chase had signed off on the research team contracts. Dotty had explained in person that we wanted to hire the firms and pay them for research on financial connections to other wealthy investors. The Chase guy didn't even call anyone to check. He just told her to send him the invoices and he'd pay them.

We could have paid ourselves rather than send the invoices to Chase, but I decided this was cleaner and easier. Someone else would be picking up the tab for this research, which wasn't proprietary. It gave our silent funder a chance to more closely track what we were doing, beyond the actual investments we were making (or going to make). I had no problem with that at all. When we made our big move, I meant to be quite clear to Chase about what we intended. And then we'd know how much latitude we truly had.

We hadn't told any of the research firms what we meant to do with the requested information. But nearly all had connections in multiple industry and financial sectors. Our research requests certainly had set bells ringing in all kinds of interesting places.

Good, I thought. *That's exactly what we need. We need people to start asking questions.*

I'd assumed something like the white van would eventually show up. I made sure to check every day for the next three days. The van moved locations twice but remained close to my apartment. I assumed they could hear anything I said there and were tracking my digital signals.

The van could have been the GRU again, though I doubted it. The Russians already had their surveillance hooks into me, so this seemed like overkill. Perhaps it was the Chinese.

Or the Israelis, since our research targeted every billionaire operating inside the nations of Israel's enemies. The Mossad kept close tabs on the finances of every wealthy family in Saudi Arabia, the United Arab Emirates, Qatar, and elsewhere because any of them could easily underwrite the individual or state-sponsored terrorism operations that ringed Israel. But the Chinese or Israelis wouldn't operate so openly on a public street in northwest Washington. They'd find other ways to keep track of me.

My best guess was the van belonged to the American intelligence community. I almost called to ask my friend at Langley but thought better of it. I had no idea what might happen after we assembled our research and opened the floodgates. Until then, I would move forward in a straight line—all in, playing to win, with nothing to fear.

Next, I asked Dotty to retain the best white-collar law firm in the city and vet the legality of what we were about to do. I told her not to give them hard numbers. I only wanted them to opine on the broad outlines of our plan...namely, were we able to legally direct Chase to invest someone else's money in these ventures? I wanted to be sure we were on solid ground if Chase miraculously did invest the ten billion. I knew there would be questions, and I wanted a few answers beforehand.

I was fairly positive we'd be fine. I knew someone who managed a multi-billion-dollar fund for one of the 25 richest men in the world. We'd talked for years, and he'd told me how he made his decisions. There was no management committee, and no board of directors overseeing his activities. He simply identified the best investment targets in an industry sector and recommended them to his principal. The rich guy said yes or no—the answer was nearly always yes—and the manager was off to the races. He'd invest several billion over the course of a year in everything from startup companies with no sales record but interesting patents to established companies with a diversified portfolio of products and an actual sales track record. In every case, the decision-making tree consisted of just the two of them.

Our situation, at its core, would be no different. The firms Dotty hired would do the research. We'd seek input from incredibly smart financial advisors. But, in the end, I'd make the call about where to direct the investments, without seeking permission or explaining the rationale. The only real difference was that the principal who might otherwise be on the other end of that process wasn't making the decision to invest. I was making the call, for reasons other than strictly making money. I was looking for connections in as many places as possible, attached to clear and obvious financial investments that anyone would look at and recognize as either sound or promising.

Any ordinary financial advisor would hope to maximize profits in a portfolio. I was hoping to maximize interest from a unique set of individuals, so I could start to ask smart questions. Whether it all made money was far removed from my thinking. Frankly, I assumed the investments would never be approved in the first place. And, if they were, I never imagined that I would benefit financially from any of this. It didn't seem possible that SCT Enterprises would also own stock as part of these investments. In theory, yes, that was what we were pursuing. But in practice, it didn't make sense.

So, based on what I'd learned from John Andrews, and on the advice Dotty had gotten from others, I decided not to charge a single cash fee for any of the investments we were about to make. Every dollar a financial advisor would ordinarily charge to manage an investment portfolio would be tied up in stock that existed only on paper.

I was also going to roll the dice precisely as Andrews had. We would propose a 15 percent profit-carry fee, entirely in stock options, that grew on a sliding scale depending on the performance. I had no idea if the benefactor would balk at the investments and at the fee. But if the fee was all in stock, I could somehow give it to Chase if the need presented itself.

I know. It sounds completely crazy. There's no way any of this is real or possible. Then again, is it any crazier than a couple of graduate students at Stanford working on an intelligence community grant funneled through the National Science Foundation to start a company that would disrupt the entire global media structure and turn both of them into multi-billionaires almost overnight? Or a kid developing an online dating profile based on photos of incoming freshmen at a few elite colleges that made him one of the richest people in the world by the time he was 25?

Here's the weird, sobering truth: People like Albert Einstein should have been billionaires. Anyone who can prove time exists outside the three dimensions we're all familiar with should also be able to figure out how to make a lot of money. But Einstein never pursued wealth and might have failed if he had. Most people inherit their wealth and pile more on top of it throughout their lives.

So even if this seemed crazy or *was* crazy, I'd let the chips fall where they might. I had no family to protect. No plans for what I might be doing later in the year. No interest in making gobs of money. No sights set on a retirement bungalow in Cabo or the Maldives or Palm Beach.

A colleague of mine retired at the end of an illustrious career at one of the federal agencies that commanded respect in the town. When he left, a whole slew of consulting firms swooped in and offered him a ton of money to consult. He said yes to one, but on a single condition. They had to allow him to go on a four-month world tour at the start of every year. They agreed, and he has now visited every country with a shoreline. He's seen everything possible to see in a lifetime…provided you can reach it from a port and on a guided tour.

I had no plans like that. When I traveled, I didn't even take pictures. I'd walked along the Great Wall in China, the cobbled streets of Paris, and the dusty roads of the old city in Jerusalem and didn't have a single photo to show for it. It never occurred to me to memorialize those trips.

I'd written stories based on someone's private conversations with presidents that someone, potentially risking a prison term, had leaked to me. I'd written about con men who should never have been allowed to succeed but bamboozled everyone they talked to. I'd discovered individuals so blatantly evil that everyone in their presence should have instantly recognized who and what they were, yet no one did until it was far too late to prevent the woeful results of their depravity.

What I was embarking on now didn't seem any crazier than what I'd already done. The only difference was that, this time, *I* was the person inside the story. I was the actor attempting what made no sense, instead of an observer of someone else's insanity. This time, I'd own it if it all went south. It was my crazy.

But I didn't care. I'd see it through to the end, whatever that might be.

As I entered my dimly lit apartment, I jangled my keys in the door. Ignoring the dishes piled up in the kitchen sink, I tossed the keys on the counter. After donning a sweatshirt draped over the table, I removed a beer bottle from the refrigerator, twisted the cap off, and chucked it into the sink with the dirty dishes.

Moving to the window, I again spotted the white van across the street.

"Hello, guys," I called out loudly to the empty apartment. "I'm back. You can turn on the tape recorder. I'll try to spice up your life a little. I've been meaning to watch that new crime series on Netflix with Jason Bateman, the one where he washes hundreds of millions of dollars for a Columbian drug cartel. You know, the one about money laundering and organized crime. Make sure you capture those phrases. It'll help with the warrants."

After flicking the TV on, I plopped on the ratty couch, ignoring the dust that wafted out around me, and took a long swig of the beer.

For a second—but only one—I felt sorry for the poor souls stuck in the white van forced to track my miserable existence.

CHAPTER 19

"Go find that analyst, for goodness' sake," a thoroughly exasperated Dotty instructed me. Can't blame her. I was hovering over her for the fourth time that morning to peek at her incoming email.

I was antsy, waiting for the research reports to come in. Dotty kept telling me, "Be patient. They take time. Sit tight. I'll be able to start pouring through them in no time. Relax."

But I couldn't relax. It wasn't that I was nervous. I was impatient. I was fully prepared for the benefactor to balk entirely when we made our pitch to Chase, and then to pull the plug as they had with John Andrews. I was convinced the game would end soon.

The safe bet would have been to ease into everything precisely the way Andrews had, and then hope not to make a fatal mistake. But I had no desire to ease into anything. I wanted immediate answers...and quick entrance into the center of the maze.

I'd already walked to the nearest Starbucks for a cup of coffee three times that morning. I was so jittery from the caffeine that I couldn't sit still. I'd read online profiles of some of the members of the club. But they all seemed so...antiseptic. No amount of background information would matter until I had something to pursue. I needed to be in their orbit, not staring down at their empires from 30,000 feet above.

Now Dotty shooed me out the door verbally. "Just go," she said. "Find her. The research reports will be finished when you get back."

"I can't find her. Jasper said—"

She cut me off. "You're not Jasper. You can find anyone. Put your mind to it. Make some calls."

"Yeah, and so what? I already know the basic contours of this thing."

"You might get new angles from her. Get answers to questions you don't even know to ask."

I leaned up against the wall. "You just want me out of your hair, don't you?"

"Damn straight I do," Dotty said without even looking up from her computer.

She and I had grown comfortable with each other. She no longer had any qualms talking to me like this. I trusted her. She was no mere assistant. In another line of work, I could easily see Dotty running things. I'd never pressed her on the professional choices she'd made, but it seemed obvious she could handle any job.

Dotty had mentioned, obliquely, that she'd made a choice in a much earlier era to focus on raising her children after completing a master's degree in international finance decades earlier. She had stopped working at an investment firm and focused on her kids, all of whom were now successful professionals with young families. Out of sheer boredom, she'd decided to start temping.

I'd never told her, but I believed it was no accident someone with her background and demeanor had shown up on my doorstep as I began this adventure. Dotty was uniquely qualified to deal with everything coming at us. The benefactor knew precisely the types of people to approach, both to lead the way and support. Dotty was a perfect partner. She was an extraordinarily talented and gracious human being who could handle any task that came her way. Despite my best efforts to remain aloof, I was more thankful with every passing day that she'd entered my life.

I occasionally caught myself staring at Dotty in awe. When I'd first come to Jackson Place, I'd thought of her as a receptionist. But she was hardly that. She handled the research firms and financial advisors with the tact and diplomacy of someone who'd been in the financial sector for decades. My guess was that she'd kept up with her reading over the years, even as she devoted her life to her family.

And in addition to all that, she was a much better person than I was, in fact. I didn't deserve the level of care and professionalism she was putting into this enterprise.

I couldn't quite bring myself to tell her any of that, but I believe she knew. Whenever our eyes met, she managed a smile. She was happy to dive in and didn't appear the least bit worried about the insanity of what we were attempting. If I had to guess, it was because she no longer had any personal responsibilities to worry about. Her children were grown, healthy, happy, and prosperous.

She enjoyed visiting her grandchildren whenever she could. But after her husband passed away, she hinted at wanting to take a big, extraordinary risk on something. She wasn't about to start skydiving or drag racing. This was as close as she'd ever come to cliff diving, she once joked.

I knew the impulse almost as well as she did. The only difference was that I was more than willing to jump off the cliff, and then, while on my way down, try to figure out where I might land. Dotty at least did her homework about the depth of the water below, the nature of the swirling winds that swept in across the cliff, and the proper posture you needed to assume before hitting the water—and then she was willing to jump.

"All right, I'll find her," I grunted.

"Good. Then I can get some work done around here."

"But what about…"

"Call Jasper!" she barked. "Ask him what he remembers about the analyst. Then go find her."

***

Jasper was more than happy to tell me everything he could remember about the woman who'd come to Reykjavik. He was also delighted to hear I'd tracked John Andrews down in St. Barts and had filled in more of the story. Jasper was especially eager to hear details about Andrews' job at FinCEN and his subsequent decision to leave it all behind and try his hand at investments. Because we were using Zoom on the video conference, I could tell Jasper was genuinely excited to be looped in.

"So he actually spent two years investing the money?" Jasper asked.

"He did. He made a lot of money doing it, in fact. Before it blew up on him, he had about $200 million invested. By the end, he owned about 15 percent of that in stock from the net profit. It allowed him to settle in St. Barts."

Jasper whistled. "That's…"

"A nice chunk of change," I said. "Yeah, I told him that. But he still had regrets."

"Regrets?"

"That he'd never gotten close to understanding the source of the funding. He tried, but even when the funding went away, he still didn't know."

"Wow," Jasper said. "If a FinCEN agent can't get close to that, I'm not sure how anyone can. He has resources no one else in the world has. When I was trying to unravel what happened with the banks in Reykjavik, I would've killed for the type of database he had."

"Which reminds me," I said, "Andrews said the funding disappeared suddenly after two years of investing. It was gone, like what happened to the money offered to the big banks in Iceland and then pulled back. You think that's what this is—Russian money?"

"Some complicated scheme through a circle of oligarchs around Simon?" Jasper added.

"Yeah, there are similarities."

"There are," Jasper mused, "but there's no way they're connected. The money that came into the banks here was clearly dirty, or at least grayish—money that needed to be laundered. It was obvious where the money was coming from. The Russians didn't try to hide it. When they pulled up their stakes, it was because they'd created an inflated risk bubble that was about to burst. They left before it collapsed. It sounds like Andrews had clean money and also a stable, seemingly profitable investment portfolio under management. Those are two very different things."

"But the money dried up for Andrews just as it did in Iceland?"

"Yes, but it sounds like it dried up for a very different reason—because he was too conservative and prudent with his actions. That's nearly the opposite of what happened here."

I'd come to much the same conclusion, but it was good to get a second opinion from Jasper, one of the few people in the world who could wrestle intelligently with these sorts of questions.

"So this financial analyst you met with…tell me about her. Where'd she say she was from?"

"Goldman Sachs."

"Which is the biggest, and would make the most sense to lie about," I said. "That means she was either from KKR or Warburg Pincus."

"That's what I assumed."

"Did she ever say where she worked...you know, geographically?"

"Not really, though she mentioned something in passing during one of our two calls, before she came to see me. She said she could see a pickup game from her window. I had the impression she was looking down on a park."

A bell jangled in my memory. I opened Google maps on my laptop and clicked on Goldman Sachs. It was near the new World Trade Center complex, in the southern part of Manhattan. I found Warburg Pincus, on the East Side. Then I clicked on KKR. They were right on the southern end of Central Park, where people gathered when it was nice outside. It was one of the most iconic vantage points ever captured on film. I'd once interviewed a billionaire whose view matched that of KKR. He'd bragged to me how film crews used to shoot footage from it.

"I'll bet she works, or worked, at KKR," I said. "At least it's a place to start. Anything else you remember...maybe about the portfolio of investments she specialized in?"

"Well, she did complain about how she hated working on leveraged buyouts, but that she had no choice."

I started nodding. "Then it's got to be KKR. They're the leveraged buyout kings. The original Barbarians at the Gate. They've managed nearly all the multi-billion-dollar deals since the 1980s. You have a big, hairy buyout, you go to KKR. Has to be them."

Jasper was nodding right along with me. "Yeah, yeah. That would make sense. It's an interesting background. She'd be a lot like Andrews at FinCEN...someone who'd seen the biggest of the big schemes up close and personal and wasn't afraid to work with huge financial ventures."

"And someone who wasn't cowed by billionaires, either."

"They've made a whole slew of them over the years," Jasper agreed. "It's the place where huge fortunes are made."

"And lost. Like some of the people you investigated in Reykjavik. There are big winners in these games...and big losers."

"Right. I can tell you this," Jasper added. "She seemed world-weary, jaded, and even cynical about people's motives. It didn't surprise me she lied about where she worked or that she later dropped off the grid."

"Do you think she lost a ton of money somehow? Rolled the dice in a big way and lost so much that she had to go in hiding? Like that guy who single-handedly caused that Asian bank to lose a billion dollars overnight?"

"You'd have to find her and ask her that question," Jasper said. "But there could be other reasons. Maybe she got closer to finding the source of the funding, and it scared her. Maybe she made so much money she could just walk away. Or maybe she decided none of it was worth it and never tried her hand at it the way Andrews did."

"Which of those possibilities makes the most sense?"

Jasper blinked twice. "She was an aggressive investor, no question. I can't see her walking away with a small stake or not trying for a huge return. She was a gambler—not spooked by anything, including big numbers and the unsavory types rolling around in those piles of cash."

"So she either lost big or won big…"

"And then walked off into the sunset," Jasper added.

"Of those two, I'd put money on the second. If she'd lost big, my guess is she'd still be at KKR or in the business somewhere else. But if she won big, she had every incentive to vanish, or at least to surround herself with enough anonymity to escape any fallout."

"Right."

"So, I need to find out who this person might have been at KKR once upon a time, and then go find the sunset she walked toward when she left."

Jasper wagged an approving finger toward the video camera. "I think you've got a plan," he said with an easy smile. "Go find her. Let me know what she has to say."

"Will do. And, Jasper, thanks for talking this through with me."

"My pleasure. I love a good mystery, and this one is unlike anything I've ever seen."

"That, my friend, is the understatement of the year."

CHAPTER 20

It didn't take long to hone in on a likely suspect at KKR, now that I was no longer looking for a needle in the haystack. Because the analyst was a woman, it had been easy to narrow the field to one of three.

One was still there. She'd been a partner and the head of their leveraged-buyout division for years. I wasn't about to call her up and grill her. I didn't want to spook my target. I wanted to find her on my own, without sending ripples into the pond. I didn't think she was my person but, to make sure, I sent her photo to Jasper. He told me he was fairly certain it wasn't her.

The second person had managed their signature hedge fund for years. She'd been responsible for dozens of their big bets and was comfortable with risk and huge numbers. She was no longer at KKR but remained a known and respected figure in the financial world. When I sent her photo to Jasper, I got the same answer. No dice.

Therefore, it had to be the third senior woman in KKR's ranks. She'd left a few years earlier after rising through the ranks to run their "alternative investment" operations—a sideline bet they'd ultimately franchised out. The group streamlined management at KKR portfolio companies and found ways to squeeze more profits from them. They occasionally forced management to fire people en masse and found ways to force companies to move laterally into other businesses to expand their sales reach. The group also made unusual bets on emerging companies and businesses.

This division, ruthless when it needed to be, had also been at the fringes of the cryptocurrency and blockchain craze. No big fund, including KKR, had jumped in that water in the earliest days. They'd only dipped their toe in once cryptocurrency looked like it might be real, and financial regulators were surrounding it with their usual death grip. Like every big fund, KKR kept their hand poised over the wheel with small acquisitions to ensure they were ready for a future breakout.

But this third woman, Michelle Searle, had been all over cryptocurrency for years, largely because of her background as a math geek with serious coding skills before joining KKR. The only female among a group of male coders now recognized as the real creators of blockchain technology and crypto, she'd made a bit of a name for herself in the underworld of cryptocurrency long before anyone in the mainstream media had started talking about it... partly because it was so unusual for a female to knock heads with her male counterparts.

Her name popped up every so often in technical articles. She was always extolling the possible virtues of blockchain and how crypto might go mainstream someday. It seemed likely she'd personally purchased crypto early on. Maybe even a great deal of it. In fact, it was possible she'd bought bitcoins throughout 2010 and 2011, when you could pick them up for only a dollar, and salted them across tens of thousands of databases. There were no names attached to these bitcoins; they existed merely as complicated, encrypted numbers.

In fact, Satoshi Nakamoto, the secretive founder of this first decentralized cryptocurrency, allegedly owned nearly a million bitcoins spread across hundreds of thousands of databases. Forums raged constantly about how much Nakamoto actually controlled.

Myths and legends cropped up everywhere in the crypto world about Satoshi Nakamoto's true identity. Some likened him to Batman, a philanthropic billionaire by day who saved the world from the forces of evil at night. Others believed he was a syndicate rather than a real, live human being. Still others claimed Nakamoto was entirely fictional and created by the NSA to create a back door into every nefarious aspect of organized crime.

His words on the early forums had been analyzed without much success for clues. Nearly every tech journalist I knew believed Nakamoto didn't exist, and that those early bitcoins had been created by first one and then several computers with no expectation it was anything other than a stupid math game with no inherent meaning. The keys had been lost because no one at the time believed they'd be worth anything.

Nakamoto had never revealed a single personal detail about himself during the two years he was active on the Cryptography Mailing List at metzdowd.com. Then in Spring 2011, he'd faded from the scene with the enigmatic statement, "I've moved on to other things"—his last known response from his GMX email account.

As far as anyone could tell, Satoshi Nakamoto had never spent a single bitcoin. No one could trace his ownership back to him. When the price of one bitcoin hit a high of $20,000 in late 2017, *Fortune, Forbes,* and other financial magazines playfully jumped Nakamoto into the top 50 richest people in the world—though no one knew who he, she, or they were, or how many bitcoins were involved. Columnists speculated that Nakamoto would become the world's first trillionaire if the price hit a million dollars.

When the price of bitcoin fell back down to Earth, and Satoshi Nakamoto was worth a mere $6 billion or so on paper, the myth-making efforts died in the mainstream press. Nakamoto was once again consigned to the conspiracy stuff of crypto forums.

Reading through Michelle Searle's personal and professional history, it seemed obvious she'd been in from the beginning. Searle had promoted crypto's potential long before the infamous Winklevoss twins went all in with their settlement money from the Facebook lawsuit. Most likely, she'd bought a lot of bitcoin at the very start.

Amazingly, though, her name had never shown up on any lists of those who made it known they owned a large number of bitcoins. As far as I could tell, she never publicly acknowledged owning even a single bitcoin, probably because her own firm, KKR, and every other major institutional investor had denounced cryptocurrency either as a fad or fraud for years.

Searle had left KKR at least two years before bitcoin fell back to Earth. Her name was still faintly associated with crypto. A few forums even regularly tagged her as Nakamoto, if only because it seemed so outrageous that a woman could have taken her place in the great bitcoin-coding pantheon.

Nakamoto started using SHA-256, a cryptographic hash function, as his proof-of-work scheme in 2009. But two years in, Satoshi Nakamoto vanished, allegedly with a lot of bitcoin, and dropped off the forums, never to be heard from again. No one had ever proven his identity, though many had tried. He could have been a lone individual, or a group of developers with a front person.

I was convinced that Searle wasn't Nakamoto (though it was possible she might have been part of a small group popularizing crypto to the small blockchain community at the time, a group that came to be known collectively as "Satoshi Nakamoto"). But clearly she had the technical expertise. Back then, she was a big money analyst, adept at looking at different ways of making money.

One thing was certain: Searle had vanished after leaving KKR. She didn't change her name, as far as I could tell, but I still couldn't find her. Evidently, she'd paid a lot of money to scrub all traces of herself from the internet. That wasn't easy, I knew. There were no references to her and no publicly available photos taken within the last three years—only a few pictures tagged to old Instagram posts from years back. There was no way to trace her in the present day.

When I emailed Jasper one of the old pictures I'd pulled from an Instagram post, I already knew what I'd hear. This was our person.

"Yep, that's her," Jasper emailed back.

"You're sure?" I emailed back.

"Positive. That's her. Where is she?"

"Gone. She left KKR a few years back and scrubbed the internet of every current reference to herself. She did just walk off into the sunset."

"Michelle Searle? That's her name?"

"It is," I wrote. "Or at least it once was. I can't find a Michelle Searle anywhere. I've found a small handful of people with the name, but none is our person. She's way, way off the grid."

"What if she got married and changed her name?"

"That would have shown up in my searches."

"So how will you find her?"

"I have one other route," I wrote back. "I'll let you know."

***

I sent a note to my friend, Silas, at Langley, with a link to Searle's old bio and profile at KKR, plus a couple of old links to the crypto forums from years back. I asked him if he maybe had a line on her. I got an immediate call back, from a blocked number.

"What in the world are you wandering into?" Silas asked without preamble when I picked up the call.

"Can you talk, by the way?" I asked him. The image of the white van outside my apartment loomed large in my mind. I was worried about tarnishing the professional reputation of folks like Silas I'd dealt with over the years.

He sighed. "Sure. Why not?" he said after a brief pause.

That pause told me everything I needed to know. The call was being recorded. He'd be careful, much more so than I'd be. In fact, he'd use the call with me to absolve himself from being implicated in anything I was involved with. I'd help him with that, if I could.

"You know I'm asking a straightforward question, right? Just curious if you had a line on this person?"

"Maybe. But first, I have to say folks here know that I talk to you. It's been in my after-action reports for years. I always record it."

"I know, Silas. You've always been straightforward. You never speak out of turn. You've only ever been willing to help me understand what I've already learned. You know how the Kremlin works, what motivates the leadership there. Nothing more, nothing less."

"Exactly. When you ask me about things, it's always been in that capacity…"

"As a Russian expert," I said, smiling at the game we were both engaged in. "I know. You're a good analyst. That's it."

"Yes, good. So, now, I have to ask you, what are you thinking, engaging with Fedorisky? Why are you anywhere near that guy? You know who he is, right?"

This would be a bit tricky. "Yes, I know exactly who he is, but I wanted his take on something. I'm interviewing him for a story."

"You've done more than that, Seth."

"Yeah, I have. But it's all part of the story."

"It must be quite a story," he said. "I'd like to hear about it someday."

"Yeah, I'm sure you will," I answered, somewhat truthfully. "But look, that isn't why I pinged you. I'm trying to find this person, Michelle Searle."

There was another long pause. It made me think he had people in his office looking over his shoulder. For all I knew, they were instructing him on what he might reasonably say to me.

"I can probably help you with that. She left American soil three years ago and hasn't been back since. She's still hip deep in cryptocurrency, as far as we can tell. Not publicly, but she still has friends in the community she keeps tabs on. But her actions are above board, at least as far as we can tell. She's nowhere near the crypto black market. Her interest seems genuine. She seems to be all about the potential for the currency price to stabilize, or at least not fall into the ocean."

"That's good to know," I said. "Where is she?"

Because I was now certain this was a recorded phone call, I decided not to verbalize my suspicions that Searle still had a large stake in the crypto scene, and thus, understandably, kept her hand in it. I also decided not to ask him how he knew about her crypto history, considering that his expertise was Russia and that Michelle Searle had nothing to do with Russia.

I knew why he had this information at hand. A task force was in place, tracking my movements, contacts, and everything I was touching. That task force would be following close behind as I tracked Searle's whereabouts.

"New Zealand," Silas answered quickly. "She's in the city of Napier, on the east coast, halfway between Auckland and Wellington. No idea if she stays there, or just has correspondence sent there."

"Interesting. New Zealand, huh?"

"Yeah, it seems to be the place of choice to wait out the coming apocalypse."

"Is that what she's doing—waiting out the apocalypse in New Zealand? Or is she perhaps engineering it?"

"We're all engineers of the apocalypse in one way or another, aren't we?" Silas gave a nervous laugh. "You seem like you're hard at that yourself."

"Let's get together for coffee soon. Lots to catch up on."

"You bet. I look forward to it," Silas said. "And good luck finding Michelle Searle. I hope she can help you with your story, whatever it might be."

CHAPTER 21

They make it look so easy in films and on television. A character travels from Washington, D.C., to some other part of the world. Whoosh, you're in a cab to Dulles or Reagan, and then, in the very next scene, you're hailing a cab in another part of the world.

If only…. It took six hours to fly across the United States, and then another 13 to fly direct from Los Angeles to Auckland. I'd foolishly booked the flights together. Had I thought it through, I'd have spent the night at a cheap hotel in LA, and then flown direct to New Zealand the next day.

I was so sick of watching movies on a tiny screen that I could hardly see straight by the time we landed. And my back was killing me. The only saving grace was that I'd had a chance to read quite a bit about the legend of Satoshi Nakamoto and the origin of bitcoin. It really was the birth of cryptocurrency. Even though there had been earlier versions, it was Nakamoto's mining (likely on just one processor) that created the 256-bit block hash in 2009 that represented the genesis of bitcoin.

Bitcoin experts had spent years analyzing those very early days. They estimated that Nakamoto was responsible for roughly two-thirds of the 1.6 million bitcoins mined that first year—2009. Charts showed a third of those had been "spent" by their anonymous holders. The rest of the million bitcoins were all "unspent," assumed to be controlled by Nakamoto across the 250,000 bitcoin data banks in existence, and were never circulated. It was possible a second computer had been involved, but most believed one computer had been responsible for all those first coins, and that they belonged to Satoshi Nakamoto, or whoever was behind the pseudonym.

Now there were roughly 12 million bitcoins mined and sitting in those bitcoin data banks all over the world. The smart bitcoin owners spread their coins—encrypted data that had never been hacked—across as many banks as they could find to hedge against their theft. Because they were anonymous, and not backed up by a government third-party, if someone hacked your bitcoin, they "owned" it. So it was better to spread the wealth.

Efforts to create a regulatory system consistently failed. Still, there were lots of ways to buy bitcoins. You could even buy partial bitcoins with your credit card if you wanted. Your partial bitcoin was then stored in whatever data mining database you subscribed to. It was worth whatever the "market" declared, should you ever decide to sell it.

In its wild ride to the moon at the end of 2017, one bitcoin had reached a value of nearly $20,000. That put Satoshi Nakamoto's wealth, on paper, in the neighborhood of $20 billion—theoretically right behind Steve Jobs' widow, Laurene Powell Jobs, on the list of the wealthiest people in the world.

Of course, it was all make believe. Laurene Powell Jobs was, in fact, worth $20 billion. She owned stock in Apple and had investments all over the world. It was real wealth. Satoshi Nakamoto's wealth was based on a bunch of encrypted numbers spread out across thousands of databases all over the world. Everyone wrote, without proof, that Nakamoto owned more bitcoins than anyone else. Truth is, no one knew if this pseudonymous entity actually owned a million bitcoins or if it was the biggest single-entity ownership of the 12 million or so bitcoins in existence.

For all any journalist or crypto analyst knew, Satoshi Nakamoto was a syndicate. I knew several tech journalists who'd studied the four cryptographers (all men) cited as the most likely candidates. None of them made sense. My colleagues now believed Nakamoto either didn't exist or was actually several men working together in the crypto world who'd never anticipated their early work would amount to much.

Conspiracy buffs sometimes compared Nakamoto to Batman on crypto forums; both seemed more legend than real. The bitcoin devotees wanted a founder capable of saving the world but didn't need to cash in his bitcoins because he was independently wealthy and fully capable of strong, independent action. Nakamoto was, in many respects, the 21st century embodiment of Nietzsche's Ubermensch. But no such real man existed.

The original million bitcoins mined in 2009, and not used, could just as easily be spread across a syndicate. One of the more popular conspiracies, in fact, was that the name Satoshi Nakamoto was an amalgam that mashed together the names of four big companies, including Toshiba and Motorola.

Others were convinced that, because the genesis code from Satoshi Nakamoto had its roots with the National Security Agency, the whole thing was nothing more than an effort by the American intelligence community to allow a back door into the illicit underground activities that used cryptocurrency.

As I read through the early history of bitcoin, it seemed others could have mined right alongside Satoshi Nakamoto in 2010 and even 2011 and accumulated quite a lot before everything started to go crazy. And if someone had accumulated those coins and not spent them, that person could rival or even surpass Satoshi Nakamoto in being capable of controlling bitcoin. After all, everything was anonymous.

That was one of the central tenets laid out by Satoshi Nakamoto in the very first forum post announcing crypto to the world. Nakamoto's ownership had only been identified after the fact, as others compared the spikes in mining in 2009 and attributed them solely to him. But there had been more mining in 2010 and 2011, exactly when Michelle Searle was active on the crypto forums.

As we flew west toward New Zealand, every investigative fiber of my being was screaming. I had to find Michelle Searle and talk to her about all of this. Though I still doubted she was, in fact, Satoshi Nakamoto, I could sense she knew *something* about this mythological figure. She'd been far too involved in those early days.

Midway on my flight across the Pacific Ocean, I realized why I was so intensely curious about Michelle Searle's involvement in crypto and her connection to Satoshi Nakamoto. I was one of a very small circle—including Jasper and Dotty—who knew Searle had likely been approached by my benefactor in 2010, in the early days of bitcoin.

The timeline was intriguing, because it meant the benefactor had been playing this game for far longer than I'd assumed. For all I knew, he, or she, was the mythical Satoshi Nakamoto and had made his billions *before* launching cryptocurrency. That might explain why he'd never touched his own stash of bitcoins. There would have been no need to do so.

But even as this notion occurred to me, I dismissed it. Everything I'd read about Nakamoto and his forum involvement in those early days was antithetical to the way our mysterious benefactor operated today. Before disappearing, Nakamoto had been willing to discuss things by writing under a pseudonym. The person who'd sent me the text had left no trails or clues that I could see. The two simply didn't align.

I was fairly confident the benefactor wasn't the personage of Nakamoto, though he might somehow have been part of the earliest days of bitcoin. But I sure hoped I'd get a chance to test this theory with Searle.

***

Dotty had insisted I stay at The County Hotel in Napier. I'd objected, but she booked me into the five-star hotel anyway. She said we were billing this trip to the research budget Chase had already approved.

"Stop squawking. It's where you're staying," she ordered. "Just drive there and enjoy the hotel and the restaurant. It's supposed to be lovely."

It was. The hotel, located in the heart of the city, matched the 1930s style of Napier—elegant and stylish, inside and out. I felt completely ill at ease in the place. I was much more accustomed to those ubiquitous three-star hotels in the U.S. This hotel was way out of my league. I admired that there *were* such places, and that people with lots of money never thought twice about staying in them, but I've never fully appreciated why such hotels exist around the world.

After making the drive from Auckland's airport through the central part of northern New Zealand, I parked my car at the hotel, checked in, then walked around Napier a bit to get the lay of the land. I've always found that, to understand a city, the easiest way was by walking it first and asking casual questions in different shops about places to visit. People there are always eager to boast about locations that make their city what it is.

Most people in Napier encouraged me to see Hawke's Bay. I came across Michelle Searle—or, at least, the route to find her—in a small bookstore on one of the side streets. I struck up a casual conversation with the owner to see if he had any local maps, guides, or books to help me navigate the city better. He showed me those he had for sale, pointed out places to visit, and then traced the routes to each of them from downtown Napier.

Several enormous vineyards appeared on the guide in front of us. Wine, he told me, was a fabulous specialty in that part of Napier and Hawke's Bay in general. Some of the wineries were big enough and popular enough locally to be included in the guide. You could visit each one most days for a wine-tasting, designed to encourage tourists to buy bottles or sign up for regular shipments throughout the course of the year.

One of the bigger ones caught my eye: Toshi Vineyards. The name was curious enough that I asked the bookstore proprietor about it.

"That vineyard is relatively new, I think," he said. "One family ran it as a farm for the better part of a hundred years. But it had been in disrepair for quite a while. Then a young woman showed up a few years back—part of the family, I guess—and turned it into a large vineyard. Came from New York, people say. One of those types with money who keep showing up here from other parts of the world. The vineyard isn't well known outside of Hawke's Bay, but it's popular with the locals. A good place to drink after work."

"And the owner, the woman who took it over... do you happen to know her name?" I asked.

"Can't say I do. But it's an easy drive. You could see it first thing in the morning. I'm sure they offer a wine-tasting."

"I'll do that," I said, thanking the bookstore owner. I bought the guide and traced the route to the vineyard before stashing it in my pocket.

The name of the vineyard, and the story behind the woman who'd moved here from New York, seemed more than a coincidence. It sure looked as if Michelle Searle had moved to Napier and taken over the family farm in Hawke's Bay. She was making wine but not going out of her way to sell it beyond the local community. Just like John Andrews, she'd left the scene and found a nice, quiet place where she could spend whatever wealth she'd accumulated.

I decided not to approach her directly, as I had with Andrews. I wanted to visit a bit first.

I'd just take part in some wine-tasting in the morning, and see where the day took me.

Chapter 22

I didn't want to alert Michelle Searle that I was about to show up on her doorstep. I planned to just look around, ask some discreet questions, and see how things went. If I was presented with a chance to confront her directly, I'd take it. But I wasn't going to risk her shutting me out before I'd had a chance to take the measure of her.

So, following Dotty's advice, I didn't hurry into my day. I spent a casual morning at a café near the bay drinking coffee and catching up on events from around the world.

Napier was on the eastern side of northern New Zealand, with a large, magnificent bay that jutted inland. Like the view John Andrews had on St. Barts, the one from waterfront shops in Napier was spectacular. Had I lived there, I'd grow tired of the scenery. But I could see why people enjoyed their visits to Napier, and why others wished to live here permanently.

It was a brilliant day as I set off for Hawke's Bay. The store owners in downtown Napier were right. It was a gorgeous place to visit. The hills and the farms I drove past on my way inland were serene and picturesque.

I found the Toshi Vineyard with no trouble. It was as large as the bookstore owner had said. I passed nearly a half mile of straight rows of grapes in the field before coming to the paved entrance to the winery.

The visitor's parking lot was only a third full when I pulled in. A few people were scattered about. I parked the car, then took stock of the place as I walked casually toward the front of the building. The winery looked almost brand new and offered a guided tour. Signs announced one would start in about half an hour. I also noticed strategically mounted security cameras all around the grounds and winery.

But they weren't simple cameras. They were probably capable of facial recognition. Nearly every high-end retail store in New York City now had this type of system. It allowed them to identify a customer as he or she walked in the door; upload the identity to a global database; and then send the potential customer's preferences to both the concierge and the salespeople on the floor. They could then tailor their questions to you as you walked their establishment. They could also try to steer you toward what you were already inclined to like or buy.

It was, in a physical sense, what happens when you look at a digital site on the internet. This same database matches your search history with the content you're looking at, and then displays advertisements based on that history. Some of it is better at matching than others, but the principles are the same: Identify you, and then give you what you might like.

What that meant, here, was that I'd be known the instant I walked into the establishment. I couldn't be sure how aggressive this place was, or whether they'd bother to match my limited wine tastes with my purchases over the years. When I had bought wine, it was nearly always a Zinfandel...only because someone once told me this was the smart wine to buy. I had no idea about wines, and never would.

But it also meant someone, somewhere, in the office complex sitting inside the winery would instantly have my name. Michelle Searle wouldn't be looking for me, as far as I knew. But she might be looking for *someone* like me, just as Andrews had been on St. Barts. So I needed to be even more cautious in my questions.

"May I offer you a glass of our newest Zinfandel?" a young woman asked almost the instant I walked through the front door.

She'd already poured a glass for me. The wine glass was sitting in the center of a round tray she was holding with a practiced hand. I glanced at the table behind her. There were a dozen different types of wine on the table behind her. She'd chosen the Zinfandel for me. It had all happened—the facial recognition, transfer of data, and my likely preference for Zinfandels—from the moment I'd begun to walk into the winery.

I smiled at the young woman. It wasn't her fault we now lived in a world where things like artificial intelligence, global databases, and facial recognition were both ubiquitous and banal all at once. "Yes, actually, I would love a Zinfandel," I told her. "And thank you."

I took a sip. It was quite good, though I could never really tell whether wine was truly good or not. I only knew whether I happened to like the taste or not. She watched me intently with a practiced eye to see whether I did, in fact, like the Zinfandel. I'm sure there are wine-tasting tells I'm clueless about. Whatever my own particular tell was, she could see I liked this particular glass.

"Vineyards introduced Zinfandels here in New Zealand just fifteen years ago," she said as she reached behind her to find the bottle it had come from. "The very first Zinfandel came from here in Hawke's Bay. It's become quite popular since."

"And Toshi Vineyard? When did they introduce a Zinfandel?"

"Oh, almost immediately after we opened," she explained. "We had Zinfandels after our very first growing season."

"Have you been here with Toshi since that time, when you opened?"

The young woman smiled back at me. "No, I'm a new transplant, from Australia. I've only been living in Hawke's Bay for a couple of years. But I love it here. And Toshi is a wonderful place to work. Everyone here adores the place."

I glanced around the wine-tasting room. A few visitors milled around, looking at the various wines for sale. A couple of groups sat together with multiple glasses and bottles of different wines.

"The place looks magnificent," I said. "The owners clearly put a lot of work and money into it. A bookstore owner in Napier told me about Toshi. He said its wines are popular with the locals."

"Oh, the tourists like it, too." She laughed. "But, yes, we have a good group of folks who visit regularly."

"And the name of the vineyard? Does it mean something?"

"The owner always says it's just a fun name. There's a vineyard in California with a similar name, though it's spelled with a 'c.' That vineyard has been around for generations, so people sometimes get our names confused."

"I see. Well, it is a fun name. I'll remember it, for sure."

She reached out with a practiced hand and gently nudged me

toward the back of the room where they offered wine-tasting for a small fee. "Are you interested in tasting some of our other wines today?"

"I think I'd like to browse a bit first," I replied. "Then I'm interested in taking the tour. The sign outside said it might start in about 30 minutes or so."

She masked her disappointment to the news that I was only a browser. But she also didn't miss a beat. "Why, yes, the tour starts shortly. It's a lovely tour. You'll see the different types of grapes we're known for, and the rows of oak barrels we use for our best wines. We have stainless steel barrels, of course, but I'm particularly fond of the smaller oak barrels used to age some of our wines."

"I'm looking forward to it."

"So I can't interest you in some of our Zinfandels, just to taste them?" she asked, making one final run at me. "We have several. We could, if you'd like, include a special bottle of one of the Zinfandels we're known for?"

I admired her perky persistence. Perhaps I was feeling like I was on a bit of a holiday, or maybe because I wasn't in a particular hurry, but I decided to brighten up her day a little. I didn't simply want to be a browser.

"How about I buy two bottles of the Zinfandel I'm drinking? How would that be?"

"That would be delightful!" she said, clearly surprised at the purchase.

"So, can you tell me more about it? What type of grape and why the owner chose this type?"

I joined her as we moved toward a row of bottles to one side of the store.

"This is actually one of our owner's favorites," she told me in a hushed, conspiratorial tone. "It's from her first year in the business here, after she took over the family farm and created the vineyard in 2015. It's dense and ripe. It has a slightly licorice flavor, which you could probably taste. But it also has a solid influence of American oak."

I had no idea what made a wine dense and ripe. I hadn't been able to detect the licorice. And I had no clue how to discern the influence of American oak. But it meant something that the wine had been fermented in American oak.

"Oh, so the owner... she's from the United States?" I asked as we made our way across the floor.

"Yes, she's an American," she replied in the same conspiratorial tone. "Her taste is elegant and refined. She's from New York, but they say she learned everything she could from Napa before coming here to take over the family farm from her grandfather."

"Well, I'm delighted by the taste. I will thank Ms. Searle silently as I sip her wonderful Zinfandel over dinner this evening."

The young woman didn't bat an eye. She didn't correct me about the name of the vineyard's owner. She found the two bottles and handed them to me. "So you're staying in Napier?"

"Yes. At The County Hotel."

I could almost see the wheels spinning in her head. Only certain types of visitors could afford to stay at an expensive, five-star hotel like that. I might as well have put a bull's-eye on my chest.

"That particular hotel is also a favorite of Ms. Searle's. Many of her guests who come to Napier from different parts of the world stay there," she said. "I'll bet she'd love to meet you. Perhaps I could persuade her to join you for the tour. She enjoys talking about the history of the vineyard and how it's operated today."

"Oh, I wouldn't want to be a bother."

"No bother at all," she added breezily. "If she's available, I'm sure she'd be happy to join you."

***

As soon as she joined the tour, I recognized Michelle Searle from her old photos. Only five winery patrons had signed up, so it was a small group. She stood at the back, listening with the rest of us as the guide walked us through the storage areas behind the winery's show room.

As we paused in front of some smaller oak barrels and our tour guide described why these particular barrels were used for the special reserve wines, Searle glided over to a spot immediately to my left. Apparently, with wine, bigger was not necessarily better. Small barrels, it seemed, produced extraordinarily expensive wines.

"It's remarkable, isn't it?" Searle whispered to me. "The technology hasn't changed in generations. We've been growing grapes and producing wine in oak barrels for a very long time."

"Quite remarkable," I answered.

"Who would ever think that, in today's world, where everything is digital and entire industries can rise and fall in nearly the blink of an eye, we would value something that is grown and even shipped today the way it was for two thousand years?"

I turned to face her. She was nearly a full head shorter than me. I had to look down at her as we talked in hushed tones. Our eyes met.

"Two thousand years?" I asked.

"At least two thousand years," she said. "This was the way they shipped wine during the Roman Empire. So it's at least as old as that. No one knows for sure. But wine and wood have been joined for a long time. Apparently, unlike things like currency or communications, old is infinitely better than new."

"Well, good." I laughed lightly. "I like old much better than new. I prefer a good book in my hand any day. I still read actual newspapers. So if wine is better using older methods, I'm all for it."

"Amen to that. I'm often torn between the two worlds. I like brand-new, cutting-edge stuff. But I also like the old ways. And wine-making is most assuredly part of the old ways."

"Not me. I've never really been good at the 'cutting-edge stuff.'"

"Why, if I may ask?"

"I'm not afraid of it," I explained. "I just don't particularly go for it. I like to take a straight line toward things. Find out for myself. I'm not comfortable allowing technology to do my work."

"I can see that. Makes sense, up to a point. But we live in a world where technology surrounds us. It's so infused in our daily existence that we hardly notice anymore. For instance, I could tell you a lot about yourself, even though we've never met."

"Like the fact I prefer Zinfandels, when I drink wine at all?"

"Yes, that," Searle said. "But I doubt you're much of a wine connoisseur."

"Can't say that I am," I answered truthfully. "I'm fascinated by it, though. Especially the fact that wood and wine have been used together for two thousand years."

"It's one of the pieces of history that drew me to this way of life here in New Zealand, away from the fast-paced worries that consume us in other parts of the world. And you're right about something else."

"What?"

She leaned in closer, so only I could hear her words. "The oak barrels. I deliberately brought American culture with me when I arrived here several years ago and distanced myself from my previous profession. But you likely know that already, Mr. Thomas. Don't you?"

So this was where the day had taken us. Things moved quickly when technology like artificial intelligence, big data, and facial recognition was at the heart of things.

"Yes, I do," I said slowly. "And am I also right about something else, Ms. Searle? That the name of the vineyard is part of a name that you hold dear?"

"It is," she replied, still standing close to me.

I nodded. "I thought so. Can we talk somewhere, in private? Might that be possible? I believe our discussion will be…fruitful."

Searle smiled broadly. "That's good. I like that. Mind if I steal it?"

"All yours," I said, matching her smile. "I have no plans to open a vineyard anytime soon."

CHAPTER 23

We found a quiet, dry, intimate place in an adjacent storage area. There were only three oak barrels—smaller than any we'd seen on the tour—sitting in the middle of it. Nothing else. The area was self-contained. No closets. The door sealed behind us as it closed. The temperature inside was pleasant.

Michelle Searle had brought two chairs into the storage area with her. I heard a barely perceptible noise above us and looked up, wondering.

"Ventilation," she said as she placed the chairs next to the three oak barrels. "We control the temperature here so it never deviates. We also control the circulation of air. Hardly anyone comes in here, other than to check on these three barrels."

I glanced at the three barrels as I took my seat. "So, I'm assuming these are your reserve wines? What are they? Or, should I say, what will they be when it's time?"

"Yes, they're special reserve wines. But not just any wines. New Zealand is largely known for its Sauvignon Blanc wines. Two-thirds of the grapes grown on both the north and south islands end up being Sauv Blanc. It's largely what Kiwi wines are known for. But they aren't the most expensive wines."

"What's the most expensive from New Zealand?"

"No one has been able to make a wine that sells for more than $300 or so a bottle on a regular basis… at least not yet. We can't compete with other wines from grape-growing regions that have been around for hundreds of years. The most expensive wines from this part of New Zealand, here in Hawke's Bay, still can't go for much more than $100 a bottle."

"If I remember correctly, don't some of the most expensive wines from France go for thousands of dollars?" I asked.

"That's right. The most expensive wines in the world can go for that. But not here. The best bottle of wine you can buy from these parts is a Bordeaux red blend. It sells for just north of $100 a bottle. Hawke's Bay isn't known for its red wine, so a blend is about the best you can hope for."

I smiled. "Let me guess. You aim to change that, and these three barrels are part of that?"

"Yeah, they are." She laughed. "They're destined to be a Cabernet Sauvignon. The maturation here should take place more than a year from now in these American oak barrels, which were new when I bought them. We'll age these wines for another three years before we put them out for sale under the Toshi brand, and see if we can't sell them for $500 a bottle and expand the New Zealand market."

I did a quick mental calculation. "You've been here for a few years. So is this the second round for you, in these barrels?"

"Yep. The first batch went into a blend. It wasn't … precisely what we'd hoped for. But we're hopeful about this second round. With a bit of luck, and decent marketing, the wine maturing in these oak barrels will become the Cabs that establish the Toshi brand name beyond Hawke's Bay."

"Will it, do you think?" I asked, genuinely curious.

Searle laughed heartily. "Oh, who the hell knows? Only fools try to make money in the wine business. It's a lot like the racehorse business. You spend all of your time trying not to lose your shirt and simply break even."

"Why do it, then?"

Searle leaned forward in her seat and placed a loving hand on one of the barrels. "Because I can, and because it's a challenge. At this stage of my life, I have more money than I ever imagined. I can afford to try to make the most expensive wine in New Zealand's history. If it fails, it makes no difference at all to me financially. I can simply start over, or try something new. So why not try to reach the top of the market?"

"Why not indeed, though I can't say I've ever had the kind of money that would allow me to just try something with no fear of the financial consequences."

140

"But that's about to change, isn't it, Mr. Thomas?" Searle studied me closely.

I had no idea whether Searle knew I'd been contacted by the same person who'd approached her. Most likely, she was making an educated guess. But it made no difference. *Might as well jump right in with both feet*, I thought. *We'll wind up in the same place soon enough.*

"May I ask you a question first?" I said. "I'm assuming the facial recognition cameras installed in this place kicked out everything there is to know about me."

"Yes. I know a lot about you now."

"And you have some idea why I'm here? Especially if I tell you that I was able to find my way here after talking to Jasper Olaffson in Iceland?"

"Ah, yes," she said with a frown. "I've always regretted my decision to deceive him about who I was. At the time, I wasn't sure who was behind anything. There were too many loose ends, from the NSA to KKR to the new tech I was looking at. I didn't know whom to trust. I was being far too cautious. I needn't have been. I know that now. But at the time…"

"No worries," I assured her. "Jasper's fine about it. I'll tell him you're sorry next time we talk."

"Thank you for that kind offer. And, yes, I know why you're here. May I assume, then, that you're trying to decide what to do, much as I wrestled with that very question years ago?"

"I am. I haven't quite decided whether I'm doing this or not. But I'll tell you where I'm leaning. I may go all in, and see how far I can take it."

Searle nodded. "You're making the right decision. Go all in. Don't be cautious. It's not like there's a rulebook. So you might as well make your own rules."

I looked directly at Searle. "So we're clear, can I state the obvious here, just between the two of us?"

"Please, do."

"We were both contacted by the same benefactor," I said. "In my case, I received a text message from an unlisted number that I mistakenly thought came from my editor. It told me to visit an office across the street from the White House. There was a receptionist in the office who'd just been hired and had no idea why she was there. I then learned there was an account at Chase Bank with what seemed like a nearly bottomless well from which I could make investments. I tested it, and it worked. But I have no idea who that person is, what he or she might want out of it, or why that person picked me."

"But you have some guesses?" she asked quietly.

"I do. I've begun to assume that it's all a rather unique, risky investment plan from someone who has so much money that they can afford to try whatever they like—not unlike your willingness to throw money at a costly wine business here in New Zealand to see if it works. But I'm no closer to discovering that today than I was when I began. Sound familiar?"

"It does," Searle said. "Quite familiar, with a slightly different twist from my own experience."

"Which was?"

She looked away, as if she rarely, if ever, talked about her own memories. It made sense. Who could she talk to about them, any-way? Only a few in the world had ever been let in on the game. There was a sad wistfulness to her demeanor that reminded me of John Andrews.

"It was more than a decade ago," Searle said. "I was quite happy in my job at KKR—rising through the ranks quickly and headed toward a partnership. Most of the alternative investments I was making were paying off quite well. I had a knack for looking over the horizon to see the next big thing. The leadership trusted me. I could do no wrong."

"You were becoming a barbarian at the gate," I joked.

She smiled. "I was. I liked the hunt. I enjoyed everything about it. At some point, I started to hear about this revolutionary new blockchain tech that couldn't be hacked. It was exciting and differ-ent, way outside the lanes of what KKR usually invested in. I knew a great deal about it, though, since my background was precisely in what they were developing and talking about. There was no invest-ment opportunity in the beginning. Only the rumor of something from someone who'd created the genesis code."

"You were involved with bitcoin from the beginning?" I asked.

"Yes, from the very beginning. But it was all tangled up. Then I got an invitation from what I thought was a colleague to join him at a Lucius concert at Madison Square Garden. I was supposed to pick up the tickets from a guy named Fox at Will Call. At the time, Lucius was only a local group from Brooklyn, so they were opening for someone else. I loved the group's music. Someone clearly knew that about me."

"So you went to pick up the tickets, but things didn't turn out exactly as you expected."

"No, they didn't. I picked up a ticket for an exclusive box seat. When I got there, my colleague wasn't present. But there was a handwritten note on the chair, inviting me backstage to see Lucius after they'd finished their set. I was to meet Fox there with Lucius as well."

"Was it legit? Did you meet the band members?"

"I did, and it was fun. I really liked the band. I knew they were going to make it big. But then one of the band members told me he wanted to introduce me to their manager's friend. That's when it became interesting."

"How so?"

"They handed me off to a guy even shorter than me, with a tangled mess of long black hair that covered his eyes and partly obscured his face. We talked in a side room, just the two of us. He was shy and had trouble looking me in the eye. He constantly ducked his head, fixed his glasses, and occasionally cracked the index finger on his right hand. His voice was so low and husky that I had to lean in to hear what he was saying. He was dressed in white pants with side loops."

"Like painter's pants?" I asked.

"Yeah. The type of pants a builder or construction worker or painter might wear. But I remember thinking it was odd. No one wore pants like that. His shirt was also white and loose-fitting, and he wore sturdy walking boots. The entire wardrobe seemed like a uniform—the kind you slip on every day and never deviate from. Like something a monk would wear. There was no color to it, nothing that stood out against the backdrop. He just blended into the scenery."

"Did he introduce himself?"

"Not exactly. He said he was a friend of the band's manager, and that he was looking at backing it. I had no way of knowing if that was true, but I was there so I listened to his pitch."

I leaned forward. "So, what was the pitch?"

"He asked if I was interested in an unusual venture. I tried to put him off, but he insisted. When he started describing this 256-bit block-chain technology that NSA couldn't crack, I was intrigued, because I'd actually coded some of what he was talking about. Only a few of us were paying attention to it at the time, so it was highly unusual for an alleged potential investor in a Brooklyn band to know almost as much about it as I did."

"Cryptocurrency, you mean?"

"Yes, as I soon discovered. He gave me a business card. It had no address, no phone number. Just an AOL email address that was a random set of letters, and his name above it. The name meant nothing to me at the time. It was only a couple of years later, after we'd begun to correspond and he'd walked me through the process to mine bitcoin from my own computer in 2010 and 2011, that I put pieces of the puzzle together."

I stared hard at Michelle Searle. She cracked a thin, sparse smile as she watched my reaction. "You can't be serious," I said finally. "You met Satoshi Nakamoto? That's who the guy was?"

"That was the name on the business card. That's who I allegedly was corresponding with back then, in 2009. It was the same name that started showing up occasionally on the crypto forums I was on."

"But it had to be Nakamoto, right? Who else could it have been?"

"Maybe it was Satoshi Nakamoto, maybe it wasn't. All I can tell you is that it was a different email address than the famous GMX account everyone associates with Satoshi Nakamoto from the early days. As far as I can tell, no one else has the AOL address I have. I can't be certain who it really was. It might have been him. But it might just as easily have been the same person who contacted you."

She sighed. "They might be the same person. They might be different people. Our benefactor might have informed Nakamoto.

I honestly don't know. I've never seen him again. I have no idea how to find him. That AOL address stopped working years ago. Facial recognition software turns up nothing because I have so little to go on."

"You met him only the one time, back stage at Madison Square Garden?"

"Yes, just the one time. I eventually got around to asking the band manager about him. He didn't know the guy at all. The whole thing had been set up through boxes within boxes within boxes. There was no chance to trace it back to the guy."

"You only had the business card? Nothing else?"

"Nothing else. But here's the important thing: When I began to correspond with him, he didn't just set me up with the same genesis computer code for bitcoin that he told me on more than one occasion would eventually scale to handle a worldwide payment system. He also introduced me to the very same investment opportunity now being presented to you.

"Once I was onto the bitcoin play, he told me to visit an office in midtown Manhattan. He wrote that he'd been given the address by someone else, who asked him to pass it on to me. I discovered much the same set-up there as you. What I can't determine is whether Nakamoto was the person who found us, or whether the guy I met back stage was simply connected to him in the way that you and I are."

I shook my head in awe. "Wow. That's quite a story. Whoever our benefactor is, he—"

"You're making an assumption that it's a man? And just one person? You know there have been rumors—substantial ones—for years that Satoshi Nakamoto is, in fact, a syndicate?"

"Yeah, I know, and my assumption could be wrong. I have nothing to base it on. Do you?"

"No, I don't," Searle replied.

I nodded. So she was still in the dark as much as I was. "One thing we *can* know is that he was obviously experimenting back then. You may have been one of his earliest efforts."

"I don't know if I was the first, but I do know this person approached someone else about the same time as me."

"Someone else?"

"I met her while I was at KKR. She was the lead researcher at a white-hot human genome startup launched by a Taiwanese businessman in London who later made billions when they cracked the human genome. They came to KKR for their IPO, which made the founder a billionaire, and I got to know her. But just as they were about to take it public, she left abruptly."

"How did you know she'd been approached?" I asked.

"Basically, she told me. I got to know her well during the grueling IPO process. I don't remember how we got to talking about it, but at some point we both realized we'd been approached by the same person. I tried to help her with her decisions, even as I wrestled with my own demons. She said she'd decided to go in a radical, new direction. Two months later, she left the company and went off on her own to start an HIV research company in Nairobi."

"Interesting. But that isn't what happened with you. He didn't merely offer an investment path. He also pulled you into bitcoin."

"He did. I have no idea why, other than the weird combination of my background and my work at KKR. But I didn't hesitate. I pursued both as hard as I could. I made some interesting investments on my own, outside KKR, through that little office I visited in midtown. It grew into quite a portfolio, all on its own. No one ever questioned my investments because I carried the KKR imprimatur. But I also allowed that computer to run nonstop in 2010 and 2011..."

"Hold on," I said softly. "So you were mining bitcoin right alongside Nakamoto almost at the same time?"

Searle nodded. "I was, but not in 2009. I've never corrected the crypto analysts who attribute the 2009 spikes to Nakamoto. They're right. It was that guy I met, or someone he designated. There's no way to know for sure. But I was the second computer."

"Did you tell anyone?"

"No. Remember, I had my KKR job and my side investment activities. I was letting the bitcoin run all through 2010 and 2011. I didn't let on that I'd met someone who professed to be Satoshi Nakamoto, or that I'd been involved almost from the very beginning. I had no way of knowing who was tracking me. So I kept it to myself."

"Did you ever use any of that bitcoin you mined?" I asked.

Searle smiled. "No, not for a long time. I didn't need to. I made a lot of money from my investments. In the beginning, the bitcoin mining was just something I did. I paid almost no attention to it. But after two solid years of mining after Nakamoto stopped, I held more in tens of thousands of data banks all over the world than he did."

"Wait. You held more than a million bitcoins?"

"I did at one time. I don't today. You know all of those bitcoins that went on the market in late 2017, the ones that allowed the market to spike up to $20,000 per bitcoin before falling so dramatically back to Earth? Most of them were mine, spread out strategically all over the world through dozens of legitimate companies so they could be used for partial bitcoin sales to ordinary investors."

I tried to run the numbers in my head. "So you…"

"Made an awful lot of money right around Christmas in 2017," Searle said. "Yes, I did. Nearly 500,000 bitcoins were available through all of those data banks, though not all of them sold for $20,000 apiece. There was a sliding scale over the course of about four months. But it allowed me to enter the Billionaires' Club in 2017."

I'd finally been able to tack zeros onto the end of 500,000. Michelle Searle was now worth somewhere in the neighborhood of ten billion dollars from the sale of those bitcoins. And she still had more coins that she hadn't used. "You're worth, what, $10 billion from those bitcoins?" I asked.

She waved a hand. "Something like that. I'd been quite comfortable when I moved to New Zealand. But now, thanks to that encounter all those years ago at Madison Square Garden, I have more money than I reasonably know what to do with. I could add another few billion on top right now if I wanted to, despite how much the price of bitcoin has fallen from that peak in 2017."

"You know, if Nakamoto had sold his million bitcoins that fall, he'd have made $20 billion or so."

"Yes, something like that."

"That means he either no longer has the data keys to those million coins, for whatever reason…"

"Or he doesn't actually need the money," Searle said quietly.

"Right. He doesn't need the money," I mused. "But who doesn't need $20 billion?"

"Satoshi Nakamoto, apparently."

I was stunned by it all. It was more than the fact that Michelle Searle had, quite possibly, met the mythical Satoshi Nakamoto, and that she'd been one of the earliest devotees of bitcoin, and that she had made billions from it. She herself was now a significant part of world financial history.

The situation reminded me precisely of what Winston Churchill had once said in a famous 1939 radio broadcast, speaking of Russia's interest in siding with the allies against the Nazis in World War Two: "It is a riddle, wrapped in a mystery, inside an enigma; but perhaps there is a key. That key is Russian national interest."

The key here was self-interest. But determining that self-interest? I had no way of discerning that. At least not now.

"Have you ever told this story to anyone—about Satoshi Nakamoto, the bitcoin origins, or our benefactor?"

"No," Searle said. "You're the first. And, if you don't mind, I'd like this to stay between us. I have no way of knowing where my vulnerability might be. But I know enough about agencies like the NSA and the FBI that track bitcoin's subterranean uses that I'd prefer to stay off the grid."

"No one knows you're a billionaire?" I asked, incredulous.

"How would they? I haven't told anyone other than you. I have no desire to be on those lists that places like *Fortune* and *Forbes* are constantly assembling. As far as anyone knows, I did quite well with investments in the States, then moved back to open a winery on our family farm in Hawke's Bay near Napier. End of story. There are lots of people with a bit of wealth just like me in various parts of the world. I have no need to let anyone know I'm part of a very small, exclusive club. The money I made over the years, and then in 2017, is now sitting calmly in a number of boring places where it collects even more money."

"You do realize, don't you, that you are, most likely, the wealthiest self-made female billionaire in the world? If you told people, you'd be instantly famous everywhere. That's something."

"Is it?" she fired back. "Or is it an unwanted invitation for every celebrity-seeking journalist on the planet to come knocking on my door?"

"I get your point. But you really have no desire to let the world know about Satoshi Nakamoto? For years, every investor in crypto and bitcoin and every tech journalist I know has been dying to know why he's never done anything with the million coins he mined in 2009. People would kill to hear this story."

"Precisely," Searle said evenly. "There are people who might very well *kill* to hear it. We both know how organized crime works, and how it's using cryptocurrency now. So, for that reason, I believe it's safest to let the myth remain just that...a myth. I see no good reason or real benefit in telling my story merely for the sake of some prurient fascination with the legend of Satoshi Nakamoto."

"I understand," I said slowly. I wasn't entirely convinced she was right, but I'd honor her request to keep her secret safe. "I won't talk of this with anyone else."

"Good. I appreciate it." She shifted in her chair. "Now you've heard my story. You know how it ends. But what of your intentions? You're at the beginning. What's your plan, if I might ask?"

I eyed the small oak barrels beside us, the liquid inside maturing until it was ready to become something more than grapes from the vine. I had no intention of waiting to see what might mature inside small, exquisite oak barrels over time.

"I've decided to go in the exact opposite direction as you," I told her. "I'm going to invest everywhere, all at once, with as many members of the Billionaires' Club as he, or she, or they will allow."

"Shock and awe in the financial world, eh?"

"Yes, shock and awe," I answered. "Then we'll see what emerges."

CHAPTER 24

On my flight back to Washington, I was still reeling from my conversation with Michelle Searle. I'd hoped our conversation would clarify things. They had, somewhat. But they'd also added new layers to the puzzle.

Was the person who'd contacted us Satoshi Nakamoto? Was the bizarre little man in white painter's garb that Searle met backstage the mythical founder of bitcoin who'd never cashed in on his math invention? Was it because he was an extraordinarily wealthy billionaire already? Or perhaps he had another goal, one that would be disrupted severely if he cashed in, or a parallel motivation that neither Searle nor I could discern.

I knew I was shooting in the dark about all of this. I was no closer to understanding who was behind everything than I was before going to New Zealand.

I did have some theories. But they were only theories.

Was the person who contacted us, in fact, a syndicate of extraordinarily wealthy individuals, much like the syndicate most crypto analysts believed was really what made up "Satoshi Nakamoto" and who had chosen to develop cryptocurrency for their own mysterious purpose? Had that group developed a radical new game for their own amusement, tapping interesting players like Searle, Andrews, and me to play the game under a set of rules that only they understood?

There was some logic to this theory. Wealthy individuals had constructed elaborate games for their own amusement for hundreds of years. The Colosseum in Rome was evidence of that. You could argue that the first Olympic Games, traced by historians all the way back to 776 BC, when it was dedicated to the gods and staged on the ancient plains of Olympia, was an elaborate game for the amusement of society's elite.

Virtually every hugely expensive professional sports franchise in the soccer, football, baseball, and basketball worlds was further evidence. Nearly every team in these leagues was owned by one or more members of the exclusive Billionaires' Club that collectively controlled over half the Earth's wealth. The stock market, or ownership of companies, was further proof. There was only one real game, some argued. Amass as much wealth as possible and win the game. Whoever has the most toys at the end wins.

I had my doubts about this theory. It seemed too simplistic. The game I found myself in was far too elaborate and private to merely be entertainment for a syndicate of wealthy individuals. Sure, they might have retired to a private island somewhere to observe the playing of their game and discuss who was winning or losing—a game to pass the time.

But I didn't buy it. This game seemed to have a guiding principle at the center. John Andrews knew he'd made a foundational mistake in his investment strategy and been punished for it. Michelle Searle had exited on her own terms, with billions in hand. But Andrews, Searle, and I all believed there was some innate purpose at the heart of the game we'd been drawn into.

This notion made my second theory more plausible—that a group of uber-wealthy individuals had cleverly constructed a game to mask an investment strategy that pushed the envelope of business in a way nothing else could. Every venture firm on the planet essentially chased the same strategy: Find things to invest in that will pay off so handsomely that they cover all losses elsewhere. Constantly look for diamonds in the rough that you can pluck, polish, and turn into things of beauty that pay off.

The game I was in would then be some version of that, employing risk-takers like myself to find those investments that might pay off nicely. We were the two-percent risk pool. And if it didn't pan out, or if we made a mistake by being too cautious or too selfish, we were cut off. It made sense…sort of. But I had serious doubts about this theory as well.

If it was only about making money, even risky money, then why construct something so elaborate? Why shield it in such secrecy? There were plenty of firms willing to hire talented individuals who could take big risks and make big bets. You didn't need to construct a game like this if that was your ultimate goal. Making money appeared to be at the heart of the game, but I didn't believe it was the central aim. Perhaps it was, instead, only a means to an end. But what end? That was the question I couldn't answer.

I had a third theory, one that hadn't formed well in my mind yet. I'd read Ayn Rand's *Atlas Shrugged* in college and been profoundly affected. I'd carried in my head the notion of John Galt and a cast of libertarian capitalists shaping the world behind the scenes for years…at least until I'd had a chance to re-read Rand's work later in life, as an adult.

Ayn Rand was a truly awful writer. Though her novel had become the bible for the modern libertarian movement, it was an abject mess. Rand had strung together ideals about unfettered capitalism as the central, driving aim of humankind and attached them somewhat haphazardly to a cast of characters who wandered through an apocalyptic landscape that formed the plot's backdrop. John Galt was mostly a ghost. He wasn't even close to being a real, three-dimensional person.

That, perhaps, was Rand's point. John Galt was the embodiment of libertarianism and what any good capitalist should aspire to be like. She certainly succeeded in that regard. Any number of capitalists, and more than a few billionaires, secretly and fervently wished to be their generation's John Galt. Decades earlier, several had banded together to capture the Republican Party in America … and largely succeeded. Rand's messy, incoherent philosophy written about ad nauseum in *Atlas Shrugged* had taken root deep inside America's pro-business national political party.

The lyrical strains of libertarianism, which inspired out-of-the-box economic theories and radical capitalism, were evident in the companies that straddled Silicon Valley and drove America's national security complex. They were evident in the origins of the infamous Silk Road, where an inventor deliberately constructed a radical way to bypass the traditional banking system in a way that paid homage to libertarianism.

My third theory revolved around this notion of radical capitalism and libertarianism as a way to order political and business life in America and around the planet. I knew just enough about the origin of the libertarian political movement in America to be dangerous…and to somewhat inform this third theory. The father of my first wife had been the chairman of the American Libertarian Party. We'd had raging philosophical discussions when he and I were much younger, until we'd both grown weary of the verbal jousting. I knew the party's central aims, and they did have something in common with the game I now found myself in.

Perhaps there was a secretive cabal of libertarian billionaires who'd banded together to create the game. But why? What purpose would it serve? John Andrews and Michelle Searle didn't seem like Ayn Rand devotees to me, and I certainly wasn't one. Plus, the game didn't have a clear aim, like taking over a national political party in America in order to seize and hold power.

Clearly I needed more data. The aims of the game were still beyond me. There was only one way to gather the information I needed.

It was time to roll the dice.

CHAPTER 25

Dotty was so prepared for the launch of our insane plan it was scary.

"So what'd you learn in New Zealand?" she asked me when I finally came into the office mid-morning after an uneasy night's rest. "Did you figure it all out? Get some clarity?"

Her desk was still uncluttered, but my office in the back now overflowed with cabinets. So many file folders were piled on my desk that I could see the stacks even from here. All the research from the half-dozen research firms had evidently been delivered and assembled.

I hesitated briefly before answering. I truly felt I knew Dotty now and could trust her implicitly with just about anything. My hesitation wasn't due to lack of trust. It was more an instinctive, knee-jerk thought that perhaps I should shield her somehow from information that might cause her trouble down the line in ways I couldn't yet anticipate. I was, despite my usual way of treating others, thinking about her welfare.

"Well…"

Dotty sighed. "Out with it, Seth. We can't have any secrets between us. You're not doing me any favors if you do. I'm in this every bit as much as you are now. We're both in the deep end. So spill it."

I smiled. I sure did like this woman. "OK, fine. You know who Satoshi Nakamoto is, right?"

"The mysterious creator of bitcoin, who has never cashed in a single one of his million bitcoins? Sure, of course."

"Michelle Searle believes she met him 10 years ago, right at the very start," I said. "Or, at least, she met a person who was either Satoshi Nakamoto or speaking directly for him."

"Or her," Dotty corrected me.

"Yeah, right. Or her. But the person Searle met, back stage at Madison Square Garden, was a bizarre little man who wore an all-white uniform. He and Searle created the first two or three million bitcoins together."

Dotty stared at me. "She really met Satoshi Nakamoto?"

"Looks that way. And it made Searle wealthy. Her bitcoins served as the backbone of what happened in the fall of 2017. She's worth at least $10 billion today, though she's never told anyone that."

"That's … crazy." Dotty shook her head. "That would make her the wealthiest woman in the world who didn't inherit her money. So might she be the benefactor here?"

"No chance," I said firmly. "Until quite recently, she didn't have the kind of wealth that allows you to lose a billion dollars and not genuinely lose any sleep over it. What's more, she was pulled into the same game we're in, right after she met Nakamoto."

"So she made investments like we're about to go after?"

"Yes, and she succeeded with some of them, though it seems like bitcoin was her big success."

"And she just walked away afterwards? She wasn't cut off the way John Andrews was when he made a wrong move?"

"By all appearances, she just walked away. She's living on the eastern side of New Zealand. She said I'm the first person she's ever told about her wealth, or the role she played in the creation of bitcoin."

"Why, do you think?"

"She doesn't see the need, she said. She has more than enough wealth to do whatever she wants for the rest of her life. She doesn't need the publicity, or the recognition."

"What about doing good for the world with philanthropy, or creating new businesses?"

"Good question," I said. "That doesn't seem to be a motivation. She's trying to create the most expensive wine in New Zealand's history. She seems content with that pursuit. I'm not sure she has any interest in going beyond that."

"How odd. That doesn't exactly fit the profile we've been building about the rationale and thought behind all of this, does it?"

"No, it doesn't. But it looks like Searle may have been one of the very first experiments. Maybe even the first. The benefactor was clearly trying things out in real time. He may have misfired with Searle. Or, perhaps, he got it right. Maybe Michelle Searle provided exactly what he needed, or wanted, at that moment in time."

"Yeah, it would help if we knew what the ultimate aim for all of this was, beyond trying to create wealth or investing," Dotty said.

"It sure would. And speaking of investing, what are all of those files on my desk back there?"

Dotty smiled mischievously. "I took the liberty of weeding through all of the proposals we got back from the firms. I pulled out only the ones I thought you really needed to look at. I put the ones that didn't make a whole lot of sense off to the side—in file cabinets and inventoried by country and cross-indexed by both last name and industries."

"You've been busy."

"I have. Pretty much nonstop since the research files started coming in."

"I imagine it was…intense."

"That's putting it mildly," she said. "It may be the most extensive financial portfolio of emerging companies, industries, sectors, and products ever assembled in one place."

"So you said you decided on the ones you wanted me to look at? What were your criteria? How'd you sort through them?"

Dotty took a deep breath. She was clearly nervous about the decisions she'd made while I was away in New Zealand. "So here's the thing. There are some truly interesting opportunities in here, directly tied to every one of the 2,700 or so billionaires on Earth. The firms provided almost exactly what we'd hoped for."

"Except…?"

"Except they didn't know how to decide why one might matter and another wouldn't. We now have an investment opportunity that's near and dear to every billionaire, as much as could be reasonably provided for each of them. We have a substantial file and rationale for each of the files in your office."

"But you didn't put all 2,700 files on my desk, did you?" I asked quietly.

"No, because here's what started to become clear as I went through them. I know you, and what I believe you're actually looking for. You aren't looking to just make money for someone else. You aren't trying to pick winners from a sea of potential losers or long shots. You aren't trying to become wealthy yourself."

"So what am I looking for, then?" I asked, bemused.

Dotty hesitated. "Before I answer that, I should also tell you I hired another firm on top of the research firms. I hired the Money Exchange after our guy at Chase recommended we take a look at them. We paid a lot for that report."

I was somewhat familiar with the Money Exchange. Coming out of the Great Depression, a young journalist named Napoleon Hill spent almost 20 years studying the wealthiest people on Earth—from the great industrialists like Henry Ford to the oil industry barons like John D. Rockefeller. His book, *Think and Grow Rich,* was the great work of his lifetime. It described a philosophy that appealed to the masses—that if you had a plan, worked at it relentlessly, and caught a break or two, you could become as wealthy as the Rockefellers or the Henry Fords of the world. It became the quintessential self-help book and guide for everyday Americans who wanted to become rich.

There was just one problem. At the time Napoleon Hill wrote his book, hundreds of billionaires had inherited their great wealth and were only piling money on top of it.

Today, more than half of the billionaires in this exclusive club were self-made, yet still relied on massive family and social connections. With such a wide gulf between the world's haves and have-nots, a book like Hill's seemed not merely quaint, but downright obscene. No amount of strategy or relentlessness allowed a common man or woman to enter this club. It simply wasn't possible. The gap between the obscenely wealthy and the poor who lived paycheck to paycheck had created a populist revolt that allowed just such a "self-made" billionaire to seize the presidency in America by promising to return some of that wealth to ordinary Americans.

Similar anti-wealth political revolutions were creating tectonic shifts in other countries around the globe. It was obvious to everyone that there was no magical secret to great wealth. It certainly didn't come from discipline and the relentless pursuit of a winning strategy, as Napoleon Hill had insisted.

But there *were* strategies that could be gleaned from the world's wealthiest individuals who had not inherited their wealth. Studying that and compiling data on them was precisely what the Money Exchange did. They had dozens and dozens of really smart people who did nothing but study the world's billionaires. The Money Exchange knew the habits, strategies, proclivities, and tendencies of every member of the Billionaires' Club. And, like any successful firm in the era of big data, they made reports on their findings available for a steep price. Many members of the Billionaires' Club secretly bought its products so they could see how their lives and strategies compared to those of their peers.

The Money Exchange rarely, if ever, released anything publicly about their core research findings. They didn't give away their knowledge for free. But I knew they'd identified one important characteristic that separated self-made billionaires from all others who had great ideas but never turned them into massive businesses like Ford Motor Company or Google.

They were incredibly and relentlessly focused. They created a finish line for themselves and never deviated from the race to it. That was the secret of great wealth, if there was one, the Money Exchange's leadership had said on a handful of occasions at public forums. Everything else—family, personal life, community, religious ties—was secondary to that single-mindedness. People set out to become wildly successful, and did nothing else during the pursuit.

Now, however, in the era of big data, I wondered if the equation was changing. Input enough data, allow it to work for you, and you bypassed the need to be so relentlessly focused on your pursuit of success. Michelle Searle certainly hadn't needed to be so focused. She'd simply been in the right place at the right time to become a member of the club.

A new path to great wealth was emerging, and our benefactor seemed to be part of it, though I had no clue how or why at this point. But it had something to do with a willingness to risk failure, even on a grand scale, in the pursuit of something other than the finish line for your great idea. That willingness to bet on yourself, and to take great risks, appeared to be one of the common factors.

One person, it seemed, could change the world if they were relentless, positive, and, like a storm, tried to make sure their ideas proliferated everywhere all at once. That characteristic was certainly on display prominently in the Billionaires' Club.

It did help, though, to be a man. Every year for the past decade told the same story. Roughly 90 percent of those who made it to the Billionaires' Club every year were men. It was much harder to make it into the club if you were a woman. While there was no real secret sauce, what did seem to help, the Money Exchange executives had hinted at over the years, was a willingness to read widely in order to see the world from a variety of perspectives.

"So what did you learn from that Money Exchange report?" I asked Dotty. "And, can I say, that was a great call. I should have thought of that. I'm glad you did."

Dotty smiled sheepishly. "The research firms' reports all kept referencing the Money Exchange, so I decided to go straight to the source and pay for everything they had. We paid an awful lot for it, but their custom research director is now essentially on call to us as a paid consultant. She's available to answer any question we might have about the reports they've given us."

"Makes sense. So?"

"What became obvious is that we only need to pay attention to a relatively small subset of folks and zero in on who might behind all this," Dotty explained. "I mean, assuming that's really what you want..."

"You don't think I'm serious about making money here?" I laughed.

"Oh, I think you're serious, but you don't care about money at all. What you want to discover is who's behind this, and why. Then you might, just might, tell that story. Everything pales in comparison. So, if that's your aim, we only need to focus on connections to a much smaller playing field."

I nodded. Dotty, as usual, precisely understood my aims and thoughts. "And that's what's on my desk back there?"

"It is," she said. "First, I put aside everyone on the list who'd inherited their wealth and were no longer actively doing anything with it other than playing around, according to the Money Exchange report. They had no strategy beyond managing their wealth."

"That seems like a good call as well. It's an efficient way to rule out a whole cast of characters."

"Then I took out everyone who's made the club in the past 10 years. They wouldn't have been around to start this. I didn't know about Michelle Searle, exactly, but from Jasper's timeline, she got started a decade ago at least. That narrowed the list substantially. There were only about a thousand billionaires in 2008. That was the year Mark Zuckerberg made the list as a self-made billionaire."

"Did you include Zuckerberg?"

"Yeah, I did," she said. "But that raises an interesting proposition. I added another criterion that winnowed down the list even further. A decade ago, there weren't nearly as many people who had enough money—say, above $10 billion or so—to play around with a game like this. Zuckerberg is a good case. Though he made the list in 2008, he didn't really have then what he has now, to take such a risk. Others are like that as well. So I made some judgment calls. I included some who were poised to grow considerably wealthier from 2008 on. I also included family members who had inherited the wealth, talked to each other, and collectively added up to a considerable sum of money."

"And the grand total is?"

"Less than 100 people," she said confidently. "There are really just 100 people or so who might have been able to pull this off a decade ago and who are still around. If you narrow it further to those who have even greater wealth now than they did back then, and aren't just fooling around with what they have, the list starts to move closer to only 50 or so."

"That's a small list."

"Yes," she agreed, "but I believe it's the right list. And I also don't think I've overlooked anyone. I've included every possible billionaire who could have started this a decade ago, including those like Alexi Simon in Russia who are in the club but aren't recognized as such. I've also included a handful of organized crime figures, like a few of those at the top of the illegal drug trade. I doubt they're our target, but you never know."

"You're right. You never know. But I think you nailed it. You narrowed the playing field so we're no longer looking at everyone in a cast of thousands." I glanced toward my office. "So that's the list of investments, aimed squarely at this list of 50 or so?"

"It is."

"Well, then, let's get started. I have a lot of reading in front of me." I started to move toward my office.

"Wait," Dotty said. "Once you've finished with that reading and identified the investment plays we're going to talk to Chase about, may I make a suggestion?"

"Of course."

"Pay a visit to the custom research director at the Money Exchange. I've talked to her three times now. She's amazing. She knows more about this club than anyone on Earth now. And I know how you like to talk to the actual experts rather than just read about it."

"You don't think reading is my thing, either?" I said, laughing.

"I *know* you don't like to read. So talk to the Money Exchange once you've finished with those files. I'll take care of Chase and get the ball rolling. Then we'll see if they blink."

***

Dotty was right again. I didn't enjoy reading. It was odd to admit that out loud, considering I crafted words, sentences, and paragraphs for a living and hoped others could make sense of an issue by reading what I'd written.

But the truth was that writing and reading were byproducts of what I liked the most—asking questions of experts until I could unravel a puzzle. This particular puzzle was insanely complicated. Asking experts about it seemed far easier than consuming tens of thousands of pages of reports to find patterns. That's what supercomputers and artificial intelligence algorithms were for. An AI machine could "read" all of that data and make sense of it. I was content to ask other human beings questions.

I did, however, sit for hours and hours, diligently reading the 50 or so files as Dotty waited patiently in a chair beside my desk. When I finished a file, she answered my questions about the investment strategy that had emerged and which she then refined.

After the first half-dozen, I could see Dotty had taken the research reports, analyzed them in her own mind, and then come up with an approach that made perfect sense. She knew exactly what she was doing. There was no need for me to read over her shoulder.

I thought about simply telling her that and turning the project over to her. But I didn't. Only the two of us were in this thing together now, and I didn't want her to feel isolated, unprotected, or overwhelmed. I wanted her to know that I was in this with her, and that meant reading through what she'd created to provide a second pair of eyes...and a second person's opinion.

Once we'd talked through all the strategies she outlined, I was certain the guy at Chase would sign off on every one of them. Dotty had created a thing of beauty—an investment portfolio that would pay off lavishly in multiple directions. Every opportunity was sound. More importantly, it would bring us right into the orbit of the billionaires we'd put on the list.

Extremely wealthy people kept making money on top of the piles they already had ... for one significant reason: They had access to precisely the kinds of investment opportunities denied the other seven billion on the planet. No strategy or lucky break could get you into this exclusive club...only the kind of money controlled by a very small group.

Dotty had focused on the investment strategies, including a streamlined way in which SCT Enterprises could take some portion in stock as a success fee, while I focused on how it might bring us within reach of the club members.

Once we finished, I told her to call the guy at Chase and make the pitch.

We argued about it for a bit. She wanted me to make the call.

I said there was no need for that, especially since she'd already established the relationship. Plus, I added, the benefactor wasn't going to make a decision based on the pitch. It would be on the merits and whether we were still on the right path...or had touched a tripwire that kicked us out of the game.

I won. She made the call and followed up with a data transfer of the most relevant portions of our research.

I expected Chase to take days to get back to us and then ask us a slew of questions about each of the strategies. I also expected them to at least decline some of the investments, which added up to several billion dollars even though we'd narrowed our target to roughly 50.

By the next morning, they'd approved every investment.

I was shocked. It wasn't that the investment opportunities weren't good. They were. I was certain they'd hold up under scrutiny from almost anyone in the financial world. But I couldn't fathom how we were able to tap that level of money so swiftly. No one could have analyzed our investment portfolio overnight to make an informed decision. Even a team of financial advisors couldn't have done it. This meant that the benefactor had authorized the investments, either directly or indirectly, without analyzing them. They had to have been approved on faith.

Dotty and I were truly in it now. For better or worse, we had transferred billions of dollars of someone else's money into investments near and dear to the hearts of dozens of the wealthiest people who ever walked on Earth.

We had turned the dogs loose. They were now off and running through the woods, tracking the trail of the mysterious benefactor who dwelled in the cabin deep in the heart of that forest. It was time to start tracking the inevitable howls of discovery as they came across something.

CHAPTER 26

I almost waved at the white Mercedes-Benz Sprinter van parked across the street as I left my apartment to walk to the Metro stop.

But I didn't. There was no need, and it would just be mean. They knew that I knew they were there, monitoring my phone calls, internet searches, and general whereabouts. I figured they'd already followed up on my visit to New Zealand. I wondered what they'd make of Michelle Searle. Would they care? Did her story matter?

I doubted it. While the NSA, especially, had an intense interest in crypto and blockchain technology, I couldn't imagine they didn't already know everything about Searle's history. The only new entry in their logbooks was the fact I now knew her story as well. The Nakamoto angle might be of interest to them, unless the dark conspiracy theories were true—that the American intelligence community was, in fact, the syndicate behind the myth and had fed it intently to turn up rocks all over the world.

So I only offered the white van a wry smile as I walked past it, knowing they were watching me closely from inside.

As I made my way through the subway system to Union Station, I checked to see who might be physically following me. I spotted at least three likely candidates—two older men carrying newspapers and coffee cups, and a young woman casually dressed and carrying an overflowing bag. What gave all three of them away was that, while keeping a careful eye on my movements, they kept a respectful distance from me as I stepped onto the subway platform but made sure to enter another car on the same train.

I thought about making their lives a bit difficult by stepping off the train at the last minute and catching the next one. But I knew such an act was pointless. Whoever they were working for—and by this point I assumed I had Russian, Israeli, Chinese, and U.S. intelligence operations tracking me—they'd just assign the next person in the chain to pick me up at the next public place. So I stayed on the train and didn't make any sudden moves. I didn't even bother to see if they'd handed me off to anyone when I boarded the Acela to New York to get to my meeting at the Money Exchange. I assumed they had.

To pass the time on the train, I read up on two special cases on Dotty's list. Neither was on any public lists of billionaires, but the Money Exchange had identified both as members of the club. Both were quite interesting.

The first was Jessica Savage, the wife of Supreme Court Justice Michael Savage. Jessica Savage had inherited a considerable sum of money from her parents, who had once owned nearly every paper mill in the country. Jessica had married Michael while he was still at Harvard Law School and had guided his career ever since. While Michael Savage, the most conservative justice on the High Court, had focused on the law, Jessica had focused all her time and wealth on building the largest conservative media empire ever assembled in America. That privately held media empire was now valued at close to $20 billion by even conservative estimates.

The Savage family business now owned a local television affiliate station in every major market in the United States. At one point, the Savage family also owned dozens of major newspapers. But she'd sold most of them off over the years as the newspaper business collapsed in the face of competition from Google and Facebook. She transferred the money from the sale of those newspapers into a far right digital media propaganda network now responsible for more than half of all political coverage in every state capital in the United States.

What I found interesting about Jessica Savage was the fact that her fortune had *increased* considerably in the past decade while her husband served a life term on the Supreme Court—even as the newspaper dynasty her family had built nearly collapsed. The Savage fortune, by all rights, should have cratered. But it had prospered. Neither she nor her husband had ever said much about how that fortune had increased, other than to point to some timely investments in emerging tech companies and big bets on the currency exchange markets. She kept her business separate from her husband's. No one had ever seen her tax returns. She was a private citizen, even if her husband held one of the most important jobs in the American government.

Over the years, Jessica Savage had also built a network of conservative political allies who constantly ruffled the sensibilities of liberal critics in the national media. Several of them now occupied leadership positions in Congress, including Samuel Jenkins, the majority leader in the House of Representatives. Jenkins clearly had made quite a bit of money from investments that tracked with Jessica Savage, based on his own financial disclosure forms. No one had ever pinned anything illegal on him. But it was obvious that Jessica Savage had helped Jenkins, both professionally and financially, over the years.

Was she the benefactor? There was virtually no chance of that. But since the Money Exchange had clearly identified her as someone capable of playing the game, she was at least worth a look. I had no interest, one way or another, in Jessica Savage's politics. I was, even now, from the old school in journalism. I had never voted in a presidential election—for anyone. I'd believed my entire career that a journalist's job in Washington was to hold politicians' feet to the fire, whether they were a Democrat or a Republican. I believed in this principle fiercely and lived it daily. That included not voting or even trying to sort through where I might be on the political scale. But I had to admit, Jessica Savage's story was a curious one.

On the other hand, Russia's president, Alexi Simon, was near the top of my own list of possible candidates. Though he'd never made any Billionaires' Club lists, he was possibly the richest man in the world. It wouldn't surprise me in the least if, someday, someone proved Simon was worth as much as $300 billion. The Panama Papers certainly provided a host of clues and a potential road map to show this.

I also knew that no journalist, anywhere, would ever try to run this down. There were sporadic efforts here and there to highlight parts of his personal finances in various places around the world. However, Simon's wealth was intricately tied up with both the affairs of the Russian state and a highly organized syndicate of legal and illicit financing made up of the oligarchs who'd plundered Russia when the Soviet empire fell. No one would ever be able to truly unravel any of it in a meaningful way. What's more, it was far too dangerous. Those who looked into these types of affairs almost immediately placed themselves in harm's way.

I had no desire to do that. But I did need to look into the possibility that Alexi Simon was connected to our benefactor. My experience with Fedorisky had already convinced me that Russia's president and the various oligarchs around him who might have enough money to play such a game were as much in the dark as I was. They wanted to get to the bottom of the story too. It's why the GRU was tracking my movements. Still, like Jessica Savage, I needed to look at Simon, and that meant investing in something as close to his central interests as possible.

The Money Exchange's New York headquarters was deep in the shadows of the taller buildings in the Wall Street corridor at the southern end of Manhattan. From the building complex where the Money Exchange was located, you could just make out the famous "Fearless Girl" statue near the New York Stock Exchange. I had plenty of time before my meeting, so I skipped the cab ride and walked there from Penn Station.

I didn't bother to see who might still be following me. It didn't matter. I was all in now, for ill or good.

I'd checked in with Dotty during the train ride. We were starting to secure the investments. They would all be in motion, one way or another, in the next 48 hours. We were sending a very loud signal in multiple directions all at once. Not only did I have no interest in hiding my intentions or masking my movements, I fully intended to see what our actions flushed out into the open.

Like so many of the office buildings in this part of New York, where the rents were up to $200 a square foot, there was no requirement to check in at the front desk in order to be ushered up to the floor of the office you were visiting. There were multiple facial recognition cameras in the lobby, tracking every visitor who walked in the front doors and toward the elevators. Like others in the city, this building had an immediate lockdown capacity if a threat was detected.

I wondered what threat profile my face scan registered now.

The Money Exchange's custom research director was waiting for me in the foyer of the entrance to the offices. She was standing beside the receptionist's desk as I entered. Stepping forward briskly, she extended a hand as I approached the desk.

"Mr. Thomas, I'm Erica Silva. We spoke on the phone. I hope you had an uneventful trip here."

I'd done my homework before the meeting. Unlike Sergei Brin at Google, she'd finished her doctoral work in computer science at Stanford on a National Science Foundation graduate fellowship. Before joining the Money Exchange, she'd spent several years as a post-doc in an AI institute that Elon Musk and several other billionaires had established to build guardrails around AI research. Her family was originally from Mexico, but she'd grown up in the foster care system in the U.S. after being separated from her parents when they tried to come to America.

"I did, Dr. Silva," I said, shaking her hand.

I'd long ago trained myself to meet a woman's eyes with a level gaze. I never let them wander even for a moment from there. But it was still hard not to notice how elegantly dressed she was. I felt substantially underdressed in my jeans and light blue, long-sleeved cotton-blend shirt that was fraying at both sleeves. I doubted she'd factor that into the equation, though. Even billionaires dressed like bums these days.

"I was able to get quite a bit of reading done on the ride here," I added. "I vastly prefer the train between D.C. and New York."

She smiled. "I couldn't agree more. It's much more civilized."

"So where should we meet?"

She gestured toward a door at one end of the hall. "We have a discreet conference room here. No windows, and it's quiet. I've reserved it for us."

I nodded, impressed. They certainly knew their clientele. I had no doubt the quiet conference room was also soundproofed, much like our office at Jackson Place in Washington. The intelligence agency operatives keeping track of me would just have to cool their heels for a while.

She allowed me to take a seat at the end of the small conference table once we were inside. After closing the door behind her, she took a seat off to one side of the table.

"Thanks so much for taking the time to meet with me, Dr. Silva," I began.

"It's my pleasure. I must admit, I was more than a little curious about your data request. My entire research team was."

"I can imagine."

"We get…unusual requests from time to time. But never anything quite like yours."

"And I can't imagine you have clients who pay for such a big data report, either?"

She clasped her hands in front of her. "Oh, you'd be surprised at the nature of the requests we receive. I can honestly say there are other clients with big data appetites."

"That's a nice, polite way of saying the members of the Billionaires' Club like to spy on each other?"

Dr. Silva leaned forward. "In a manner of speaking, yes. But we produce results, regardless of the nature, intensity, and complexity of the request."

"Which is why they keep coming back, I assume."

"Yes, that, and the fact that we now fully lease and operate Frontier 2," she said matter-of-factly. "But I would have assumed that you, of all people, would know about that."

I couldn't help myself. I stared at her, speechless, for several seconds. "Wait," I managed finally. "There's a second Frontier supercomputer? Here? At the Money Exchange?"

"Not here, at least not physically. It's upstate in the Adirondacks, where we can assure its safety in the event of a terrorist attack or an extreme weather event. Hurricane Sandy taught us all just how vulnerable this part of the city is to a breach of the floodwall. We also need to control the temperature and other aspects of Frontier 2's physical security. It's easier to do that north of the city."

I was having a difficult time processing this news. The Department of Energy had unveiled the first Frontier supercomputer at Oak Ridge National Laboratory in Tennessee less than a year ago. It was the world's smartest, most powerful, scientific supercomputer. I'd been obsessed with Frontier when it was announced. I'd begged the science desk at the newspaper to let me cover the unveiling. They'd indulged me for the hell of it because the science desk was so woefully understaffed.

Some of the mind-boggling facts about the Frontier supercomputer were still hard-wired in the recesses of my brain. It was eight times faster than any other supercomputer in DOE history, which was saying something. It could process 200,000 *trillion* calculations a second under ordinary circumstances. But it could handle even more for certain scientific applications...on the order of three *billion billion* precise calculations per second. There was a name and a number for that—three exaops—that no human being could possibly grasp. Our brains were physically incapable of contemplating an exaop.

Frontier was taking on the most advanced energy, physics, and artificial intelligence tasks conceived in the history of civilization. If any supercomputer could push AI toward the tripwire that people like Elon Musk and others feared, the Frontier was it. Persistent rumors circulated that it was, even now, starting to approach what was often said to be the holy grail of AI—human-level intelligence—that could signal either the next stage of human evolution or the end of us all.

And it could happen literally in the blink of an eye, the world's leading computer scientists had told me when I reported the story. Under that AI theory, once a supercomputer like Frontier reached human-level intelligence, it would instantly leap to super-human level intelligence. We had no idea what happened after that.

The current White House had tasked Frontier with leading its high-profile AI initiative that encompassed every federal agency using supercomputers. That included NSA, which had its own supercomputer complex in the desert out west. But AI wasn't all that Frontier was working on. A supercomputer with that sort of computing speed and power made the impossible possible, so it was now tackling previously impractical tasks in theoretical and high-energy physics. It was an IBM system made up of thousands of individual servers, each of which contained massive core processors in their own right. All were linked together and attached to a half dozen super-accelerating graphics processing units that allowed the supercomputer to seamlessly handle even the most complex visualizations. Frontier could visualize our universe. It was that powerful.

I hadn't heard that IBM had built a second Frontier. But it made sense. Once it had built the first Frontier, a second one was infinitely easier and a great deal less expensive. IBM, after all, was in the business of selling computers that could make the impossible possible. It had done so since the Second World War. It was an IBM subsidiary that had developed the precursor to the modern computer, which enabled the Nazi regime to accurately track the six million Jews they exterminated during the war.

"May I ask...," I said hesitantly, "do you...handle quant investing or high-frequency trading for some of your clients with your Frontier 2, or perhaps some bitcoin mining? And how in the world can you afford it, if I might ask?"

Dotty and I had looked closely at quant investing and high-frequency trading. From the outside, both looked like magic. Quants were now using machine learning to create trading algorithms that no longer required human input. It could make trades that lasted mere minutes and might someday merge with high-frequency trading (which processed trades in milliseconds, anticipating stock price surges or declines so fast that it was able to essentially print money for those willing to bet vast sums). In my view, quant computing would inevitably make human stock trading obsolete. It was close to doing so right now.

Dr. Silva didn't hesitate. She'd probably heard this question before from clients. "You must know I can't divulge what our clients ask of us here," she said politely. "You wouldn't like us to do that with your own requests, would you?"

"Of course not."

"So, likewise, I can't comment on what our clients ask of us here. But I can tell you there is literally nothing Frontier 2 can't handle, in my experience. If you can imagine it, Frontier 2 can do it."

"Like quant investing," I interjected with a wry smile.

She ignored that. "As for your second question, we are able to afford it because we have a roster of clients who sub-lease it, with our direction. It's not unlike what happens with the original Frontier at Oak Ridge. The National Science Foundation, NASA, even NSA—all take portions of their own budget to pay for time on Frontier at Oak Ridge. We have a similar arrangement here. But our clients aren't federal agencies. They're private entities with the means and the data requirements for a supercomputer that has the computing power and sheer speed of Frontier."

"So I could sub-lease it for a task if I'd like?" I asked.

"You could. If you'd like me to send a portfolio on pricing, I'd be happy to do so."

"I'd like that. So, yes, send me that package."

Dr. Silva made a mental note. Then she shifted gears. It was like watching a precision watch tell time. "But can I clear something up first? Our general counsel and media team want to make certain of the ground rules before we proceed."

"Please."

"I want to make sure that what we discuss here is off the record, and simply for your own information. You paid a large sum of money for an interesting data report. But our wish—my wish—is that our conversation here is to answer your questions about what's contained in that report. Not for publication."

I nodded. There was no need to explain the gradations between off the record, on background, and on the record for her. I knew what she wanted, and I intended to honor her request. "Yes, this is off the record. I will not use any of the information we discuss in whatever I might or might not publish in the *Post* or anywhere else. This conversation is simply to inform and add to the report you provided us."

"And if some day you decide to utilize information from the report we provided…"

"I will not quote from the report, or from our discussion here," I said. "You have my word. Those are the agreed-to ground rules."

Dr. Silva nodded, satisfied, and leaned back in her chair. "That's acceptable. So, how can I help you?"

"You might have noticed a pattern in my requests."

"I did. Or, to be more precise, I should say my research team did."

"Would you mind telling me what you think that pattern might be, if I can ask? Just curious to see what your research team's take on this is."

She studied me intently. "I believe you're deliberately trying to get the attention of some of the wealthiest individuals on the planet through an investment strategy that will speak to each of them personally," she said firmly. "Am I close?"

I glanced at Dr. Silva's hands, which she'd re-clasped in front of her. There were no white knuckles on either hand. She was relaxed and in her element. She likely enjoyed this sort of repartée about her firm's research. "Close enough," I answered.

"Good. May I assume you'd like our help, from the data, ascertaining *precisely* the additional steps needed to make your way inside that circle? You'd like to explore the connections to the most important C Suite members. If possible, you'd like to see if there are overlapping board memberships, or family connections in some potential investments that signal an intense interest on the part of the principals."

I stared back at Dr. Silva, slightly in awe. Big data conferred all kinds of advantages on its recipients in settings such as this. But she was taking leaps beyond the data, likely based on years of trying to ascertain the real motives behind a client's request. "That would be enormously helpful," I said. "But even more than that, what I'd really like to know is a bit...outside the scope of what you usually provide for your clients."

"What might that be?"

"Beyond those connections—which are helpful, as I said, and what I was hoping for—I'd also like to narrow the list we sent you even further."

"How so?"

"I'd like to create a pathway list that includes those worth more than $10 billion a decade ago and who haven't signed the giving pledge. Oh, and who have considerably more than that today. I don't want anyone who owns a large toy, such as a professional sports team. Or the guy who's killed every large animal for sport on the endangered species list. Or the guy who's won America's Cup four times. Not interested in any of them.

And you can ignore the men who've bought private islands for themselves so they can set up a libertarian utopia where they can serve as little emperors in their own fantasy. I have no interest in the members of the Billionaires' Club who are deluded, venal, cruel, or narcissistic. I'm also less interested in those who inherited their wealth, though I'm not ruling them out."

"And that's all...you just want that list, which is quite simple to process? You realize you're likely to end up with a relatively small data set of individuals—perhaps no more than two dozen candidates or so?"

"If I'm lucky, yes. I'd like to narrow the target a bit."

"Anything else?" she asked. "That request is rather straightforward."

Now it was my turn to lean forward at the table. "I'm looking for unusual, even quantum, leaps in wealth growth or decline that don't make any discernible sense," I said casually. "Also for trends in their investments that don't track with what might otherwise be in their wheelhouse. I'm only interested in people actively doing things off the beaten path."

"You want the unusual, then? The things that don't fit an obvious pattern?"

"Exactly. I don't care about lucky Series A-round breaks or outsized short bets that did or didn't pan out. I'm looking for something else. The leaps or falls that don't make any sense."

"Anomalies in the data?" she asked.

I smiled. "Precisely."

CHAPTER 27

Dotty had the investments well in hand. She was making steady progress with all of our targets, especially the core ones on our list that was growing smaller by the day. And, while I professed not to care about it, Dotty said a few of our investments were already starting to pay off. SCT Enterprises had cash flow and might have considerable value soon. We could, if we wished, develop a line of credit against the value of the stock we now held as the manager of the investment portfolio she was growing.

I had no interest in leveraging the value held on paper, I told Dotty. But it was interesting that the possibility existed.

Dr. Silva, my new best friend at the Money Exchange, had sent me both her package on what it would take to sub-lease Frontier 2 there as well as the much smaller list of the Billionaires' Club members who were worth more than $10 billion a decade ago, were still alive, and had not spent it on expensive toys. She'd narrowed the list even further to active investors with a penchant for at least trying new things.

She'd been right. It was a small list. There were only about two dozen people on it. Only two were women, both heiresses from the same family that had created the largest retail chain in history. The rest were men.

It made sense that the list was that small. While the number of billionaires in the world was growing at a clip of about 150 or so a year, that trend was relatively recent. The total number of billionaires globally had been steady at or around a thousand or so until 2009, when it began to grow consistently. The rise of a brand-new tech industry had changed the equation. Google, Facebook, and Microsoft took their place alongside industry titans like ExxonMobil, Bank of America, and Johnson & Johnson as the world's biggest, most profitable companies.

For the longest time, there had been a relatively small, stable list of men who were all billionaires and a very small subset of women who'd inherited great wealth from their industrious, entrepreneurial husbands or fathers. In fact, in 2008—the year I was arbitrarily using as my baseline year for when I believed our benefactor had begun to experiment with this highly unusual game—there were just six women among the 50 wealthiest billionaires. All six had inherited their considerable wealth. The disparity wasn't surprising. The more things change, the more they stay the same, as Jean-Baptiste Alphonse Karr might say.

But that did make it easier to focus my efforts. It certainly appeared that I was looking for a man arrogant enough to believe he could single-handedly change the course of the world through individual wealth and industry while also playing a complicated, hidden game. My working theory was still that this man was mostly bored with wealth creation and had created the game as one more way to move chess pieces around the board. Perhaps he'd enlisted other men in his quest, much as the mythical gods of Olympus sometimes wagered among themselves about the course of human events.

Dr. Silva had added a special category at the end that contained just three files. Her research team had placed them under the subhead of "anomalous data." All three men were known to me, though not well known to the global public.

The first had essentially combined the concept of Amazon and Google into one entity in China and was now building a competing internet that allowed government censorship. It had made this man extraordinarily wealthy. I had no doubt there would be two internets within a decade, with this man responsible for the creation of the second. He appeared to have the full faith of the six men who controlled China with an iron fist. There were persistent rumors he held assets for China's premier, Zheng Li, which further consolidated his wealth and power inside China.

The second man was someone the world had not yet heard much about, but almost certainly would before too long. His parents were Taiwanese, but his parents had moved the family to London when he was very young. He had a doctoral degree in genetic engineering and started several companies that had made him billions. He was an early pioneer of human genome research and had created companies based on that research well before anyone knew they would work.

The file contained information I'd never seen in published peer-review science literature or newspapers like my own. His companies were clearly working on aspects of cloning research in clinics—from organs to full human cloning—that the United Nations and global medical societies were profoundly uncomfortable with but had not yet banned. I'd read through the file twice before I made the connection. The woman in Nairobi whom Michelle Searle had mentioned to me, who had also been approached by our benefactor, once worked for one of this man's companies in London.

The third person surprised me. Aleksandr Petrovich wasn't on any of the billionaires' lists but had climbed to the top of Russia's organized crime syndicates from the moment Alexi Simon seized power. His own ascent had tracked seamlessly with Simon's rise. Just as Simon had profited from the deliberate looting of the former Soviet Union's state industries, so too had Petrovich profited from that larceny along the way.

It wouldn't have occurred to me to include Petrovich in my search, but I knew it made sense. While Dotty brought our investment portfolio into line with the small group Dr. Silva's research team had identified, I figured I should at least consider Petrovich, who was among the world's wealthiest men, easily in command of tens of billions of dollars. But he would never confess to such wealth, nor would anyone in any publication ever acknowledge that wealth. And, yet, his wealth and reach existed nevertheless.

Petrovich had steadily risen through the ranks of Russia's complex organized crime syndicate from the earliest days of the collapse of the Soviet empire. He'd gotten his start with prostitution and money-laundering in several Soviet satellite states but moved up the food chain to seize control of big, legitimate businesses like national banks and natural gas companies.

He was known as the "boss of bosses" in Russia. Justice Department task forces had seized assets from Petrovich shell companies on two occasions when they were exposed in North America. The

FBI had kept Petrovich on its "10 Most Wanted" list for years, until finally giving up when it was obvious Petrovich would never set foot in any country that had an extradition treaty with the United States. Petrovich had developed a knack for never being in the wrong place at the wrong time. He'd survived several assassination attempts. Any number of lieutenants were vying for control of his organized crime empire but, by all accounts, Petrovich still ruled with an iron fist.

I did wonder why Dr. Silva's research team hadn't identified the other significant organized crime figure in their report to me. Yakuza chief Akio Sota was a peer of Petrovich. The Yakuza's ranks had grown smaller in recent years, but it was still the largest organized crime syndicate in the world. The Yakuza had close to 100,000 members around the world and operated under a strict code and a rigid hierarchy.

Sota was at the top of the hierarchy, likely controlling the assets the Yakuza commanded. No one knew how much was Sota's personal wealth. I doubted any Yakuza chief had the freedom to color outside the lines, but you never knew. Perhaps that was why Dr. Silva's team hadn't included him.

Of the two organized crime chieftains, I had a path to Petrovich through Ivan Fedorisky. It would take work, but I was confident I could at least start the conversation there. I had no way, at all, of getting to Sota. That would take considerable work, and I wasn't sure if it was even worth the effort. So I figured I'd start with Petrovich and see how far I could get.

***

Dotty immediately tried to convince me that I was out of my mind. She was pacing in "my" office at Jackson Place, where all of the many research piles had been reshuffled or filed.

"No way," she said. "I won't allow it. You can't seriously think you can arrange a meeting with someone like Petrovich? Even if you can, it's *dangerous*."

"I can," I argued, "and I don't really believe it's as dangerous as you're making it out to be. It's not like I'm trying to threaten his livelihood or business. I only want a meeting. How dangerous can that be?"

"Incredibly dangerous!" Dotty flung back. Fear showed in her voice and in her face.

I was touched by Dotty's genuine concern for my safety, but I'd interviewed folks like Petrovich throughout my career. I'd even managed to work background interviews from some of them into stories about political corruption. It took work to gain their trust and to assure their advisors I intended no harm to their business.

I believed I could convince Fedorisky I wasn't any threat to Petrovich. Even if there was some danger to me personally, I was willing to take the risk. Now that I was getting closer to the center of the maze, I needed to rule actors and players like Petrovich out of the picture for good. I had to know the big organized crime syndicates weren't involved in the game I was playing. I still had serious questions about the role cryptocurrency had in tracking the massive, hidden wealth secured in every dark place on Earth.

"I don't think so," I countered with as much confidence as I could muster for Dotty's sake. "I only want to talk. I'll assure Fedorisky I'm not looking for information that'll harm their businesses. If anything, we're sending money their way—not the other way around."

Dotty was having none of it. She kept pacing. Her hands were shaking. Even the thought of me going to Moscow, or wherever Petrovich called home these days, was troubling her deeply. "But he's done awful things, hasn't he?" she asked plaintively. "Hasn't he?"

"Yes, to his enemies, or to those who get in his way. But I'm not his enemy, and I have no intention of getting in his way. I'll make that clear."

"But…"

I held up a hand. "Dotty, it's OK. I'll be fine. You just keep doing your thing. Let me do mine. Petrovich is a key player around Russia's president. That entire network around Simon is important, for any number of reasons. I have to take a run at this."

Dotty stopped pacing. She was incredibly stubborn and didn't let go of things easily. But she also knew me well enough now to realize I wasn't letting this go, either. "Can you at least take some precautions? Bring some bodyguards with you? Take a private jet with you to Moscow in case you need to get out of there quickly?"

"The bodyguards won't help," I said. "In fact, they'd make things much worse if I actually get a meeting with him, which is highly doubtful at any rate. My safety is more assured if I show up by myself, with nothing to protect or shield me. And while a private jet would be nice, I can't imagine that our benefactor would like that very much. It's precisely the kind of luxury that could get us kicked out of all this immediately."

"Actually, I don't think so," Dotty insisted. "We're not buying a private jet; we're leasing it. And while that's going to be more expensive than flying commercial, I genuinely believe it isn't the type of expense that would disqualify us. I think it's worth the risk, especially now that you're going to be visiting multiple sites around the world to test the investments and meet with people. It's a necessary expense."

"Our benefactor might not see it that way."

"Perhaps," she said, "but I still think it's worth the risk. We've been testing the boundaries every step of the way. This is just another guardrail. We're going to need to do essential things like this soon regardless. We've been paying for expensive infrastructure, research, and consultants. Leasing a jet is a necessary expense. You can visit multiple places, even in a day, this way. You aren't nearly as limited in your movements."

Crossing her arms across her body, she added, "And, need I remind you, this makes it considerably harder for the white van crowd that's been following you around to keep tabs on you. I've already spoken to several leasing companies who assure me they can procure private planes with every security measure we might require to keep you safe from prying eyes and ears."

I no longer kept anything from Dotty. She knew everything I knew, and I kept her apprised of what I was seeing and hearing. I'd told her about the van outside my apartment, and my hunch that we were being tracked by three or four intelligence agencies. Dotty hadn't blinked at that news. The more I got to know her, the more I was impressed with her ability to hide her natural fear of what we were trying to pull off, as well as its implications.

"But it would be awful if leasing a private jet is the move that crosses whatever lines our benefactor has drawn," I tried.

"I don't think so," Dotty said firmly. "I think we have more freedom with those kinds of decisions. It's the *big* ones that are going to cause us trouble, where we are really flying blind. We thought the investment ask to Chase would end it, and it didn't. It would be one thing if we were buying yachts, mansions, private islands, and pro-sports franchises all over the world. But we're not. We're leasing a jet, which will make your movements easier and more secure. Just take the risk. If it ends things, it ends things, and I'll restart my retirement."

I knew Dotty was right. It was more that I was actually uncomfortable with the thought of flying on a private jet. *That* was what was really bothering me, not whether it might be the tripwire that ended the game. But I knew I needed to get past that. I couldn't let my own hang-ups about the trappings of wealth stop us from solving the puzzle.

"Okay, do it," I finally agreed. "And if it ends things, it ends things."

Chapter 28

Dotty procured a small private jet that seated four comfortably and secured a spot at a hangar at Reagan airport.

It didn't end things. There were no hiccups from our guy at Chase.

So I called Fedorisky. He didn't balk at the question. If anything, I got the distinct impression he'd been expecting the request, or something like it. Evidently, they wanted to test me and what I knew.

While I was waiting for Fedorisky's answer, I got another call at home—one I'd been expecting for some time.

"You *do* realize how colossally stupid this is, right? What can you possibly hope to gain from a meeting with Petrovich?" Silas asked me.

I didn't answer right away. I picked up my first cup of coffee that morning and walked over to the window. It was still a bit gray outside. The sun hadn't come up yet. But I could still make out the silhouette of the white van. It was parked in yet another location on the street.

I thought about making a joke to Silas that they really didn't need to keep moving the van—that they could just park it in one place for their 24/7 surveillance of my apartment. But I didn't. They were playing a game, much as I was. There was no need for either of us to acknowledge the game. And if I did make a joke, things could get ugly. The intelligence community had no right to spy on a journalist pursuing a story, even if they had serious questions about what else I might be up to.

The agency task force was now probably substantial, with a combination of analysts, field agents, and Kremlinologists hoping my efforts would give them a window into the tight circle around

Simon and his oligarch pals. They were allowing me to do some of their work.

What I couldn't possibly know was whether they disapproved my even considering going into business with Simon's crowd. The Series A investment with Fedorisky was one thing. Quite some time ago, he'd washed the grime off his relationship with the Russian oligarchs who'd staked him initially. But investing with anyone directly in Alexi Simon's shadow was something else altogether.

"I just want to ask him some questions, Silas." I didn't even pretend to show surprise that he knew about my efforts to get to Petrovich.

"But what do you want from him? From his network? What exactly are you pursuing? A story?"

"Yes, of course, a story," I said quietly. "It's what I do. You know that. I find things, and then I tell people about them."

"But what kind of story? A connection between Petrovich, Simon, and the White House, perhaps? To Howard Phelps—the vice president's business interests? What have you found so far? You've got fishing lures in all sorts of waters right now. I'm just wondering about your motivations."

I paused. That was a dangerous question for Silas to ask, especially because our conversation was being recorded and would be sliced and diced at multiple levels. I knew how this worked as well as Silas did. The transcript of our conversation would circulate inside the agency and other levels of the intelligence community. Snippets would make it to the National Security Council staff at the White House. A summary might even make it to the President's Daily Brief if they could inflate the value of the intel and tie it directly to some Russian action.

Most likely, someone had prompted Silas to ask me that question. That told me the task force now had at least one or more people at the NSC involved. It was interesting, though not surprising, that NSC staff were sensitive to the financial connections between Simon's circle and officials in Washington, D.C.

"I haven't found any connections, Silas. I haven't asked anyone about it," I answered finally. It was true. I hadn't asked those questions. But I would, if I got the chance.

"But that's what you're looking at, isn't it?" he pressed.

"Listen," I said firmly, more for his handlers on the call than anyone else, "I haven't asked about any connections to the White House. None. I'm pursuing a story about the ways in which money moves around the world through traditional and non-traditional means, and I'd like to talk to Petrovich about it. I've taken a special interest in the Panama Papers, offshore banking, and crypto. But I seriously doubt I'll get an audience."

"If you do, what will you ask? What can you possibly hope to learn from someone like Petrovich? We gave up on him years ago, once it became obvious he'd never set foot in a country where we have extradition rights. He's completely protected by Russia's president. We can't ever touch him. No one can."

"I know that. But I have real questions about how much he and his network rely on non-traditional forms of money, especially cryptocurrency. They move way too much money to rely on cash. They have to be using something else."

"He'll never tell you that," Silas scoffed. "Never. You're dreaming if you think you're going to get any answer to that question."

"Perhaps, but you never know until you ask. That's the one thing I've learned over the years. Sometimes people are waiting for someone to pose the right question, in just the right way, at just the right time, to them."

"Good luck with that," he said. "I can't imagine any of it will pan out. I don't know anyone who's ever gotten the kind of audience with Petrovich that you're seeking. You'll be lucky if you get an academic in some think tank on their payroll who says he has a connection, or a lawyer who's pretending to represent a legitimate client inside his network."

"You might be right, Silas. I guess we'll see."

***

The second call that morning surprised me a bit, though.

"Hey, dude, you didn't tell me you were trying to become a master of the universe," Tom Kyle said loudly when I picked up. "What in the hell are you up to, anyway? I've got CEOs calling me right and left."

"I'm just asking questions," I told my colleague at the Chamber of Commerce. "That's all."

"You're doing more than ask questions, my friend. Half the oppo research firms in the city are already whispering about you. No one can figure out what you're up to. They can't tell what type of fishing expedition you're on, or who your target might be. The speculation is all over the map, from the White House to half of my members."

"Let me guess," I said, laughing. "They all want to make sure they're not in the crosshairs, and they decided to sic you on me."

"Yeah, pretty much. I mean, that's what I do."

I grinned. "You're the guard dog. I know."

"So, look, Seth, some of the D.C. offices for these guys—the ones that go in and out of the White House on a regular basis—say that even some of the NSC types are spooked by what you're up to. They're wondering, not altogether quietly, whether you have something on the White House that you're trying to run down. Seriously, what in the bloody hell are you up to? And my offer still stands if you need to talk to the president's chief of staff. I can make the connect to Admiral Symons."

"Thanks again for the offer on Symons. I'll let you know if I need to take you up on it. And before I answer your question, as much as I'm able, may I ask you something?"

"Sure."

"Are any of these CEOs from private companies? Ones like that spook software firm that runs the NSA from Silicon Valley and is valued at $20 billion? Or companies that bought stock back like the big chipmaker did when they were sick and tired of the quarterly earnings dance with public investors? I know most of your members are from the publicly traded companies. But I know that Cargill and Koch have worked out of the Chamber in the past. So any private groups like them wondering about me?"

"A number of them," he said. "None of the public companies—the ones who have to file everything with the SEC whenever they make any sort of significant move—have called. You aren't on their radar. And even if you were..."

I grimaced. "They'd just run me through their PR shop endlessly until I coughed up what I was doing. I know. I've been through that drill more than I care to remember."

"Yeah. The public companies don't give a rip about much, other than what might affect their stock price. So, if you're investigating one of them and it might move the price…"

"I'm not," I said quickly. "Really. And I'm not focusing on just one company."

"Then what, exactly, *are* you looking at? Does it have anything to do with that Jackson Place office, the one you came to see me about?"

"Yes, it does. So tell me this. Have some of them specifically asked you about the Jackson Place office? Not just what I'm up to, but specifically what might be coming out of that office across the street from you?"

Tom hesitated, but only for a moment. We were both pros in trading information. "Yes, a few," he answered. "And they were very specific in their requests."

"Would you be willing to send me a list of those who're asking?"

"Sure, but only if you give me some idea what you're looking at so I can call off the dogs. I have to go back to them with something. None of them want to be part of the next Seth Thomas special report that lands you your next Pulitzer."

"I'm not winning a Pulitzer off this thing, Tom. I'm pretty sure of that. It's…way more complicated and, quite frankly, pretty dull stuff."

"Okay, fine. How dull? What is it?"

I knew I had to give Tom something. I also knew that whatever fishing lure I gave him needed to be something that would cause a very small crowd some level of anxiety. "I'm looking at cryptocurrency, and financial transactions in different parts of the world. I'm getting close to the real origins of bitcoin, why it really got started. It might surprise some people."

Tom grunted. "Man, I never took you for a tech journo type. Trying to hunt down the elusive Satoshi Nakamoto. You know a whole lot of your colleagues have gone down that rabbit hole and wished to god they'd never made the effort. Those crypto math guys are all dark lord wannabes. They sit in their cave writing code and never come up for air."

"Tell me about it. I once watched a coder on a trip to Hong Kong. He kept his hoodie on, over his head, for the entire flight.

Never looked up. Never left his seat. Never even glanced over at me sitting in the seat beside him. Just sat there, writing code, the whole time. Line after line."

"Yep," Tom said. "They lock onto their code to build something. And then they take over the world and become the newest addition to the billionaires' crowd. The Instagram guys who hit 30 million users, get bought by Facebook, then watch their crowd of onlookers and users jump to the moon and hit a billion almost overnight. So you're looking at *that* crowd?" He paused. "That's not like you. It's way outside your lane. You're the corrupt politics guy."

"Well, maybe I'm the crypto guy now. Maybe I want to be a dark lord, too. I mean, if all it takes is to chain yourself to a desk for a few years, write some code, and then become a billionaire at the end...jeez, who wouldn't do that?"

"Right. You and all your mad math skills. But it's one thing to give up your life in your twenties so you can live large the rest of your life. You're a little late in the game to get started, aren't you?"

"You never know," I said. "It's never too late to try something new."

"So, look, you gonna tell me what you're really up to or not?"

"I told you already, and I meant it. I'm taking a serious look at financial transactions, cryptocurrency, offshore banking, and the way wealth is moved all over the world. I truly am looking into that. And I'm getting close on the cryptocurrency question."

"And you really don't have any single target you're going to land on and ruin their lives?"

"I promise. I'm not planning on going after one target to pull them down," I said truthfully. "That's not what I'm looking at. It's the system. It's not necessarily one specific actor over another. So will you send me that list of those asking specific questions about Jackson Place?"

"I will. I'll tell folks that you don't have any one target. You give me your word that you aren't going after one specific company? That it's really and truly about the crypto craze and the financial system more broadly?"

"I give you my word," I said. "I don't have one specific target. I'm looking at the financial and banking system much more broadly."

"And if you do wind up with a target that you're going to go after hard—which is what you do, as we both know—then you'll call me and give me a heads-up in case it's someone connected here?"

"Yes, Tom, I will. Though I really don't think that will ever happen. It's not what this is about."

"All right, if you say so," he said. "The list will be in your inbox later today."

"Good," I answered.

I knew that Tom would share most, if not all, of what we'd discussed with the Chamber members who'd called him to check up on me. But that was fine. Those who cared about the narrative I was quietly weaving would take additional steps. I didn't really care about those who wouldn't try to take the lure in the water. Tom Kyle was *exactly* the type of inside player I needed to flush targets out into the open. He traded in inside information. It was what he did. It was what all of Washington did. The only commodity in D.C. was information.

Tom's list would be immensely valuable regardless. If someone was asking about the Jackson Place office, with very specific questions, there was a good reason for it. There was an excellent chance they were either connected to the benefactor somehow, or had been once. Either way, it would narrow the playing field even further.

CHAPTER 29

Fedorisky surprised me. He got back to me in less than 24 hours. But he didn't call me back. He made an appointment with Dotty to meet at Jackson Place. He was sitting calmly in a chair next to Dotty's desk, chatting with her, when I arrived a couple of hours after talking to Silas.

"Can I assume we have privacy here, in this office?" he asked me as soon as we were seated at the table in the back office.

Dotty had closed the door behind us. I knew she was dying to sit in on the meeting. Under ordinary circumstances, I would have asked her to join us. But this was not an ordinary circumstance.

"You can," I said. "This entire townhouse has been swept and secured. Your guys can't hear us. Ours can't. No one can."

Fedorisky nodded. "Good. I'd assumed so. That's why I wanted to meet here."

I noticed he'd come to the meeting without any materials. He was dressed casually by D.C. standards, in jeans and a dark sports coat over a v-neck tee shirt. He was wearing argyle socks, with expensive loafers, though.

"How's your Series A round doing?" I asked.

He smiled broadly. "All done. Give it two years and you—and your mysterious investor—will thank me profusely. They're about to sign a massive joint venture deal with American Standard that will closely resemble a precursor to an acquisition by the largest oil and gas major in the world."

"Which means what, exactly?"

Fedorisky laughed. "You really don't read the *Wall Street Journal*, do you? American Standard execs hinted at it in their last quarterly call. When they announce the JV in the next few days, your stock will balloon. I mean, really take off into the stratosphere. Everyone will start talking about it like it's the next billion-dollar unicorn, maybe even the first big renewable energy giant."

"But it'll still be private?"

"Sure. But you could re-sell your private stock once the news hits about the American Standard interest. All sorts of private investors would snap up your preferred Series A stock, even before an acquisition. Everyone knows there will be a big alternative energy play at some point. This could be it. You'd make a ton of money that way. But if you hold your preferred stock from the Series A round, it'll be worth even more down the road. I'm talking about *serious* money—enough to make you want to sit on their board for 10 years."

"You always seem to have the Midas touch," I said. I avoided the urge to ask him just how much money this particular deal might make him. Dotty would know, and I'd ask her later.

"By the way, you wouldn't mind telling me who, exactly, your mysterious investor might be, would you?" he asked casually. "It's the talk of the town. I'm sure you know that."

"I do know that. But you wouldn't expect me to break a confidence, would you?"

He leaned forward. "So, have you been asked that? Has your investor told you not to break their confidence by sharing that information with anyone?"

It was an interesting question. It simultaneously tested whether I knew yet who the benefactor was and what I intended to do with that information once I had it. "I have my investor's confidence, and I don't particularly wish to break it."

"I see," he said. "That's probably wise on your part. Those who tell tales out of school often get tossed from school when they try to come back inside."

"I don't tell tales out of school. When it's time to tell tales, I generally like to tell everyone all at once."

Fedorisky sat back in the chair, folded one leg over another, and studied me for a few moments. I could tell we were about to enter new, uncharted waters.

"I'm sure you know by now why I visited your office here on Jackson Place when it opened," he said. "As you well remember, I was the first one to show up at your doorstep. I wasn't shy about my aims, or what I was offering."

"You weren't shy, and you were the first," I agreed. "And, yes, I *do* know now why you came here."

"Very good. I wanted to make sure that we'd established a baseline."

"We have. I have a pretty good understanding of what you're trying to find."

"And have *you* found it?" he asked.

"You asked that already, in so many words," I said quietly. "And you have my answer."

"I do indeed," Fedorisky replied. "So here's the thing. There are more than a few in Moscow and other parts of the world with considerable, intense interest in what you're pursuing. I'm sure you can appreciate that interest. There are...people with very large stakes in both non-traditional financial and banking practices that you've been asking about."

"Like the offshore accounts exposed in the Panama Papers?"

"Yes, like those papers, among other things. They also have an abiding interest in the true origins of cryptocurrency as well, for obvious reasons. They may be just as interested in its origins and real use as you are at this point."

"Really? They don't see it as a fad?"

"Currency exchange that can scale to cover the entire world and doesn't need third-party validators or intermediaries?" he asked. "No, they don't see blockchain as a fad. They see it as the inevitable future, depending on its origins and who genuinely controls it."

I nodded. "That *does* seem to be the question everyone is asking: Who really holds the keys to this particular kingdom? The owner would wield considerable control over all kinds of people, institutions, industries, and even countries if it scales worldwide in the manner that you and others anticipate someday."

"Precisely," Fedorisky said. "I daresay they have a critical need at this point to understand *exactly* who holds the keys to this kingdom. They intend to take whatever action they need to assure themselves that someone—say, the U.S. government—hasn't established a Trojan Horse for its own needs. They would make just about any move necessary to answer that question." He paused for emphasis. "And I mean *anything*. They are willing to roll the dice and risk quite a lot for the answer to that question. Non-traditional banking holds enormous potential, but only if it's not a government creation. It has to be private *and* anonymous as advertised."

"Well, it certainly would make it easy to move vast sums from one place to another without any trace," I said slowly. "I can see that. Anyone can see that. It would make the need for offshore banking almost obsolete. It would make it infinitely easier to convert rubles to dollars, for instance."

"I like that word—*convert.*" Fedorisky smiled. "It's a much nicer word than…"

"Wash, launder, or clean?" I offered playfully.

"Yes, words like that. So you can see why people have an intense interest in the ways in which money is moved from one place to another, outside the reach of the regulated banking system. Of course, provided it's what it purports to be, and that it isn't a back door creation of your NSA or a complicated way for private interests to control things remotely."

"Oh, come on." I tried to keep a straight face. "You don't actually believe that idiotic conspiracy theory that the NSA created it, do you?"

"I don't. But that doesn't mean others don't have their doubts or believe it might be a real possibility."

"Then they're living a fantasy," I said. "From what I can tell, it's quite legitimate, and it's already made its way into the mainstream."

I wasn't about to tell him about Michelle Searle, even though he and his colleagues were probably aware of her role. I also wasn't going to talk about what I knew of Satoshi Nakamoto's identity.

"Yes, it's definitely mainstream," he answered. "Many, many transactions are now possible. It has, as they say, made the impossible possible."

I smiled. "Indeed. I imagine it's one of the many reasons Mr. Petrovich is perfectly content to keep his movements confined to Russia and a handful of countries where he can't be extradited to the United States. It means he can even safely move money in and out of countries like North Korea or Iran despite strict sanctions."

"Yes, of course. So let us speak of Mr. Petrovich. I have news in that regard, which I believe you'll like and appreciate."

I masked my surprise. "Glad to hear it." I had never actually believed that someone like Aleksandr Petrovich would meet with me. *They must really want to know what I'm pursuing, and what I've learned,* I thought.

"He is willing to meet with you, at his dacha in Rublevka just outside Moscow," Fedorisky stated, turning quite serious. "He has information he's willing to discuss on background and with all of the usual caveats that it did not come from him. Information I believe you will find quite interesting. Definitive, in fact."

"And I'm sure there's a quid pro quo. So what is it? What does he want?"

Fedorisky moved his chair close to the table and leaned in. "He wants assurances from you, beforehand, that you *will* publish the information he provides, even if it causes considerable trouble for your government."

"You know I can't categorically make such a promise until I've talked it through with my editors. But *will* it cause considerable trouble for the U.S. government? Perhaps for this White House specifically?"

Fedorisky took a deep breath and then exhaled slowly. "Yes. It will cause trouble for this White House. It will cause quite a lot of trouble, in fact."

I had a decent idea what they wanted to discuss and to give me. I wanted to ask why any of them—Fedorisky, Petrovich, or Simon—wished to take such a precipitous step. If it was what I thought it might be, the move would create a permanent rift between Russia and the United States. But I'd learned over the years not to question a source's motives too closely beforehand. It was better to get the information first and ask questions later. The stakes seemed considerably higher here, but I would still follow my own rules about sources and their motivations. I'd deal with the consequences, and the motives, after I saw what they had to offer.

"All right," I answered. "Here's the assurance I can give you: If the information is legitimate and what I believe it is likely to be; if I can verify it; and if I can prove to myself and my editors that it can be safely reported without compromising American national security interests, then I am quite confident that my newspaper will publish it. It will not compromise U.S. national security interests, right? I can make that assumption?"

"It will not compromise your country's national security interests. Quite the opposite, in fact. It should answer some rather important questions—definitively so, in fact. But it *will* make the White House profoundly uncomfortable."

"Good. I'll need to separate out those two questions."

Fedorosky nodded. "Understood. I believe Mr. Petrovich can live with that assurance. I will proceed with the arrangements for your visit. I'll provide the details shortly." He stood to leave.

"Before you go," I said, "do me a favor. Tell the security around Petrovich that I'm coming by myself, without any protection whatsoever. I have your assurance that I will be safe in Moscow and when I visit him at his dacha?"

"You have my assurance," he said. "We need each other, Mr. Thomas. We all know that. You will be perfectly safe as Mr. Petrovich's guest. You will have no worries—none at all."

CHAPTER 30

"So you really *are* going to Moscow to meet with this man, even though you know exactly who he is and the things he's done?" Dotty asked.

After Fedorisky left, Dotty wouldn't let me leave the office until I told her everything. She made me sit at my desk chair until I recounted every last detail. She sat across from me, her hands folded nervously in her lap.

Dotty rarely got emotional. But she was emotional now. Everything about this clearly bothered her in a profound way.

I pulled the special file off my desk—the one Dr. Silva's research team at the Money Exchange had created for us—and handed it to Dotty. "Read this again," I told her. "It's pretty obvious that we need to take this meeting. Dr. Silva's team flagged it for us specifically, because there are some 'anomalies of data' attached to what Petrovich is doing."

"I don't need to read the file to know that a man like this is at the center of some very awful, corrupt things everywhere in the world," she fired back. "We should not be doing business with this man. Not ever. Not for any reason. There is no justification for going into business with anything this man does. It's just..."

I could see she was on the verge of tears. "Dotty," I said gently, "we will never go into business with this man. I give you my word."

"Then why are you going to meet with him? He's a horrible, horrible man. He's done hideous things. I...I don't think I could even be in the same room with someone like that."

I'd never talked to Dotty much about what I was really good at—namely, finding out things that people didn't want exposed to sunlight and then writing about it. She and I only ever really talked business. Or, I should say, Dotty explained to me how the financial and business world worked while I listened. I wasn't about to try to start now, not with her so worried.

"Here's the thing," I explained. "It became quite clear just now in my conversation with Fedorisky that they…and I mean the entire crowd out of the Kremlin, from Alexi Simon through Aleksandr Petrovich…have something important they want to share with me. They are desperately trying to flush our benefactor into the open, much as I am. For that reason, I'm willing to go there, see what they have to offer, and then evaluate what, if anything, we should do with it."

"And this terrible man, he has something valuable he wants to give you?"

"Yes, and it's evidently something the entire leadership in Russia is willing to give up. What I don't know, at least not yet, is why they're doing this now. They clearly have their reasons. I just don't understand them. But first things first. I need to meet with Petrovich and see what they're offering."

Dotty stared at her hands folded in her lap, then lifted her eyes to meet mine. "I trust you, Seth. I do. We're in this together. I know you'll do the right thing. If you have to meet with this…person, then I know it's for the right reasons. I honestly don't understand this—any part of it. But I'm just worried. You'll be safe, right? And you won't do anything with what he gives you until you come back and we've talked about it? Okay?"

"I won't do anything with it until we've talked it through. I promise. Now, can we talk about something else Fedorisky told me?"

I could tell Dotty wanted to keep pressing me on my decision, but she was also resigned to the fact I was going to do this meeting regardless. So she let it go. "Fine. What did Fedorisky tell you? I assume he told you that our Series A stock is about to be worth, oh, I don't know, maybe 100 times what we paid for it, thanks to what American Standard is doing?"

"You know about that?" I asked, stunned.

Her pained expression was almost comical. "Seriously? You really don't read the *Wall Street Journal*, do you?"

"Fedorisky said exactly the same thing," I said, smiling.

"Well, he's right. You really should read it. You might learn something about what we're trying to do here."

"But why, when I know that you have it all under control?" I teased. "Why do I need to know anything about that world?"

Dotty rolled her eyes. "You're ridiculous, you know. Hopeless. I mean, you *should* want to know what's happening, because your investments are starting to get quite serious traction, and we are only beginning with what Chase authorized. On paper, at least, we're starting to look like a big concern. The American Standard acquisition alone will move our little venture into the big leagues financially. You're going to have one whale of a tax bill at the end of the year."

I waved her off. "It's still on paper. It's not real, at least not yet. We can still pull back. We don't have to accept that stock. We can always still roll it all right back to our mysterious benefactor. There's still time."

Dotty looked at me quizzically. "I suppose we *could* do that. But why would we? What would make us decide to retreat and give back everything we've fought to build here?"

"I'm not sure," I said, being honest. "I just know it's still a possibility I'd like to reserve. I've been willing to let this whole thing ride, much like the way the FBI or other government agencies take financial positions to get inside organizations they're investigating. But I still want to make sure we can end things if we need to."

"We're getting close to the end of the runway. We'll have to take off very soon before we run out of runway and fall off the cliff. A lot of important people know about us now, including people a block from where we're sitting. They're asking questions."

I sighed. "I know. That's the point. Money is power. That's what all of this is about, after all, and why so many care about it. That was behind all the moves we've made. We *wanted* people to start asking those questions."

"Well, they are. Take the list that your friend, Tom Kyle, sent over from the Chamber. We have investments now in every private company that's connected to prominent men who sit on top of massive hedge funds or investment funds or private equity firms. That group is now asking some pointed questions. We'll need to provide answers soon, even if they're somewhat general. The integrity of our portfolio will demand it."

"So what *does* our portfolio look like now?" I asked. "I mean, if we had to pull the rip cord for whatever reason—like, say, intense pressure from the White House through the Treasury Department—what would it look like? What would we be giving up?"

"You really don't know, do you?"

"No, I don't. Not in any great detail. I wouldn't be asking otherwise."

She started to speak but then changed her mind. Getting up from her seat, she commanded, "Wait here," and walked out of the office to her desk. Returning with her laptop, she opened it, typed in a few commands, then handed the laptop to me. She watched me as I silently processed what was displayed on the screen.

It was a spreadsheet with only a few columns. One was our investment amount. The second was the type of investment. The third was the principal—the name we were pursuing with the investment. The fourth was the financial activity to date, up or down. The fifth column was our stake in it or, more precisely, an estimate of what our stake was projected to be.

"Scroll to the bottom of that fifth column," she told me.

I did. I stared at the number at the bottom of that column. "That can't be right. It says we're approaching $100 million in value."

"Why wouldn't it be real? The starting point was 15 percent in stock from the net profit someday as a profit-carry, which we learned from John Andrews would likely work. But it *is* almost entirely on paper at this point because the exits are both estimates and years away. A significant portion of the projected increase is due to the American Standard joint venture and several other investments quite similar in nature because they're obviously inside plays where the preferred stock investors are closely following a private company."

"But it's real?" I was astounded.

"It *could* be real, if everything matured or advanced as our own financial analysts tell us they might. I've had all of them go over this portfolio closely. I knew you'd ask me this question at some point. I wanted to be ready."

I glanced again at Dotty's spreadsheet. "You certainly came prepared."

"This isn't a game any longer, Seth. This is quite real, whether you happen to like it or not. That's why, if you're going to walk away, you don't have much more time to do so. You'll have to make some important decisions quite soon."

"I can see that."

"And at the top of that list would be this question, which I doubt you've even considered: If we were to give all of this back, who, precisely, would we give it back *to*? Who is our benefactor?"

"We can just give it back to Chase. Let them deal with it."

"We could, I suppose," Dotty said slowly. "But how wise is that? We'll never know what we were ever involved in if we do that. If someone ever decided to challenge us—you know, really come after us in some fashion because we've done something that causes them to pursue us—we wouldn't even know how to protect ourselves. We wouldn't have any resources to pay for that defense. We wouldn't even know where to start or who to blame. And, in the end, we'd have nothing whatsoever to show for any of it."

I started to fidget in my seat. "All the more reason for me to get to the bottom of this, then. I need to find out who our benefactor is. That knowledge might well be the only thing that protects us at some point, regardless of what we decide to do."

"Well, decide quickly," Dotty urged.

"I will. I promise. But first things first. I need to see Petrovich in Moscow. See what he has to offer. Then I'll turn my attention to the question you're really asking. The research from Dr. Silva's team is a good start. I'll talk to her and see if I can't find some common threads to start pulling on."

CHAPTER 31

The nice thing about having your own private jet at your disposal is that you aren't limited in where you can visit. Your timetable belongs solely to you. So I decided to visit Nairobi first and then fly to Moscow immediately afterward. I wanted to see the fourth person who'd been approached by our benefactor.

It wasn't difficult to find the woman Michelle Searle had told me about. She'd made a modest stir five years ago. I found several blog posts on the Skoll World Forum site and elsewhere that told at least part of her story.

Sandra Oakes had grown up in Taiwan with a British father and Taiwanese mother. Both of her parents still lived there. She'd come to the United States for her undergraduate studies and later graduated from Harvard Medical School. Her residency at Boston Children's Hospital was in pediatrics with a specialty in life-threatening genetic disorders.

But she'd surprised both her colleagues and family by choosing not to practice medicine. She decided instead to work for the hottest human genome startup in history, whose founder also had roots in Taiwan. She made the move to research based on her belief that understanding genetic disorders passed along to children from one or both parents was the key to disrupting their impact on children. She believed companies combining intimate knowledge of the way the human body worked with big data research in supercomputer networks was the future.

But only a few short months before that London start-up issued an IPO that would ultimately make it the most valuable human genome derivation company in history—with stock valued in the billions for its small circle of investors and core staff—she left abruptly to start her own company in Nairobi, Kenya.

Her company, Moyo Laboratories, discovered a novel way to outrace HIV mutations. It was as close to a HIV vaccine as anyone had ever come, using some of her human genome research platform.

Dr. Oakes explained in interviews that she'd left to start Moyo because she wasn't content doing only research. It bothered her that nearly 20 million people were still living with HIV and dying from AIDS because they didn't have access to antiretroviral therapy. What the world needed, she said, was something that could compete with nature and the way in which the HIV virus mutated and evolved. Moyo set its sights on that and largely succeeded.

Dr. Oakes explained that collaboration with computer science experts had allowed her to fully explore every possible mechanism for transmission of an infectious disease like HIV. Using the most sophisticated supercomputer modeling in the world, Moyo developed a way to anticipate mutations faster than the HIV virus could mutate.

After several years of small trials, she found an unconventional method that used supercomputer models to engineer synthetic antibodies from the receptors the HIV virus uses to affect T cells. It required a combination of powerful computer modeling and synthetics to outrace the way in which the HIV virus mutates.

But the really shocking part of what Dr. Oakes had done was to make the synthetic antibody treatment Moyo discovered virtually free to anyone who was in a family, community, or setting where they might be infected with the HIV virus. It was like open source software, only for clinics trying to keep the HIV virus from being transmitted to others.

It required regular monitoring, but her Nairobi company was now on the frontier of keeping the HIV virus and its possible mutations from traveling further in populations that had grown weary of the AIDS fight.

I set up an interview with Dr. Oakes through her informal media advisors, based in London. I told them that I'd be in Kenya, and that I hoped for about 30 minutes of her time for a story I was working on. They were happy to accommodate my interview request.

The other thing I learned about having your own private jet is that it's an incredibly efficient flying office. Dotty had booked a takeoff time for me with a leased jet for mid-morning. I took a cab to a private hangar at Reagan National. We were airborne almost immediately. I called Dr. Silva once we were out over the ocean and headed toward the African continent.

"How can I help you today, Mr. Thomas?" she asked.

"Well, I'm flying to Moscow to meet with Aleksandr Petrovich," I said. "Thank you so much for your file on him. It was enormously helpful and made my decision to seek an audience with him an easy one. But I had a question about the file you sent me. I was curious about one of those anomalies you found."

"My pleasure. Happy to help. So you'll visit him in Rublevka after your stop in Nairobi to see Sandy Oakes?"

I paused for a long moment. "How did you...?"

"Know you were visiting Dr. Oakes?"

"Yes, that."

"She told me, of course. We're friends and colleagues. We have been for years. I assumed you'd already made the connection, Mr. Thomas. It was in several of the stories written about her work. I was her collaborator on the computer science research side in the earliest days of her own work, when she set up her company in Nairobi."

I stared out the window of the jet as we flew 10,000 feet above the Atlantic Ocean. There were no clouds anywhere beneath us. I had an unobstructed view of the ocean far below, stretching as far as the eye could see. It was breathtaking.

I blinked a couple of times, processing the implications of what she'd said. "I guess I missed that while I was reading up on Dr. Oakes."

"That's surprising," she replied. "I'd assumed that you, of all people, would not miss a connection like that. After all, that's what you do. You connect dots. That was a relatively easy one to connect because she's mentioned our collaboration in interviews. So I assumed you'd already made the connection."

"Well, I have now. Thanks, that's helpful. Is she still a client of yours there at the Money Exchange?"

"You know very well I can't comment on that," she said, laughing lightly. "But we still are friends. Now, about Mr. Petrovich?"

I wanted to press her a bit more about her research collaboration with Dr. Oakes. There was something here that I just wasn't grasping. I knew that very smart people in the world collaborated all the time. But it seemed a bit strange that these two, in particular, had somehow managed to intersect. I knew there was some connection I wasn't seeing. But it would have to wait.

"Yes, thanks," I said a bit absentmindedly. "One item in particular in your research file on Petrovich really struck me. You called it out for me. I wanted to ask you a bit more about it."

"Absolutely. What would you like me to expand on?"

"Well, it has to do with Petrovich's unusual entry into speculative land development and real estate. Everyone knows that real estate is a damn near perfect way to launder money. You announce projects or renovations, then never actually spend any real money on it. The money comes out clean on the other side.

"Or you just get all of your pals to buy condos, mansions, or apartment complexes at hugely inflated prices that don't reflect the market and move money from illicit to perfectly legal that way. Petrovich has clearly done that, all over the world, based on your research. But he went above and beyond that…"

"By launching dozens of high-end real-estate build-outs all over the world, financed by cryptocurrency ICOs through a small, networked maze of private companies that pyramids up to just one holding company?" she said, finishing my sentence. "That anomaly?"

"Yeah, that one. Who in their right mind would do that? Why would Petrovich need to do that, when there are tried and true methods to buy existing real estate through inflated prices with real cash? Why try to build something new with a complicated scheme of ICOs like the one you've called out?"

There are only a few ways for traditional companies to raise funds for things like sales forces, or new construction, or new lines of merchandise. They can attract outside investors through a series of regulated methods. One of those is an Initial Public Offering (IPO), which allows the public to buy a piece of a company that's matured to a point where people will understand it well enough in order to invest.

But a new form of investing had grown up alongside the bitcoin and blockchain technology Michelle Searle and others had developed—something called an Initial Coin Offering (ICO). An ICO looked a lot like an ordinary IPO, with one critical exception. ICOs are fundraisers like IPOs, but the investors who buy into them (either with real money or pre-existing digital tokens) receive new cryptocurrency tokens specific to that ICO.

The opportunity for a startup company is obvious. It bypasses the exceptionally rigorous, time-consuming, and highly regulated capital-raising process that's required by the banking system, venture capitalists, and governments. The company holding the ICO can start using its capital raise immediately to try new things. The opportunities for investors are twofold: They can make more money if their digital tokens increase in value, and they can see the value of the company increase.

But there are also huge downside risks for investors. If they buy into something that isn't ready for a capital raise, the company falls on its face and becomes worthless. Or the digital tokens collapse as well, regardless of how well the company might or might not be doing. I couldn't see how any of these downside risks might appeal to someone like Petrovich.

"There are a couple of ways to think about Mr. Petrovich's motives here," Dr. Silva said in that clipped, deliberative monotone I'd still not grown accustomed to. "First, as you know, cryptocurrency is an incredibly useful way for his own business interests to move money around without prying eyes. And, second, some of the capital in his network is simply too large to move in traditional ways."

"Like asking couriers to carry bags of money from one place to another?"

"Exactly. Put simply, he and his partners have too much money. They have the luxury, perhaps even the need, to try big, new ventures that they can try to capitalize."

"Fine, but why do so with an ICO?" I asked.

"Because it allows them to truly build a pyramid scheme. They bring in all manner of smaller investors from all over the world, who have no idea what they are actually investing in when they get their digital tokens. And at the top of that pyramid is Mr. Petrovich and anyone else he chooses to reward as part of the management of the holding company controlling it."

"Do you mean to tell me that no one investing through these ICOs knows that they are, in effect, washing money for a Russian organized crime syndicate? And, by the way, what in the hell does the big LLC holding company mean? What, exactly, is 'Pozolochennyy Limited'? I've seen the name before, on a new investment firm in Reykjavik."

"To answer your first question, no, they don't. And this appears to be the point—that, and the fact that none of the funds are accountable or traceable in any banking system anywhere on Earth. And to answer your second question, roughly translated from Russian, it means 'gold-plated.'"

"Seriously? What is this, the Roman Empire?"

"No, just another type of empire," she said.

I couldn't tell if she was joking or not. I never could tell with her.

"OK, so what about the people at the top?" I asked.

"Mr. Petrovich and whichever partners he's invited in to manage the overall strategies of the collective deals are well aware who is behind it. Each of the individual ICO companies might be in the dark, though I doubt it. But those who are involved with all of them…the partners who have a stake through all of the various LLCs and the like…they certainly know. It would be impossible for them *not* to know."

"I see," I said thoughtfully. "So the real question is, who knows about *all* of those LLCs—the ones involved with all of the individual ICOs that scale up to the holding company?"

"Yes, Mr. Thomas," she answered. "That would appear to be the question."

CHAPTER 32

From the window seat of my private jet, it was interesting to watch our landing at Nairobi's airport. It had been years since I'd flown in a smaller plane, and I enjoyed watching the runway rush up to meet us.

The pilot turned our jet away from the commercial plane gates and made his way to a private hangar toward the back of the airport. Dotty had arranged for a car, and it was waiting for me when the jet arrived. I quickly learned the other extraordinary thing about flying a private jet to another country: The customs official immediately met us at the hangar and cleared us into Kenya after inspecting the plane to make sure we hadn't brought anything with us.

This is the way to fly, I found myself thinking as the car pulled out of Nairobi, past a row of Air France planes at commercial gates and toward the airport exit.

Jomo Kenyatta International Airport is about 10 miles southeast of Nairobi's central business district. But the traffic in Nairobi is notoriously bad, and today was even worse than usual. Despite the short distance from the airport to downtown Nairobi, we were stuck in traffic for nearly two hours. It took all the patience I could muster not to lose my mind as we idled in traffic on the way to the headquarters of Dr. Oakes' nonprofit medical company, located in the heart of Nairobi's bustling business district.

I admit, I was a bit surprised at downtown Nairobi. It wasn't huge compared to some of America's largest cities, but it had its share of tall buildings. What surprised me most was that, while the city wasn't especially green in its public spaces, I spied plenty of green spaces inside the gated communities as we inched along from the airport to downtown. I immediately liked the place.

At last, the driver pulled onto a side street off Kenyatta Avenue and parked in front of a smaller building. There was a sign out front with an inscription in Swahili: "Na inahitaji moyo na akili kunjufu." I thought about asking the driver what it meant but typed it into my iPhone to translate it instead. "And it requires an open heart and an open mind," Google's translator said.

I smiled to myself. *So that's what Moyo Labs stands for.*

There was no receptionist when I entered. In fact, no waiting area at all. I immediately walked into a big, open space with high ceilings and doors along the hallway on both sides. Most of the doors had a top and a bottom. The tops were open. A shelf sat atop the closed bottom-half of each of the doors. People lined up in queues at all the open doors.

I made my way slowly through the long lines, waiting patiently at each of the open doors, and looked into each room. Women in all-white outfits took requests at each door. Rows of medicines were aligned in an orderly fashion on shelves in each room.

I stopped at one of the open doors, made a gesture to apologize to people at the front of the line, and asked somewhat loudly: "Dr. Oakes?"

I got a blank stare from the young woman handing out medicines, but a second woman behind her pointed toward the other end of the hall. When I didn't understand immediately, she gestured again and said loudly enough so I could hear her, "Outside. Dr. Oakes. Outside."

I nodded once to thank her and continued to make my way toward the end of the long hall. Most turned to stare as I made my way past. A few whispered to each other, pointed, mouthed "mzungu" to each other, and then giggled a bit. I wondered what the word meant.

I pushed open the two glass doors at the other end of the hallway and was a bit startled to walk into bright sunlight again. In the center of the open courtyard was another throng of people. Some were off to one side, waiting patiently in small groups. A larger group gathered around someone in the center of the courtyard. I made my way to the edge of this larger group. A young Asian woman was examining someone while the rest waited patiently and listened to what she was saying.

"Dr. Oakes?" I asked again.

The woman looked up from her patient and squinted at me. "Seth Thomas, the reporter from the *Post*?"

"Yes. Do you have a few minutes to talk?"

"Let me finish with this patient first. You can have a seat at the back of the courtyard. I'll join you there in a moment."

"Wonderful." I moved away from the crowd in the center of the courtyard. Finding a stone bench at the opposite end of the courtyard, I sat down to wait.

I watched Dr. Oakes as she went about her work. She was calm in her demeanor, and the patients seemed intent on listening to every word she spoke. After saying something to the group in Swahili, she walked toward me.

Wrapping her stethoscope around her neck, she took a seat beside me on the stone bench. "I only have a few minutes," she said.

"No worries. But I have to ask. I'm just curious. I didn't think that you practiced medicine?"

She smiled. "I don't, as a rule. But there is always a chronic shortage of trained medical professionals capable of offering free, specialist training. There are plenty of free clinics in Nairobi but hardly any with specialists. I do my best to help with that, and I've encouraged other specialists to come here at least one day a week. I hold free clinic hours myself two days a week. People come from quite a long distance, in some cases. I don't like to turn them away."

I glanced at the rather large group still waiting patiently to see Dr. Oakes. "But you'll be here for hours."

"Yes, most likely."

"And it will be dark by the time you finish seeing them?"

"Also true," she said. "But it's such a small thing for me to take the time to answer their questions and help them. It's the least I can do. And I enjoy it—the break and the chance to do what I was trained to do. It can be such a chore taking care of all of the logistics and distribution for Moyo Labs."

My plan had been to ease into the conversation before working my way around to the question that I'd flown all this way to ask. But seeing her in her element, helping people in this fashion, I decided not to waste her time with a preamble.

"Dr. Oakes, do you mind if I just get to the point of why I'm here? I don't ordinarily do this, but I feel like I can be direct. Erica Silva told me on the flight here that the two of you are colleagues."

"Yes, she was my research colleague in the beginning of Moyo," she said with a soft smile. She looked past me briefly at her patients to make sure they weren't getting restless, then swiveled to face me again.

"Well, given that I can trust her, I also feel like I can get right to the point, if you don't mind."

"Yes, of course," she said. "Ask away."

"Why, exactly, did you leave the human genome research company when you did?" I asked. "I don't mean the sound-bite answer you've given to everyone else. I mean the *real* reason."

She raised a brow. "That's an odd question. You don't believe the answer I've given in the past, I take it?"

"To be honest, Dr. Oakes, no, I don't. Sure, I believe you sincerely wanted to start something like Moyo Labs, and then did. I believe every wonderful thing you're accomplishing here is what you'd hoped to do. But do I think it was the catalyst for your decision to leave London and come here? No, I believe there's another story behind the one that you've told. And it has something to do with what Michelle Searle told me not so very long ago."

Dr. Oakes stopped moving and turned her entire attention on me. It reminded me quite a bit of the withering look that Dotty would occasionally give me when she wanted to make sure I was paying close attention to what she was trying to tell me.

"You've spoken to Michelle?" she asked finally.

"I have. In fact, I recently visited her in New Zealand. I flew there to see her, and we talked. Now I've flown here to see you, and to talk."

"Is this actually for a story that you're working on, Mr. Thomas?"

"It doesn't have to be, necessarily. What I am hoping for is the truth, because I believe that we have something in common…in fact, the very same thing that Michelle Searle and I learned that we had in common."

Dr. Oakes eyed me for another minute, then said, "Very well. Erica did say that I could expect direct questions from you. But she also said I could trust you to be discreet about what we discussed.

So I'll answer your question directly. I heard from someone—likely the same person who reached out to both Michelle Searle and you, I suspect."

"So you heard from our mysterious benefactor in the months prior to the human genome research project going public?" I asked. "The same one I heard from not so long ago myself?"

"I did. It was actually almost a year before the IPO. It was a number of months before I did anything with the information, though."

"And what was that information, exactly?"

Dr. Oakes sat back on the bench. It seemed obvious that she hadn't talked about this with anyone for quite some time.

"We had a number of human subjects involved in our research in the two years prior to the IPO," she explained. "We weren't simply running data through a supercomputer or working on massively parallel sequencing. We needed human test subjects that allowed us to explore what we were seeing in the data."

"Human test subjects? For what?"

"It's complicated. But I will say this. I was profoundly uneasy with the direction the company was going. I'd been troubled for some time."

"Let me guess. They were laying the groundwork for human cloning?"

Dr. Oakes didn't answer immediately. She looked at me for several long moments. That was all the confirmation I needed and explained why she'd truly left. But I also knew there was more.

"For the purposes of this story," she said finally, "it's sufficient to know that I was involved with dozens of human subjects who came in and out of our lab. I got to know most of them. But there was one in particular, a smallish man with a bland, round face who was always so pleasant. His name was Al Pennyworth, and he was one of my favorite test subjects. He loved the Arsenal. He had his favorite pub in London, which he was constantly trying to get me to visit. He was a huge, sentimental sop for movies like *Mary Poppins*, which he'd seen at least a dozen times. He liked riding around the city on the big double-decker buses. He really loved plays from the cheap seats in London's small theaters."

"Sounds like a nice man," I offered.

"He was. Well, one day, during one of our sessions, he handed me a letter. He asked me to read it while we were sitting there. It was neatly typed on a white sheet of paper. There was no signature at the bottom. Research papers were included with the letter."

"And what did it say?"

"It was from what I can assume was the same benefactor who contacted you. The letter promised me access to whatever I needed financially to successfully start what came to be Moyo Laboratories. It gave me contact information to several key people who could help on the data research side, including Erica at Stanford. It contained some preliminary research on supercomputer modeling related to the ways in which antibodies attach to the HIV virus, along with some novel engineering approaches for synthetic antibodies. It was unique and intriguing. I'd never seen anything like it. It contained novel pathways I'd never considered. It was detailed and specific. Honestly, it was an unexpected gift."

"But let me guess. It all seemed too good to be true, so you didn't take it seriously?"

"I didn't, not for several months. I started looking at the research in the evening, after office hours. I asked questions online of colleagues. I contacted Erica, and she offered to help. When it became obvious there was something there, I reached out to the bank listed on the contact sheet. I asked about the funds for the lab. They said I could designate whatever I wanted for the lab. There were no restrictions, they told me. I didn't believe them, so…"

"You tried it out," I said quietly. "And you discovered they *were* telling you the truth. The money was there."

"Yes, I was able to start Moyo Labs immediately. I tried doing both—my job at both the genome company and this virtual lab—but it became impossible. The breakthrough at Moyo happened right before the IPO. The choice was easy. I'd never cared about the money, so I walked away from the IPO, left London, moved here, and started Moyo. The rest, as they say, is history."

"That can't have been easy, though. I doubt anyone understood the decision you made. It's not like you could explain it."

"No, it wasn't easy. But Moyo Labs, which took off quickly, was so clearly the right thing for me to do with my life. It's been like one constant blur of activity ever since I made the decision to leave and start this."

"And your patient, the one who gave you the letter initially? What did he say about it?"

"You know," she said with a somber expression, "I never had the chance to ask him about any of it. I never saw him after he delivered the letter that day."

"So who was he, do you think?" I asked her.

"I assume that he worked for our benefactor. I tried to find him about a year after I'd left. But there's no Al Pennyworth in London. He must have made up the name."

"Do you think you'd recognize him if you ever saw him pass by on the street?"

"Not any longer," she said. "It's been years. He was the kind of person who vanishes in a crowd. I never paid all that much attention to what he looked like. I just enjoyed our conversations. And then he was gone." She stood now, eyeing the restlessness of her patients. "So, Mr. Thomas, does that satisfy you? Is that the story you wanted?"

I hadn't taken any notes during our meeting. There was no need. "Yes, Dr. Oakes, it does. And, as you guessed, I was also contacted by that same benefactor."

"And has it worked out for you, as it has for me?"

"I don't really know, to be honest. It's like trying to put a jigsaw puzzle together without all the pieces."

"I hope I've at least been a bit helpful," she said with an easy smile.

"More than you know, Dr. Oakes."

CHAPTER 33

When my jet was about 100 miles from Moscow, two Russian MIG 29s pulled up on either side of us. They moved just off both wings so quickly it was like we were standing still.

I heard the door to the pilot's cabin click open. I looked over my shoulder. The co-pilot walked toward me and took a seat beside me.

"What gives?" I asked him.

The co-pilot glanced out the window at one of the MIG 29s. It was so close I felt like I could reach out the window and touch it. "They'll be with us all the way to Moscow," he said calmly.

"We need an escort?"

"Apparently," he said, smiling. "But the good news is that we shouldn't have any trouble landing at Sheremetyevo when we get to Moscow."

I swiveled to peer at the MIG 29s off to both sides. The dull metallic-gray exteriors were a stark contrast to the bright blue sky behind them. Both pilots were fixed on their flight path. They weren't really paying any attention to us.

I turned back to the co-pilot. "Did they say why?"

"No. They just asked about our intentions, and what we planned to do when we got to Sheremetyevo."

"So they already knew which of Moscow's three airports we were going to?"

"They did. I didn't ask them how they knew that."

"Interesting. I'm assuming that we're fine. That they're just escorting us."

"As far as I know, yes, they're just escorting us. If it makes you feel better, this isn't all that unusual for certain types of VIPs... especially those the Russian government has an intense interest in."

"So I'm a VIP now?"

"Yes, sir, Mr. Thomas, you certainly are a VIP now." He got up and returned to the pilot's cabin.

I glanced out the window at the MIG 29s again. I decided to ignore them for the balance of the trip. Despite the fact that we had two highly trained Russian military fighter pilots on either side of us, we had an uneventful trip the rest of the way. We landed at Sheremetyevo without any further trouble. Both jets pulled off and away from us before we landed.

I wondered vaguely how they knew where we were going. But it didn't really matter. At this point, I assumed we were the constant subject of chatter on multiple networks.

As in Kenya, our jet pulled into a private hangar where a car was waiting for me. A customs official was there to meet us as well. He made a quick tour of the jet, then we were on our way. But we had an easier time with traffic than in Nairobi. We were lucky, because Moscow traffic jams for people trying to make it to their dachas can be truly horrible. But we were able to make our way around the eastern edge of Moscow without much trouble before reaching the highway once known as the "tsar's road" south of the city. It took us to the mansions of Rublevka.

Rublevka is about 15 miles away from downtown Moscow. You can't actually find it on a map anywhere, but media, realtors, and government officials all know where it is. Most of Russia's elite have their second homes there. Just as New Yorkers retire to their Hampton estates during the summer, the wealthiest Russians make their way to their dachas in Rublevka whenever possible. Almost every home there is worth millions, with many worth tens of millions.

It's the most expensive countryside and dacha area in Russia. Alexi Simon's dacha was there, along with nearly every other senior official in the Kremlin. Official events, including international meetings with heads of state, often took place at Simon's country home in Rublevka. The entire area reeked of wealth and snobbery. Most Russians either envied or scorned it, but there was still only one Rublevka in the world.

Aleksandr Petrovich's dacha was grander than all the others, including even the Russian president's expansive country home.

Worth $100 million or more, it was easily one of the ten most expensive homes anywhere in the world. The house had been listed on Sotheby's for nearly $120 million before Petrovich purchased it for an undisclosed sum.

Petrovich's grand home was situated at the end of a long, meandering road to the back of the area. It was located in one of Rublevka's gated communities on several acres of land. I noticed that you couldn't drive a car in a straight line from the gateway entrance on the road to the house. I assumed that was by design. We made our way up the winding entranceway, past several roundabouts that encircled gardens and water fountains. It looked like a palace from the outside, with red and gold shutters on all three levels and a massive entryway at the front.

There was only one car parked out front—a Mercedes-Maybach S 560. It was one of the most expensive cars in the world, and cost more than I made in a year. I wondered vaguely if Petrovich had told his driver to park it out front just for my benefit.

I approached the massive front doors of the mansion, expecting to be greeted by his personal bodyguards. But when one of the doors swung open, Petrovich himself stepped through it. He extended his hand to greet me as I made my way up the steps. He held a drink in his other hand. There were no bodyguards around that I could tell.

"Mr. Thomas, how nice to see you. I certainly hope your trip was pleasant and uneventful," he said in a low baritone. His English was quite good. I had no trouble understanding him, despite the thick Russian accent. He was a big man, easily several inches taller than me and probably 100 pounds or so heavier. Dressed casually in black slacks and a red silk shirt, he seemed quite unlike the most feared mafia boss in Russian history. But, of course, appearances are often deceiving. Especially so in this case.

"The MIG 29s were a surprise," I answered. "But other than them, yes, it was uneventful."

Petrovich smiled. I couldn't help but notice that he had several gold fillings. It was likely the very smile that created terror in others, in different settings. "Ah, those. Alexi wanted to assure that you had no trouble making your way here."

"I believe we could have managed without the Russian fighter jet escort, but no matter. It's all good. I'm here now, safe and sound."

Petrovich gestured to the interior of his home. I moved past him and stood in his entryway. Two paintings flanked the enormous hall on either side. I recognized them instantly as two of the most famous paintings in Russia. One depicted a tragic moment in the country's history. The other was a portrait of the most enigmatic woman ever painted, save perhaps the Mona Lisa.

Petrovich watched me to admire them both. "Yes, they are originals," he said before I could ask the question.

"But how? These are only on display at the Tretyakov Gallery. I know, because I've seen them there myself."

"I have an arrangement with them," he said. "Whenever they require the purchase of a painting that is important to Russian history, I am available without question. I purchase it and donate it to the gallery. In return, they occasionally allow me to hold these here, in this home. I thought you might appreciate both, so I had them delivered here."

"Just for me?"

"Yes, Mr. Thomas, just for you. I hope you are suitably impressed."

"I'll admit it, yes, I'm impressed." I gestured at them both. "May I take a closer look?"

"By all means. That is why they are here. I wish nothing more than for you to examine everything you see today—from these paintings here in this hallway to other items we shall discuss in due time."

I moved over to study the paintings more closely. They were exquisite. They also seemed to be the originals, or good forgeries. But I didn't doubt Petrovich. I assumed they were just as he'd said—the originals on loan from the Tretyakov Gallery. Wealth and power certainly did have its benefits.

"These are spectacular, Mr. Petrovich," I said after admiring both for several minutes. "I have never seen anything quite like them." I glanced around the hallway. There was no one in it except us. I kept expecting bodyguards to show up and search me. But it really did appear to be only the two of us in this massive mansion. "By the way, can I ask…are we alone here at your house?"

Petrovich nodded deliberately. "Yes, it is just the two of us. My driver is here but out back with the kitchen staff. We will not be disturbed here in the main house. I give you my word. I wanted to make certain you were immediately comfortable upon your arrival."

"Yes, of course, and thank you. I certainly appreciate your hospitality."

Petrovich gestured to a sitting room off to one side of the vast hall. I could see, from where we were standing, that it was a study. "Shall we?" he asked. "And may I offer you something to drink? Vodka perhaps?"

"I've never been a vodka fan, sorry," I said with a laugh.

"So some Scotch, then, without ice? I have some 24-year-old single malt from St. Magdalene."

"Of course. Who can turn away thousand-dollar-a-bottle Scotch?"

"Exactly," he said.

As we entered his study, I looked at the books lining his shelves on either side. All of them were hardbound. I felt a slight temperature shift as we entered. I could hear the air circulating from high above the room. "First editions?" I asked.

"Yes, all of them," Petrovich answered. "And the room's temperature is controlled, as you can tell, to make certain they remain in good condition." He walked over to a spot on the shelf and pulled out a thick volume, handed it to me, and then watched as I gingerly held it in my hands.

"A first edition of *War and Peace*," I said. "Okay, I'm more than suitably impressed."

"Good." Petrovich chuckled. "I wanted to make certain you were convinced we only deliver the best."

He walked over to a mantle, pulled a bottle from it, and began to pour a drink. He handed it to me, then made his way to the center of the study. A large box rested on a heavy, round oak table surrounded by several chairs and a couch. A folder lay atop the box.

I took a seat at one end of the couch and looked at both the box and the folder resting on it. "I assume this box, and this folder, are why I'm here." I took a slow drink from the glass of Scotch. It was as smooth as any drink I'd ever had. It melted in my mouth and then burned just a bit as I swallowed.

"Yes, they are. So, please, have a look. Take as long as you like. We can discuss what they mean after you've had a chance to look at the contents of both the box and the folder."

I gently placed my glass of Scotch on a coaster on an end table near the couch. Positioning myself at the edge of the couch, I placed the folder off to one side and lifted the top off the box. I could see immediately what was inside. It startled me. It wasn't what I'd been expecting.

The box contained photocopies of quite a few files. I picked up the first batch from the top of the pile. I sat there in the quiet of Petrovich's study—surrounded by expensive first editions of the most important, profound books in the history of human civilization—staring at the very first photocopied page for the longest time before going through the rest of the documents.

The first set of documents included a copy of Vice President Howard Phelps' tax returns to the U.S. Internal Revenue Service from the years prior to the White House. I placed the first set of documents down beside the box and began to inspect the remainder of the photocopied files. The second batch included more tax returns—those of Jessica Savage, the wife of Supreme Court Justice Michael Savage. I set those to one side and inspected the third set of documents. They were the tax returns of Jessica Savage's colleague, Samuel Jenkins, the majority leader of the House of Representatives.

I began to systematically inspect each set of tax returns more closely, one by one. Petrovich said nothing. He simply allowed me to inspect the documents. Occasionally, he took a sip from his glass but otherwise left me to my review.

I had no way of knowing for certain if the documents were genuinely the individual tax returns of Howard Phelps, Jessica Savage, and Samuel Jenkins. But I was fairly certain they were legitimate copies. I was more than a bit stunned that the Russians had obtained sensitive financial information on central players with both national political parties in the United States, effectively representing all three branches of its government.

I knew the Russians were masters and purveyors of *kompromat*, but this was next level stuff. I read through several of the years, which listed out assets and liabilities and explanations of LLCs and limited partnerships inside the business interests of Savage, a Republican, and Phelps, a Democrat. They looked quite authentic.

The implications were both profound and disturbing.

I was eventually able to identify one distinct common thread running through all three sets of tax returns. One venture, in particular, had almost certainly made billionaires of both Savage and Phelps, and had nearly propelled Jenkins into the same exclusive club as well. One particular investment had suddenly and fortuitously worked extraordinarily well for all three. It was both the organizing principle of the Russians' *kompromat* on these three—and equally as likely to be the reason why Alexi Simon was now throwing all three to the wolves.

Anyone looking at these tax returns could see why none of them would ever want them made public. The connections to Russian financing were impossible to miss. It wasn't disqualifying, even for Phelps. It might not even be illegal, unless one could draw a direct connection to Petrovich's organized crime syndicate. But given what had transpired during the 2016 presidential campaign, it would have been exceedingly difficult for the American public to forgive such a deep connection to Russian financial interests around Alexi Simon, much less to Petrovich himself.

I turned to the folder next. I pulled the documents from them and studied them closely. They, too, were a surprise. The folder contained the legal documents explaining the upper hierarchy of the ICO pyramid scheme that Petrovich had put together. The documents detailed the way in which the various cryptocurrency ICOs were linked together into one holding company. Seven partners actively controlled the ICO networks inside the holding company. Petrovich was one of them. Three were Russians who were obviously cut-outs for Petrovich. The remaining three were Howard Phelps, Jessica Savage, and Samuel Jenkins.

It was this partnership that had propelled Phelps into the ranks of the Billionaires' Club after so many years of trying to scale that particular mountain. The profits from the very same partnership had more than covered the mounting losses in Jessica Savage's family fortune. And it had made Samuel Jenkins wealthy enough to self-finance his political campaigns.

The ICOs had allowed a massive amount of money to wash through the system. Some of the development companies were likely real, and valuable. Some were not. But it made no difference. The sum of the scheme was in the tens of billions, and I was quite certain that nearly all of it was laundered from the looting of Russia's public sector. All three of the American officials—who, collectively, had an enormous amount of sway over all three branches of the U.S. government—had profited from a Russian holding company entirely hidden from view. The individual ICOs were all known. The holding company that tightly controlled them all was not.

I turned finally to face Petrovich. "So this is true...Phelps, Savage, and Jenkins are all principal partners of Pozolochennyy Limited with you? I'm reading these documents correctly?"

"Yes. Those three are the principal partners."

"They are *your* partners in it?"

"Yes, my partners," he said in a measured tone. "You will find, once you do your research, that the other three names in the holding company all work for me in some capacity. One is the chairman of the board of a natural gas pipeline company that I have a substantial, controlling interest in. The others are similarly part of my business network."

"And the tax returns? They really are those of Phelps, Savage, and Jenkins?"

"They are," Petrovich answered. "And before you ask me, no, I am not at liberty to say how I obtained them. You can ask, but you will need to simply accept that they are indeed their returns. You will need to make your own decision as to whether you choose to take them with you when you leave here and what you intend to do with them once you return to America."

"But I can assume that one of Russia's two intelligence directorates obtained them, under Alexi Simon's direction?"

"As I said, I cannot tell you that. You can speculate however you'd like. But I can assure you, they *are* their tax returns."

I studied the sheaf of papers in my hand and then the box on the table. "This is not at all what I was expecting."

"And what were you expecting?"

"Certainly not this," I said truthfully. "Not anything even remotely like what I see in these documents. But I do have to ask: Why are you giving these to me? I'll be blunt. Aren't these three *infinitely* more valuable to you under your control? Why push them out into the cold like this?"

Yet even as I asked this question, I already knew the answer. In the U.S., both national political parties in the United States were now fully behind serious and substantial efforts to close down Russia's offshore financing that had disrupted several U.S. election cycles…and showed no signs of slowing down. Both parties had been moving in that direction for years.

Russia's brutal war against the Ukraine had only accelerated that process and stiffened their resolve to undermine Alexi Simon's financial positions. Cryptocurrency and blockchain were essential to Russia's future in a global banking system that had turned quite hostile to their interests, but only if that technology was not manipulated by American intelligence services, specifically the U.S. National Security Agency.

I found it amusing that Russia's GRU, of all places, was still uncertain about the conspiracy theories that code breakers at NSA had created cypto and blockchain as a way to infiltrate Russia's financial inner sanctums. Outing these three would do more than severely disrupt American democracy yet again. It would set in motion a chain of events that might very well expose crypto's lasting and legitimate ability to scale to a global financing system that could not be tracked by American intelligence services.

Petrovich smiled again. It was bone-chilling this time, given the context. "They no longer hold value for us. If we are to continue to rely on its capacity, we need to understand precisely how blockchain technology and cryptocurrency originated. We have grave questions about its utility, as do you. This is…a necessary step to reach a level of certainty. And, I might add, it is time for the world to understand the true nature of American capitalism and its political system."

"Never mind the obvious trouble this will cause all three of them, especially the vice president," I said. "You *do* realize how other world leaders will react to what's on this table here when it's made public, right?"

"We accept the consequences to both of our countries," he answered. "Russia is poised to take its place as one of the world's greatest nations. This is a necessary step. It is long past time that the world understands what motivates and drives your political leaders. The contents of this box and folder perfectly illustrate the very nature of America's capitalist system."

CHAPTER 34

I took the box and the folder with me. It wasn't a difficult decision. I'd set out to tell a story, wherever it led. It's what I did, after all. It's what I've always done. The box and folder were part of that story. I couldn't simply leave them behind inside Petrovich's house of exquisite toys.

During the transatlantic flight back home to D.C., I spent the time looking through the contents closely. Petrovich was right about one thing. It would take more research to connect the Russian financial elite enmeshed within Petrovich's crime syndicate with the ICOs, the holding company that had rolled all of them up, and the blizzard of LLCs and limited partnerships littered like baubles throughout the 20-year history of tax returns for Phelps, Savage, and Jenkins.

But the pattern was clear, especially in the years immediately prior to Phelps' run for office. He'd been worth quite a lot in the private sector, but he was not, despite popular accounts, a billionaire. The Russian ICO scheme had done that for him. Likewise, Savage's media empire had clearly been on the ropes, until the ICO scheme bailed her out and saved her family fortune. And Jenkins? He'd just hitched his wagon to Savage, for good or ill.

I had no doubt I'd be able to connect the dots between these three and the upper echelon of Russia's financial and political leadership. It was clear that all three had benefited immensely from the direct aid of Russia's elite…specifically, Aleksandr Petrovich's ICO pyramid network. The folder outlining the principal partners, combined with the tax returns, was clear and unambiguous.

After the collapse of the Soviet Union, the American public had largely ignored the slow return of the Russian empire. It had also largely ignored the merger of its political leadership with private financial wealth that rivaled what had once been the Roman Empire. Most people believed that emperors and kings were a thing of the past. But Russia and China were evidence that authoritarian control, combined with great personal wealth, was alive and well on the earth.

What I struggled with was why Russia's president, Alexi Simon, and the Kremlin's political, military, and state security leadership had chosen to make their financial arrangements with the American vice president, the wife of a Supreme Court justice, and the majority leader of the House of Representatives known at this particular time.

What I'd said to Petrovich was obvious to any competent observer. They had considerable leverage over all three. But Russia was trading that leverage to sow damaging political chaos throughout America's democracy. Even though Russia would deny everything as American propaganda, once I'd told this story, it would send a signal flare to every one of Russia's enemies. Alexi Simon was clearly playing to win, even if America's leaders were seemingly oblivious to his machinations.

Russia's leadership was taking this large, calculated political risk because they'd concluded that the chaos and ensuing damage to American democracy was worth the price. Phelps would be out of office at some point. Savage's husband would remain on the high court for life, but his status and ability to be a deciding voice on the court had waned considerably in recent years. And Jenkins had made no secret of his willingness to leave Congress and cash out rather than remain in the House. This story would simply hasten that move... or worse.

But the wholesale destruction that these documents would unleash on America—whom Alexi Simon believed was Russia's great enemy in its quest to take center stage in world politics—could create political instability that might last for many years beyond Phelps' or Jenkins' terms in office, or even Savage's tenure on the Supreme Court. It could accelerate Russia's ascendance again as a great world power at America's expense. Any reasonable observer would likely conclude that the trade Simon was willing to make did, in fact, make sense on the world stage.

Alexi Simon had made Russia's re-emergence as one of the world's superpowers, with vast reach geopolitically, his great life's work. It drove everything he'd ever done in his life, from his rise to power from the depths of the KGB to his absolute control of the Russian state. Simon had played any number of highly risky chess moves such as this over the years.

These three, though, had likely fallen into his hands unexpectedly. Russia's president had now obviously decided it was time to take advantage of that windfall, at their expense, for the greater good of Russia. And the side benefit was that it could, quite possibly, prove or disprove the conspiracy theories about the origins of blockchain and crypto that was now quite clearly at the heart of Russia's ability to operate in the shadows of the world political stage and finance its moves.

I struggled some with why Petrovich would go along with such a move. It would expose him and damage his own business empire. But he, and others in Simon's circle, had no choice. They did what Simon demanded, without question. If they did not, they didn't merely fall out of favor or political power. Life, liberty, power, and wealth were all at risk in a Russian oligarch's life, though Petrovich probably wouldn't suffer much because of the publicity. He'd be fine.

I was torn about what to do with Petrovich's gift. As we flew across the Atlantic, it became clear to me that I needed to consult with at least one or two people I could trust before deciding my own course of action. I wasn't comfortable making this decision by myself.

Problem was, there were very few I could confide in. Dotty, certainly. But I couldn't go to my editors at the *Post* with this yet. I wasn't even sure whether I *would* ultimately go to them with it, given that my own story was now so entangled with our mysterious benefactor. I needed to consider the consequences to me personally, as well as to others. I couldn't consult with colleagues. I knew what they'd tell me to do.

But there was one person I could discuss it with, who might have some insight and who would keep my confidence. While I'd only gotten to know her recently, I was certain Erica Silva could offer a trusted perspective.

I needed that perspective right now. So I knocked on the pilots' door, and asked them to re-route to JFK in New York. Having the ability to change your itinerary while you're flying across the ocean? Yet another perk of using a private jet.

***

Dr. Silva was waiting for me at the reception desk. She held a folder and a laptop. But we didn't move to the conference room this time.

"Do you mind if we talk outside while I get a cup of coffee?" she asked. "I've been trapped inside the office all day. I'd love to see some actual sunshine for a bit."

"I'd love some coffee," I said. "Lead the way."

There was a crowd in the elevator, so we rode to the lobby in silence. I had a cardinal rule, one I'd obeyed for nearly my entire career in journalism. I never talked about business in elevators or places where anyone might overhear. Colleagues of mine listened in on conversations on the Acela from Washington to New York, though I didn't.

When we got outside, Dr. Silva stopped and basked for a minute in the sudden bright sunlight. "I sometimes wish I had a job where I could work outside, where I wasn't trapped at a desk," she said. "But this is the best I can hope for, to get outside a couple of times a day in between calls and meetings."

"So where's your coffee spot?" I asked. I expected her to head toward the nearest Starbucks, where the average cup of coffee had twice as much caffeine as the typical cup of coffee. I often wondered if people truly understood why they felt compelled to wait in long lines at Starbucks for their afternoon coffee.

But she surprised me. We walked over to an outside vendor at the corner, across the street from the New York Stock Exchange. There were a couple of people in line.

"I hope you don't mind," she said. "He's local, and he makes a delightful cup of Mexican coffee. And he always has fresh pastries."

"By all means, though I didn't take you for a street vendor aficionado."

232

"He's been here, at this corner, for years. Most of his family is still in Mexico."

The coffee was delicious and hot. I tried not to burn my lip as we walked along the street to a somewhat secluded park bench. She pointed to a statue of a small girl with her arms planted on her hips, staring up at the historic NYSE building.

The mayor had relocated the Fearless Girl statue from its Bowling Green spot, where it had faced the iconic charging bull synonymous with Wall Street. Young girls were waiting in line to have their picture taken with Fearless Girl in the foreground and the New York Stock Exchange building in the background.

"I always get a kick out of seeing that statue, and the way girls love to have their picture taken with it," I told Dr. Silva as we settled in on the park bench.

"Me, too," she said. "I know it began as a marketing gimmick a few years ago. But I still like to see it as well. Someday, years from now, people will simply forget its marketing origins and think of it as nothing more than an iconic part of New York City lore here in the shadow of the stock exchange building on Wall Street."

I laughed. "Yep, everyone forgets origins after a while."

Dr. Silva placed her laptop and folder on the bench beside her and sipped her own hot coffee. "Were your trips to Nairobi and Moscow a success?"

"They were, thank you."

"I'm glad to hear it." Dr. Silva smiled. "Sandy Oakes is my hero. She has been for years. I cannot say enough nice things about her, and her work."

"I can see why. And I agree. Her work is absolutely critical. We're all lucky she made the decision she did once upon a time in London."

"It wasn't an easy decision to make," Dr. Silva said. "Very talented people like her are forced to make life-altering decisions at critical junctures. History tends to record the path taken and ignores what might have been. All I can say is, thank goodness for Al Pennyworth, whoever that wonderful little man might actually be, and the person he serves."

There was something about that phrase that bothered me. It wasn't that Dr. Silva knew about our benefactor. I'd assumed she and Sandra Oakes had discussed it at some point. No, it was more than that…the way Dr. Silva characterized that person. But I wasn't really here to ask about that. I needed to make a decision about Petrovich's gift.

"Did you know Al Pennyworth?" I asked.

"He'd left the human testing by the time Sandy found me to discuss what became Moyo Labs. Sandy has talked about him, of course."

"By the way, what did you happen to think of her idea when she first came to you with it?"

"I thought it was brilliant, like Sandy herself."

"Yeah, she's a real superhero, like Wonder Woman," I said, laughing.

A brief scowl darkened her visage. "No, she's *not* some fantasy, comic-book heroine ginned up in a trinity with Batman and Superman during the Second World War to counter Nazi propaganda built around Nietsche's Ubermensch," she said, her voice rising with a sudden anger. "She's real. She's flesh and blood, and the sort of person we should all aspire to be. She is what I would hope a real superhero would look like, if such a thing is possible."

I was startled by the fierceness of Dr. Silva's demeanor and her response. I'd only been joking. But obviously I'd hit a raw nerve. "Well, now I'm a big fan," I said quickly. "I was beyond impressed by her commitment to her work. I've never seen anything like it. She's a true hero."

Dr. Silva swiftly recovered her composure. "So, Mr. Thomas, you said on the phone that you wanted to talk about something you found in Moscow. How can I help you?"

"For starters, can you read through these documents? They were given to me by Petrovich. I assume they were obtained by Russia's security networks."

I handed my own folder to her. She placed her cup of coffee off to one side on the bench, then opened the folder. She looked through Vice President Phelps' tax returns, and then the returns of both Savage and Jenkins, as well as the documentation of their involvement in Petrovich's pyramid ICO holding company. She didn't seem especially surprised. She finished reading, then closed the folder.

"I see. So what do you intend to do with these?" she asked. "Or, I should ask first...*do* you intend to do anything with them?"

"Before I answer that, can I run something past you first? This is all in confidence, of course. Please don't share this beyond your research team."

"By all means. And please don't worry. You are our client, Mr. Thomas. What we discuss with you is for your benefit only."

"Great," I said, nodding. "What I need to do first is make certain of the authenticity of these documents. Petrovich said I'd have no trouble connecting the three principal Russian partners in the ICO holding company scheme to him. I can certainly do that with my own research. However, I was wondering..."

"If we couldn't make short work of it instead with our own information network here?" she said, finishing my query. "I can already answer that question. It's my turn to give you some documents."

She handed her own folder to me. I read through the printed documents inside. She had already cross-linked all three of the partners in the ICO network with Petrovich. They were clearly lieutenants in his network. There was no doubt of that.

I looked up. "So it's true. Petrovich was telling the truth. The three Russian partners in the ICO holding company all work directly for Petrovich."

"I asked our research team to study this shortly after I sent you the report on him," Dr. Silva explained. "It's the core of what we do here at the Money Exchange. We find the connections between people and places inside deep financial networks, even those deliberately hidden in shadows. The team found these connections without much trouble. All of it is hiding in plain sight, as long as you know where to look. Now, with what he's given you, it won't take much for you to illustrate the full picture."

"Well, clearly you know where to look," I said, impressed.

"Yes, we do. And there is one other thing I'd like to show you." She opened her laptop, typed in a command, then handed it to me. There was a query matrix open on it. A computer program had drawn direct links between Petrovich's multi-layered ICO networks and a number of the LLCs and limited liability partnerships appearing on all of the tax returns.

"What am I looking at, exactly?"

"You're looking at all the proof you'll ever need that the vice president's financial holdings are inextricably linked to Russian financial interests, along with Savage's and Jenkins' own finances. But there's even more here." She typed in a command in the query bar, and a new set of lines began to fill the screen.

"So what's this?"

"Petrovich meant to protect the identity of the ICO network's assets," she explained. "No human can track these massive numbers. No one can draw connections between various companies and concerns spread out everywhere or hope to make coherent sense of so many ICOs. It's like one giant math puzzle built in, around, and on top of cryptocurrency. No human can solve the equation and identify those at the center of the maze. There are hundreds of these, all of which are designed to make it virtually impossible for any single human being to track."

"But Frontier 2 can," I said. "It can take every aspect of every ICO, add them all up, and then draw conclusions about what it all means."

She nodded. "Which is precisely what we've done."

"And I'll be able to use the conclusions?"

"You will. You'll need to assemble how you arrived at the bottom line. But it won't be difficult. We've given you the answers. Now you only need to make up the questions and make certain the answers match."

I let out a heavy breath. "I also need to decide if I want to tell this story."

"Yes, there is that. You will need to decide what matters most," Dr. Silva said. "But I feel quite sure you'll do the right thing, once you have all of the facts in front of you."

CHAPTER 35

I was dead tired when I got back to Washington. It had been a long trip, even with the perks of a private jet and streamlined customs. I had a lot weighing on my mind, and no real idea which path to take.

Ordinarily, after such a trip, I'd stop by a bar and have a few drinks and something from the bar menu before heading back to my apartment and collapsing in my miserable bed under sheets that hadn't been washed in weeks. But I had no real desire to do that right now. I had way too many questions swirling around in my head, and not nearly enough answers.

Dr. Silva's Money Exchange research had helped. I was now certain the documents Petrovich had given me proved beyond any reasonable doubt that Vice President Phelps' recent entry into the exclusive Billionaires' Club was inextricably tied to Russia's financial elite, and that both Savage and Jenkins owed their financial success to those very same interests. That part would be easy to explain to my editors, and to everyone else. The story was almost certainly as it seemed to be. It would be the biggest story of my journalism career and would effectively end Phelps' vice presidency, much as graft had once ended the political career of Spiro Agnew, former President Richard Nixon's vice president.

I had made one other firm decision, though. I'd called Tom Kyle during the plane trip back to Reagan airport. I asked him to reach out to his friend, the White House chief of staff, to set up a meeting. I didn't want to meet with Admiral Symons at the Roosevelt Room in the West Wing, though, and I doubted he'd be willing to meet with me at Jackson Place even though it was right across the street. Tom suggested the Chamber of Commerce boardroom as a neutral corner. I told him that made sense. He tried to push me on what the meeting was about but eventually gave up when it was apparent I wasn't going to tell him. He did extract a promise from me to bring him in before I broke whatever story I was working on. I promised to do that.

But the truth was, I didn't know what to do. I wasn't simply a journalist pursuing a story any longer. I had crossed several lines. I was now *part* of that story—and uncertain whether I wanted to tell it or extricate myself from it. I also wasn't sure that I *would* tell a story. And, if I did, what parts I should leave out.

I tried watching something online. Nothing was remotely appealing. I combed through social media feeds, which mostly made me mad. I stood at the window staring at the white Sprinter van across the street. I opened the freezer door at least a dozen times but never pulled out anything to microwave. I stared wistfully at the liquor cabinet but decided to avoid that particular distraction.

It felt as if a hidden clue, or maybe more, was embedded somewhere in my subconscious. I kept going over conversations I'd had in recent days, trying to find the skeleton key that unlocked everything.

It wasn't the fact that Fedorisky, Petrovich, and, ultimately, Russian President Alexi Simon were trying to use me to further their own geopolitical aims. I was used to sources with ulterior motives. But, at the end of the day, the story always wins. If it's there, you tell it. Nothing else matters.

After my third round of pacing inside my miserable apartment, with no end to my torment in sight, I decided to call Dotty. I glanced at the clock on the kitchen stove. It was 10 p.m., far too late to call. But I had to talk to someone. I felt like I was going crazy.

She picked up on the first ring. "Hello, Seth."

"Did I wake you?" I asked.

"No, but thanks for asking. I was watching the first episode in the final season of *The Man in the High Castle*. Have you watched it yet?"

"The one about Nazi America…what it would be like if Hitler had won?" I laughed. "You do know that's fiction, right?"

"Yes, Seth, I know it's an alternate reality," she said softly. "It doesn't mean we can't learn from it."

"Maybe. But I think we all know what modern fascism looks like."

"Do we?" she challenged me. "Is it so implausible—the thought that extremism like what we saw in Germany can take root here in this country?"

"Well, yeah, people always like to believe that American democracy will never succumb to such obvious racism, hatred, and class warfare. But you might be right. It might be possible."

"I'm not sure there are enough good people in high places anymore willing to do the right thing, no matter the consequences. It's tough duty being the salt of the earth," she said. "But that isn't why you called—to chat about an alternate reality where fascism exists in America."

"No, it isn't," I admitted. "Truth is, I can't stop pacing around my apartment. Nothing makes sense to me now, no matter how hard I try. I keep going over and over things in my mind."

"So tell me about it. Maybe I can help. But before you tell me what's troubling you, remember that our conversation isn't…well, you know what it isn't."

I smiled. It's what I'd grown to adore about her. She was always on her toes, even at 10 p.m. "Yes, and thanks for the reminder. I'll be judicious. So, for starters, can you tell me about the meetings you've set up with our investments? I know we can talk about it tomorrow, but it might help me while I'm trying to wrestle with these things."

"Sure. I've set up more than a dozen meetings from the list we got from our financial advisors, research firms, and the Money Exchange. That's more than half of our short list. They all want to talk in person. The plan is proceeding exactly as we envisioned. And most of the others have reached out in one way or another."

"So you're telling me our plan worked?"

"It's working quite nicely. We're hearing from everyone we set our sights on."

"And the investments still make sense to pursue? No hiccups? Nothing unusual?" I pressed.

"It's all good. No red flags. I just need to confirm all of the meetings with your schedule."

I hesitated. "You know, I've been thinking..."

"Oh, no." She groaned. "Don't tell me you're not going to sit in on these meetings?"

"Okay, I won't tell you. But, really, Dotty, you can handle all of these meetings by yourself. You don't need me. I trust you completely."

"Well, thanks for that. But I thought the purpose of this exercise was to see who showed up so that you could start connecting dots. Isn't that still the goal?"

"It is," I said slowly. "But...something's happened that I *really* need to focus on first. There's a lot at stake. I can't afford to get it wrong."

There was no way I was going to talk about Petrovich's documents and ICO network on an open line that we both knew was being recorded. If I did, it would likely make the PDB by the next morning and start swirling around inside the NSC staff and the agencies within 24 hours. I wasn't ready for that kind of attention just yet.

Dotty sighed. "All right. I can always debrief you later, after the meetings."

"Thanks. That would be a big help."

"Fine. We have that out of the way. So why don't you tell me what's *really* on your mind?"

I'd begun pacing again. I was now standing at the window. I looked down again at the white van. "Okay. So here goes. Who do you think our benefactor is? I mean, really? Who is it?"

"I can tell you who I'm pretty sure it *isn't*. It isn't anyone in the crowd you just met with. There's zero chance it's connected to them. They're asking way too many questions. They seem quite desperate to find out themselves. They're pushing buttons, making things happen. That's not the profile of someone who's pulling strings."

"I think you're exactly right," I answered. "They are testing things, like cryptocurrency markets, to see what threads unravel when they pull on them. They're tracking people and companies and institutions, which means they're trying to find out things, not directing traffic. And they're also playing for keeps. By no means is this a game to them."

I glanced over at the box I'd brought back with me, and the folder sitting on top of it. The Russians were absolutely playing for keeps, and they'd raised the stakes considerably. They were making a play to change the world's geopolitical order.

"It's definitely not them," she said. "I think we can rule them out."

"Yes, we can. So let me try something else out on you. Who put the thought in your mind about the Money Exchange?"

"Hmmm," Dotty said while she pondered the question. "That would be...yeah, our guy at Chase."

"And has he ever made a suggestion like that—directed us toward something specific like that so we'd follow up? I know the Money Exchange is essentially the central repository of information about pretty much everyone who's on our short list."

"You know, he hasn't actually. That suggestion is outside of what he usually does, which is to accept information from me and then answer my question about whether the money is available to cover whatever it is we're proposing."

"So it's...an anomaly? Out of the ordinary?" I asked.

"Ha! That's funny. But yes, as Dr. Silva might say, it's an anomaly of data."

"That raises an interesting question. So, any other thoughts about who we might be trying to discover here?"

"I do, actually," Dotty said. "I believe it's just one person. I don't think it's a group. I also don't think it's a game. I believe there's something real behind it all...something genuine he or she would like to accomplish."

"Why?"

"Because of the type of people invited to play the game. I mean, just look at some of the people you've been able to track down. One was present at the origin of bitcoin and cryptocurrency. Another was an expert on exposing the activities of some of the most notorious criminal elements in the world."

"Right," I said slowly. "And look at Nairobi. What she's done there. Saving lives, maybe even millions of lives. I think you're right. It's genuine. These are people operating at extraordinary heights."

"Precisely. It's as if our benefactor is trying to create real-life superheroes in a very flawed, human world where awful things can happen and tragedies occur all the time. He or she is searching for specific kinds of people who can rise above it all and do what's right to actually make the world a better place. Like the MacArthur Foundation genius awards."

I stopped pacing. I stopped thinking about the white Sprinter van on the street below, or who might be listening in to our call. I even stopped thinking about the box sitting on the coffee table in my crummy apartment that might bring down very prominent politicians and alter the world geopolitical order, depending on decisions I would need to make soon.

Several pieces of the puzzle suddenly and seamlessly slid into place from the chaos that had been torturing me.

"Wait," I said. "Say that again."

"What? About trying to deal with the awful things that happen in the world?"

"No, not that. About superheroes."

"I said that our benefactor seems to be trying to create—or find—superheroes in real life who can truly make a difference. Like Nairobi."

"Yes, exactly like Nairobi," I said, more to myself than to Dotty. "Exactly like the real, flesh-and-blood people who can truly change the world if they have access to the right financial support, networks, and information."

My mind was already racing in several directions at once, making connections I'd been unable to make when the pieces of the puzzle weren't falling into place. Dotty had inadvertently cracked the code, though I didn't think she realized it. But thanks to something she said, I knew where to look now.

I didn't know who our benefactor was. Not yet, at least. But bread crumbs had been dropped in the forest. They'd been there all along. All I had to do was follow them.

CHAPTER 36

They say none of us should fear that Artificial Intelligence will truly achieve human-level intelligence and then super-human intelligence—something that would be godlike and beyond anything the human mind can comprehend—because of one simple thing: Humans can make leaps. Computers can't.

Sure, you can program supercomputers to try to make those leaps. Deep, machine-learning AI can mimic the human mind. It can try to replicate the mysterious process that sometimes occurs when the human mind makes a leap that defies logic. But can they, in fact, be taught to make the same sorts of leaps that define the human mind? I have my doubts.

When our mysterious benefactor first contacted me, he or she had sent a text message: "Get your head out of the cloud, make like Clark Kent and fly by."

It was my one and only clue. I had nothing else to go on, other than that one clue.

Like all journalists I know, we not-so-secretly harbor thoughts that we can be just like Clark Kent in the newsroom. But we don't fly around in capes under our journalistic garb. Our words do that flying for us. It's actually Clark Kent who makes the world a better or safer place, we all assume.

I hadn't tried to psychoanalyze the clue embedded in that text. I was a journalist, so of course I wanted to be like Clark Kent, or perhaps Superman, who wanted nothing more than to expose the forces of darkness and make the world a better place. What journalist doesn't aspire to that? I had nothing else to go on, though, so I hadn't thought about it much since receiving the text.

But I had other clues now. Others had been contacted, and there had been clues there for each of them as well. I'd never connected them...until now. And neither had they.

When John Andrews had been contacted, it had come in the form of a computer-generated voicemail from a company called Wayne Construction. The name of the company that had reached out to Andrews might have been either random or coincidental, but I was fairly certain this wasn't the case.

Jasper Olafsson had said one of the people who'd contacted him had wanted to establish a private, secluded island away from the rest of the world called Paradise Island. This, too, could have been a random or coincidental choice for the name of just such an island. But I didn't think so.

Michelle Searle believed that she might have met the person behind it all, and that person might even have been the mythical Satoshi Nakamoto. But her first contact had come through an invitation to a Lucius concert, where she was told to meet a Mr. Fox. The choice of that particular band name, and the last name of the person she was supposed to meet there, likewise could have been either random or coincidental. But I doubted it.

When Sandra Oakes had been handed the road map that ultimately convinced her to leave certain riches behind in London in order to start Moyo Labs in Nairobi, she received them from a man who called himself Al Pennyworth. This particular choice was certainly not random. It seemed deliberate.

And when I talked to Erica Silva recently, she reacted visibly to my suggestion that Dr. Oakes was a modern-day version of Wonder Woman. I'd found it odd at the time. But perhaps it wasn't so odd after all.

The moment I hung up with Dotty, I started my research. I began with the common thread in all five of the specific contacts with the benefactor.

During the Second World War, when Nazi propaganda convinced many of a master race of Supermen somehow better than others, a trinity of mythical American superheroes was created on the pages of comic books. They went on to become cultural icons. Those three superheroes—Batman, Superman, and Wonder Woman—were created by writers and artists at what eventually became DC Comics. The enduring superhero myths that they created continue to resonate with mass audiences today.

DC Comics emerged from the dark shadows of a world war on the backs of that trinity of superheroes. But they had not triumphed in the marketplace from the creation of those three superheroes alone. They also successfully rolled up nearly all of the other smaller comic book rivals that were likewise creating superheroes on their pages.

I quickly discovered in my research that one of the comic book rivals acquired by DC Comics near the end of World War II was a company started by a writer in New York City who had spent much of his career living on the edge of poverty. Like Edgar Allen Poe, who immortalized Publisher's Row in New York in the 19th century, this particular writer had tried to establish himself both as a writer and as a literary magazine publisher with little success.

But he had succeeded beyond his wildest dreams with a company built around his own set of mythical superheroes that he'd created to sell comic books and pay the bills. Several articles from the New York newspapers at the time said the company he sold—Bond Street Publishers—had more than pulled him out of poverty. It had given him his first real financial stake, which he parlayed into other successful publishing ventures, industrial companies, and successful real estate throughout Manhattan.

The founder of Bond Street, Mathias Sullivan, always said that every good thing that had ever happened to him was because of those three superheroes—Batman, Superman, and Wonder Woman. He always said he owed his fame and fortune to them and what they inspired in us.

"I owe everything to those three superheroes, who came into our lives at one of the darkest times in human history," Mathias Sullivan told one biographer. "They are more than just archetypal myths. They taught me how to dream. I would not be the man I am today without them, because they gave me the courage to create my own superheroes, and to build a company around them."

Mathias Sullivan repeated that story for decades after selling his company to DC Comics. He eventually became quite wealthy. But he always credited his initial success to the inspiration of that superhero trinity.

Decades later, Sullivan's granddaughter tried, unsuccessfully, to buy the company that her grandfather had sold Bond Street to after the war. In the one and only story about that unsuccessful bid, Sullivan's granddaughter, Margaret, referred to the very same story about the creation of her own family's fortune and success. She made the effort because she wanted to honor her grandfather, she said.

And in that single story were the five bread crumbs that had eluded me until now. Clark Kent was Superman's alter ego. Batman's Bruce Wayne ran Wayne Enterprises. His loyal butler was Alfred Pennyworth. Lucius Fox ran Bruce Wayne's businesses. And Wonder Woman was born and raised on Paradise Island.

I had no idea, really, why our benefactor had chosen to place such bread crumbs along the various paths. If I found others who'd been contacted by the person, I felt sure I would find more such crumbs. They'd been placed there deliberately, with the thought—or, perhaps, the hope—that someone, someday, might follow them.

Next I turned to the Money Exchange. There wasn't much in the public domain about them. That wasn't surprising. They were, after all, an exclusive global consulting business like McKinsey or Accenture that catered to the most exclusive clientele on earth. I was certain their business model was built on the best data and information and sold at the highest prices to the wealthiest, most influential members of an exclusive club on an entirely proprietary basis.

But no company like the Money Exchange could afford to remain completely behind the curtain, like the Wizard of Oz. They had to be just transparent enough about what they did, and why, to maintain their perch above their competitors. There would always be a few sporadic public comments about big topics trending in the news.

So I researched the Money Exchange. It was a privately held company. No one had ever written about private stockholders or a small board. There was nothing about owners, board seats, investors, or even the potential value or net worth of the company. I couldn't find anything on Dow Jones, *Bloomberg*, *Fortune*, or anywhere else.

It reminded me of Palantir Technologies, which had once been a very private company estimated to be worth north of $20 billion. Before going public in 2020, it had been responsible for much of the software and hardware systems of the National Security Agency, the Central Intelligence Agency, and others in the intelligence community in the United States. Prior to going public, there had been virtually nothing available on Palantir. It had been created by one of the original board members of Google, who had purchased massive amounts of land in and around Palo Alto and Menlo Park.

But who was Palantir? How broad was their reach inside the intelligence community? All that anyone really knew about the company was that it had been named after the "seeing stones" in J.R. Tolkien's *Lord of the Rings*. The palantirs in *Lord of the Rings* were crystal balls that allowed their users to communicate and see what was happening in distant parts of the world. Its name had now been appropriated for a massive technology company handling that mission for America's intelligence community.

There wasn't even all that much available publicly on the Money Exchange's lease-purchase of the Frontier 2 supercomputer. IBM had issued a press release on it. No one wrote about it, presumably because every tech journalist had already written extensively about the incredible supercomputing power of the original Frontier at Oak Ridge. I was one of those journalists who'd written about Frontier. I'd paid zero attention to the *second* Frontier.

I spent two hours reading every single story that ever mentioned the Money Exchange. There wasn't a single reference, in any of them, to its owner. The Money Exchange's long-standing president—a former partner at a hedge fund—was quoted in some of the big, trendy financial stories. But it was the usual stock quotes you find from the hedge fund and venture fund guys. The more interesting comments came from Dr. Silva, with the type of analysis about topics that I'd witnessed firsthand in my meetings with her. She knew her stuff cold.

But I did, finally, find one story. It was a tiny, five-paragraph story in a local weekly newspaper in the town of Newton, situated at the southern edge of the High Peaks Wilderness in the Adirondack Mountains. It was a funny little story about how the Money Exchange was bringing a nearby ghost town called Tanin back to life. The Frontier 2 supercomputer was located there, at the site of what was once the Adirondack Mining Company.

Adirondack Mining had once been a major source of jobs in

that part of New York State. It had been prominent in the 19th century. American presidents occasionally visited the place when they vacationed nearby in more prominent places like Lake Placid. The mining company had held on for dear life for decades but had finally succumbed to the pressures of new technologies and new industries. When the mining company folded, Tanin became a ghost town.

The Frontier 2 had brought it back to life somewhat, the local newspaper story said. A few of the locals were able to secure jobs with a Money Exchange subcontractor hired to maintain the systems that kept the supercomputer system running. There was a picture of local officials at the ribbon-cutting ceremony. No one from the Money Exchange was quoted. It was just a small, inconsequential story about a few jobs bringing a ghost town back to life in a remote part of the country called High Peaks.

But I next looked up the history of the Adirondack Mining Company. It had changed hands many times since its heyday in the 19th and early 20th centuries. Its final owner, who had made a great deal of money from its operations immediately after the Second World War, was Mathias Sullivan...the very same man who'd sold his own comic book firm to the publishing company that created Batman, Superman, and Wonder Woman. Mathias Sullivan used the wealth from the sale to create a globe-spanning enterprise, which was later passed on to his heirs. The Adirondack Mining Company had been part of that enterprise.

Sullivan's granddaughter, Margaret, had kept the mining company alive through sheer force of will for nearly 20 years. By all accounts, she'd done everything humanly possible to keep the company running so it could provide jobs for the communities around it. But it had not worked. The march of new technology had ended its useful life, and no amount of money could change the truth.

Was it a coincidence that the Money Exchange had chosen to assemble its Frontier 2 supercomputer system in the very same ghost town that had once been an important part of Mathias Sullivan's financial empire? An empire that, by his own admission, owed everything to mythical superheroes that he and others had created in the dark shadows of a world war? Was it coincidence that the

Money Exchange had located an incredibly valuable asset in the same ghost town that Margaret Sullivan had spent so much of her life trying to preserve?

I couldn't find out much about Mathias Sullivan's heirs. There was a flurry of stories after he died, with some speculation about his net worth. It was considerable for that time, though not quite in the same league as the Rockefellers. His eldest son, by most accounts, continued to grow the business. They bought several buildings in midtown Manhattan, for instance. But there had been little coverage in the financial press since Mathias' death.

Margaret Sullivan had inherited her grandfather's estate and companies, but I could find nothing at all on her net worth or what she had done with the financial empire her grandfather had built. She'd never made any of the lists of the billionaires, for whatever reason. That meant she either wasn't a member of that exclusive club, or that she was incredibly and successfully private about her family's financial state of affairs.

My last search felt as elusive as the previous ones. I tried to find out what I could about Erica Silva. Like the Money Exchange more broadly, what I found was a smattering of quotes from her in various publications commenting on trends. Her analysis was always illuminating and insightful. She was quite an asset to the Money Exchange. They were fortunate to have her on staff as their custom research director.

But I couldn't find any meaningful biographical information about her personal life. She was a virtual ghost on the internet. She didn't have a profile on any of the major social media sites. She didn't have a Twitter or Instagram account. She didn't have a Facebook page. So I couldn't query followers or friends.

It was shortly before dawn when I finally found what I was looking for. I came across a story in a local small town newspaper about 150 miles or so southwest of Mexico City. It was in Spanish, but the Google translation was straightforward.

It was a brief story about a local medical clinic that had been opened in the small town, endowed in the memory of Enriqué Silva and his wife, Sofia, who had died tragically in the crossfire of a drug cartel fight many years earlier. The medical clinic would be a godsend to the local residents in that part of the country who could afford neither the time nor the money to travel to Mexico City, the story said.

Toward the end, the article briefly covered some of the backstory. Enriqué and Sofia, while being deported back to Mexico, somehow got separated from their daughter. The Silvas had died before reuniting with their child, who was later adopted and now lived in the United States.

I finished my research in the early morning hours, just before dawn. I closed the blinds in the bedroom to shut out the light beginning to stream into my apartment. The pieces of the puzzle were no longer tormenting me.

I knew where the cabin in the deep woods was now, and who lived there.

I fell asleep almost the instant my head settled on the pillow.

CHAPTER 37

The president's chief of staff at the White House was a cautious man. He'd built a successful career in the Navy by learning how to navigate turbulent or choppy political waters that originated from Pentagon, Congressional, and White House overlords.

He'd risen to the rank of Admiral in record time. He'd caught pirates off the coast of Somalia. He'd stared down the Chinese after a near-collision of a U.S. warship and a Chinese destroyer in the South China Sea. He'd served as the chairman of the Joint Chiefs of Staff before finally retiring from military service.

But serving as the president's chief of staff was Admiral James Symons' most difficult tour of duty. He complained to colleagues in private conversations that he should never have come out of retirement to work in a cesspool of backstabbing. He spent his days babysitting young staff aides, soothing bruised egos, and dousing raging internal conflagrations.

But his biggest challenge—one he'd never fully learned how to deal with—was the president herself. She was an empty vessel, prone to taking on board the recommendations of the last person to see her. Symons had used his entire professional toolkit in an attempt to bring order to the chaos that encircled the White House every minute of every day. None of it worked. Strategies were formulated and then dismissed on a whim.

And, yet, the machine that was the national government continued to churn. Early in his tenure as the White House chief of staff, Admiral Symons had decided that the only rational response on his part was to do what he could to keep the essential elements of the government moving forward. Everything else would be whatever it was going to be.

I had partially read Tom Kyle into the story I wanted to discuss with Admiral Symons. I told Tom just enough to make sure Symons realized the import of the meeting. I'd asked Tom to convey to Symons that I really wished to meet with him alone, without someone from the White House press staff in tow. Symons agreed. As I suspected, he asked if we could meet in the Chamber of Commerce's boardroom.

I showed up a few minutes before we were supposed to meet. Tom was waiting for me at the elevator and walked with me from the bank of elevators to their cavernous boardroom.

"Is he alone?" I asked Tom.

"He is. He's waiting for you. We reconfigured the big board table so it's much smaller, just for the two of you."

"I appreciate that."

"So, you gonna tell me what kind of nuclear bomb you're about to drop in Symons' lap?" Tom asked with a crooked smile. "I know you, Seth. You wouldn't go to all this trouble to meet with the president's chief of staff if it wasn't a helluva big story that'll entangle his boss."

"As I said, it *is* a big story. I wanted to give them time to process it and respond to it."

"So what'd you find—*kompromat* the Russians have? Do you have tapes?"

I smiled. "I don't have tapes. You know me. I don't care about that sort of thing."

"But you have *something*, don't you? And it's big."

We entered the Chamber's boardroom. The chandeliers had been dimmed a bit. The huge room felt even bigger without the massive table that usually filled the room. There was a small table in one corner. Symons was seated at it, waiting patiently for me to arrive.

"Yes, Tom, it's big. But it isn't tapes. And I'm not going to tell you what I have until I've discussed it with Admiral Symons."

"Fair enough." Tom stopped at the entrance to the boardroom. "But you'll tell me, right?"

I ignored his plea and walked briskly across the floor. Symons stood to greet me. We'd never met, but I recognized him from the many photos of him in his current job. And I knew he was well aware what I looked like.

I noticed there was a folder in front of him on the table. I didn't generally like to read documents others were carrying with them unless they asked, but it was hard not to see the label affixed to the folder. It was my name.

"Admiral Symons, thank you so much for agreeing to meet with me." I offered my hand and he shook it firmly.

"Of course," he said. "I understand from Tom that it's important."

"It is. I wanted to give you a chance to hear about it first." I pointed at the folder on the table. "Can I assume that you have the intelligence community brief on my activities in that folder? There's been a van outside my apartment for weeks. I assume you have a summary of the calls they've recorded. And a summary of what the task force has been trying to piece together."

Symons shook his head. "Yeah, I suppose it's pointless to pretend I don't know anything about what you just described, or that it isn't true. So, yes, this folder is about you."

We took our seats. "So can I also assume that you have the very latest reports on me—that I flew to Moscow to meet with Aleksandr Petrovich?"

"I do," he replied. "And, I must say, the NSC staff was perplexed about the purpose and nature of the trip."

"To be honest, I was, too. I'm not in the habit of regularly meeting with someone like Mr. Petrovich. I didn't know what to expect. But the guy certainly lives like a king. That dacha of his in Rublevka is like a palace. Originals of some of the most famous paintings in Russian history. First editions of the great Russian authors. The most expensive cars in the world."

"They don't call him the boss of bosses for nothing, Mr. Thomas," Symons said somberly. "I doubt whether either of us quite comprehend the number of bodies he's buried in order to amass such wealth and power in Russia."

"You're right. I can't. And I don't really feel like thinking about it all that much."

"And yet...you met with such a man. May I ask you why you did so?"

I looked directly at Symons. I didn't want him to misunderstand my answer, or the thinking behind my decision to meet with him.

"Because I go where the story takes me, Admiral," I answered. "I always have. I have never shied away from that principle. I will pursue the story to the ends of the earth if need be. I will talk to sources I detest, or despise, or that I don't necessarily trust in order to find the appropriate finish line of a story I'm pursuing."

"And what have you found, Mr. Thomas?"

"Before I answer that, may I ask you a question?"

"Of course."

"You've seen the intelligence community files on Russia's efforts to corrupt American elections. They now span several cycles, each more insidious than the previous effort. You've no doubt signed off on the limited public statements about Americans in this administration who continue to do business with Russian financial interests, despite Russia's malignant desire to do substantial harm to our democratic process?"

"I have, on both counts," Symons said.

"So, given the fact that you know how the intelligence community does its work, and how critical it is to national security interests, do you believe that anyone at the highest levels of this administration—or in other branches of the U.S. government, for that matter—has been compromised in some way by Russia's political and financial leadership? What do you believe, personally?"

Symons nodded. I strongly suspected he'd heard some version of this question before, in the course of private conversations. "You know very well I can't answer that question. My personal views on it don't matter. In any event, I'm not at liberty to share them, nor would it be appropriate to do so. I serve at the pleasure of the president. It's that simple."

"Fine, I respect that. So let me ask you: If I were to present *incontrovertible* proof to you that the American vice president—Howard Phelps—was indebted personally and financially to wealthy individuals who surround Russian President Alexi Simon, would it change your opinion on that question? And that others, in similarly high positions representing both of America's two national political parties, were similarly entangled?"

Symons glanced at the folder with my name on top. I could

see from his body language that he was trying to decide just how deeply he wanted to enter this conversation. I assumed there was information about me in the folder that might inform what we were discussing, but which he wouldn't share with me.

"So have you found that incontrovertible proof, Mr. Thomas? Is that what Mr. Petrovich provided when you met with him at his home in Rublevka?"

"Yes, I have, Admiral Symons. I'm in the process of fact-checking everything and ascertaining the credibility of what I have. But I expect that I'll be able to verify it all. And I wanted to give you a chance to respond to the factual basis of what I've found."

"I appreciate the offer," he said. "Can you give me the general outlines of what you found?"

"Yes, I can. What I found is that the vice president is inextricably linked not only to wealthy individuals in Russia, but he is a principal business partner with an elaborate network that surrounds Mr. Petrovich himself. And you, of all people, know what that means.

"And the vice president is not alone. The majority leader of the House, from the other party, is similarly compromised. So is the wife of one of the more prominent members of the Supreme Court."

Admiral Symons said nothing for several long moments. His face remained impassive. "I'm sure you realize the seriousness of such an allegation," he said finally.

"It isn't an allegation, Admiral. It appears to be the truth, even if it emanates from someone with Mr. Petrovich's reputation. I can question his motives and history, but the documents are conclusive about the truth of the allegations. And, if true, there will be consequences— investigations, hearings, maybe even prosecutions. I'm sure you recognize that."

"I do. I'm sure you realize that the vice president will vigorously deny such a ludicrous allegation—as will the president who selected him as her running mate. He will say it's an utter fabrication by Russian military and intelligence agencies that have perfectly honed the fine art of propaganda and weaponized it against America. It will be their word against his."

"So you'll send me that response?"

"Yes, I will get you an official statement from the White House denying this scurrilous allegation against the vice president." His eyes met mine with intensity. "But I want to be clear. If, as you say, you have incontrovertible proof of this, then I can only assume you will report it. You will report it, won't you, Mr. Thomas? You'll tell this story to the American people?"

"It's hard to say no to a story like this, Admiral," I answered. "Stories like this happen but once in a journalist's life. So, yes, it's safe to assume I'm going to tell it."

Chapter 38

"So is now a good time for me to give you that democracy lecture, the one you enjoy so much?" Jacob Shapiro asked me. "America was founded…"

"Stop," I pleaded. "Seriously, just stop."

"Fine. I won't give you that lecture about the value of the Fourth Estate. But I will say I told you so," the *Post*'s hard-charging managing editor told me. "I knew you still had it in you. *Burned out,* my ass. This is maybe the single biggest story of your career. And you know what? It might actually do some good. It might clean up some of the mess. Russia has been at this game for years. Most Americans don't seem to give a damn. But this? It might change things."

"I'm not so sure about that," I said. "But it is a helluva story."

I hadn't seen Shapiro or anyone else in the newsroom for weeks. He'd been true to his word. He'd let me pick my own investigative assignment. He'd left me alone for however long it took. I never told him, or anyone else, what I was working on. The only stipulation was that I come back to him when I had a proper story to tell. So I was back.

"I have faith in you," he'd said those many weeks ago when he'd made the deal with me. "I believe you'll come across something no one else would ever have dreamed of pursuing. And then you'll tell the rest of us about it."

He'd also told me, "Don't quit on us, or what this place stands for. Go after something…and don't stop until you catch it."

Well, I'd chased the story of my life. And I'd caught it.

I'd also made my decision. I planned to tell the story to the American people, as well as I possibly could. They deserved to hear the truth about their vice president, the House majority leader, and the wife of a Supreme Court justice who served for life. I would leave some parts out, because they didn't matter to the story. No one would ever care about my benefactor, who'd set me on this path in the beginning. That was between the two of us. There was no need to include that.

I'd sent Shapiro a note after my meeting with the president's chief of staff. I outlined what I'd found, and that I was now waiting on an official response from the White House denying the truth of what I'd found. I told him he'd need to bring in the newspaper's general counsel from the beginning. I told him to fasten his seat belt, because the ride was about to get bumpy.

Then I took 48 hours and wrote what would likely be the most important 10,000 words of my life. I included Jasper Olaffson's investigation into the way in which the Russian oligarchs had nearly bankrupted Iceland's economy a decade earlier. It was useful background on the way in which the Russian oligarchs manipulated the banking systems of entire nations. It had direct relevance and bearing on the enormous bet the Russians were placing on blockchain and crypto.

I used what I'd learned from Ivan Fedorisky about the way in which those with vast amounts of wealth were able to make billions off an inside game. I used the background I'd gotten from Michelle Searle about the origin and utility of bitcoin and cryptocurrency as a way to explain why Russia's biggest organized crime network had created a network of ICOs that spanned the globe. I added some color by describing Petrovich's home. I closed with the ICO holding company partnership of Phelps, Savage, and Jenkins with the most feared crime lord in Russian history.

I'd proposed to Shapiro that we make some portion of the tax returns public. Phelps' returns were certainly fair game, as were Jenkins. Savage's were another matter, though lawyers might argue that hers were sufficiently joined with her husband's as to make them fair game for public dissemination. I'd argued that the step was necessary to buttress the central elements of the explosive story about the partnership with Petrovich and the far-reaching make-up of the ICO network. The newspaper's general counsel brought in a phalanx of outside lawyers to study the unprecedented nature of such a move.

What I *didn't* include in the 10,000-word draft I submitted to Shapiro was the game the benefactor had played in the past decade or so through her carefully selected players.

There was no need to tell John Andrews' story. I would let Michelle Searle reveal Satoshi Nakamoto's true identity—and her own newfound entry into the Billionaires' Club—when she was ready to talk about it. Her story didn't matter here.

I especially didn't include Sandra Oakes' incredible story about the true origin of Moyo Laboratories. There was no real need to tell that story. It also wasn't mine to tell. It was Dr. Oakes'.

"I do have one question for you," Shapiro asked me as we sat in the main conference room just off the newsroom. "I'd like to get it out of the way before the lawyers join us."

"Sure, name it."

"You didn't tell me how you came across this story in the first place—how you came in contact with Ivan Fedorisky, or why he connected you to Petrovich."

"Does it matter?" I asked. "We have the documents themselves. We have the tax returns, and the corporate papers. It's all locked down in those documents."

"But I just want to make sure," Shapiro pressed. "You didn't color outside the lines on this thing, right? Nothing illegal or unethical?"

I smiled. "No, Jacob, it's all strictly legal." Which was true. The pursuit had been highly unusual. But illegal? No, it wasn't that. "Petrovich offered the documents to me all on his own, after I'd asked Fedorisky to introduce me to him."

Shapiro nodded. "Good. Helpful to know." I could see he wanted to follow up, but he didn't press.

And it was true. The documents did speak for themselves.

"May I ask you something as well before the lawyers show up?" I asked.

"Go for it."

"The owner of the *Post*...he's one of the wealthiest people on earth," I said. "He's not going to have a problem with this story, right? He's not going to step in?"

"Oh, he knows quite well the trouble this story will cause, in any number of directions. But he won't interfere," Shapiro answered. "I've spoken to him about it. So has the executive editor. He supports this, and us, completely. We will publish this story. I give you my word on that."

"I just wanted to check. You know how these things go sometimes."

"I do. But it won't in this case. This story—your story—is why newspapers like ours exist. It's why we matter. You find the story, and then you tell it. We try to find the closest approximation to the truth that we can discover. And then we let the American people decide what they intend to do with that truth once they hear it."

"Good. I trust you. And that's what I believe we have before us here…the closest approximation of the truth that I could discover."

"I agree," Shapiro said. "So let's go tell this story."

CHAPTER 39

I got out of the cab on H Street, near the entrance to Jackson Place and our office. The homeless guy on the grate had a new sign today. Hung prominently from his now-permanent encampment on top of the grate, it was hand-lettered in big, broad strokes: "Giving away British pounds, thanks to Brexit madness and runaway inflation. Good old American dollars welcomed."

I loved that the guy stayed current with the latest news. I pulled money from my pocket, peeled a twenty-dollar bill from it, and dropped it into the bucket perched precariously on top of one of his grocery carts.

"Thanks, friend," he called out, peeking at me through a crack in his fortress wall.

"Stay warm," I said and started walking toward the office on Jackson Place.

I hesitated briefly on the front stoop to steel myself for the difficult conversation I knew I was about to have. I turned the knob slowly and then entered with determination.

Dotty was waiting for me in the interior office. I was pretty sure she already knew what I was going to say. She'd always known. She'd done everything in her power to keep me engaged with the work at the office on Jackson Place. She'd moved heaven and earth to ensure I followed and understood every move she'd made with the prospective investment partners who came through the office.

But Dotty didn't need me. She was fully capable of managing the various financial advisors, research firms, and outside vendors whose information informed her every decision on the world-class investment portfolio she'd built.

The truth was that Dotty was the driving force behind the investments that now made up SCT Enterprises. Every aspect of the portfolio was because of her. I may have been the name on the door, but it was Dotty who understood every aspect of the business. She knew it all. I didn't. She constantly explained the work to me, in painstaking detail. But it was her work. It wasn't mine.

We'd actually argued a bit about the job titles for SCT for a while. I'd asked her to just name herself CEO, but she always resisted. Her title as business manager was sufficient for what she needed to accomplish, she said. Nearly everyone she dealt with, and who paraded through the townhouse at Jackson Place, expected a man at the helm of SCT. They weren't comfortable with a woman running an investment portfolio of the magnitude she'd built.

Nonsense, I countered. She was fully capable. I had no real role in the business or the work.

No, she'd then explain patiently. Our benefactor had contacted me, and then brought her in as my sidekick. That arrangement suited her perfectly.

"I like being your Girl Friday," she joked in one of our many polite arguments on the subject.

"But you realize, don't you, that Hildy Johnson takes over in that movie, right? She decides that she doesn't want to be anyone's Girl Friday and takes matters into her own hands," I'd argued right back.

Dotty wasn't my Girl Friday. She wasn't anyone's sidekick. She was an amazing, talented financial analyst in her own right who obviously had a gift for going where her own particular story led her. She took the research portfolios, sorted the wheat from the chaff, and knew precisely where to go with it.

I'd never questioned her judgment. It was obvious to me that she knew what she was talking about. I would never have been able to drive to the heart of the Billionaires' Club without her guidance system. She was the reason SCT Enterprises was now poised to make a considerable amount of money for our benefactor—and for us, the managers of that portfolio.

I asked Dotty to set aside her work for the morning, after I'd met with Jacob Shapiro and the lawyers at the newspaper. I wanted to talk, I told her on the phone. I'd made some decisions.

"Just don't," she said as we sat together on the small couch in my office. "Don't tell me. I don't want to hear it."

I could see that Dotty was on the edge of tears, which was quite unusual for her. She was a tough, fearless woman. She didn't cry. She'd proven she could handle the likes of Ivan Fedorisky, and any other scary person who stepped onto her path. She'd even managed a brave smile when she realized just who Aleksandr Petrovich really was.

But this was different. She knew what I'd decided. And she didn't want to hear it.

"I can't take the money," I said. "I especially can't take it if I'm going to write this story."

"Yes, you can."

"No, Dotty, I really can't," I told her firmly. "I have to choose. I either have to take the money, or tell the story. I can't do both."

"But why not? Why can't you do both?"

"You know the answer to that question as well as I do. There will be intense scrutiny on me when this story posts. All hell will break loose. Everyone will do their best to break me down. They'll look into every aspect of my life."

"We haven't done anything wrong here," Dotty said, still fighting back the tears. "We've done everything exactly by the book. We have our own lawyers, and advisors, and researchers. Everything we've set up will pass any test. And, I'm quite sure, the person who set us up here has to be pleased with the investment portfolio we've assembled."

I smiled warmly at her. "Yes, I'm certain she's pleased beyond measure with what you've accomplished here, in this office. You've accomplished exactly what she imagined when she gave us this opportunity. In fact, I'm sure you've exceeded her expectations."

"What *we've* accomplished here," Dotty countered.

"No, what you've accomplished. This place…it's all you. We both know that. You really and truly don't need me for this. It's all yours. So I'm stepping aside. This is now your business, your office, and your money. I can't take it. I *won't* take it."

Dotty was determined, though. I could see it in every aspect of her being. "But Seth, everything here makes perfect sense from a responsible, fiduciary point of view."

"All true. But that won't matter when the story posts. They

already have a massive intelligence community file on me at the White House. I know that. You know that. Everything I've done to uncover this story will eventually come under the microscope. So I have to make a clean break of it. I need to protect you from what we both know is about to happen. And that means I can't take the money."

"Look, I get it," she said. "I do. I know what drives you. It's always the story. It's always the truth you're trying to uncover. The money, the power, the access…the rest doesn't matter to you. I get that. I know why you don't care about the money, why you only care about the story."

"That's exactly right. I don't care about the money. Which is why it's an easy decision to walk away from this and hand the keys to you."

"But I don't want you to leave."

"I'm not going far," I told her. "And I'll be back. I'll visit you here all the time. You'll get sick of me. I promise."

"I'm not sure I can do this by myself," she said weakly.

"That's not true, and you know it. You can handle all of this perfectly well by yourself. We both know you never really needed me here. I was always just along for the ride, while I tried to discover who brought us into this game. The investments we made and the money we were trying to make were always secondary to that search…for me, at least."

Dotty stiffened and blinked fiercely, as if to ensure she wouldn't cry. "Okay, I'll accept this," she said finally. "But on two conditions."

"Let's hear them."

"First, you allow me to keep this office open for you in case you ever change your mind and want to return."

"I'm not…"

She cut me off. "Just say, yes, Seth. Keep the possibility open. That's all I'm asking."

I gave up. "Fine. I accept that condition. So, what's the second?"

"Promise me you'll tell me once you know for sure who brought us here to Jackson Place at the very beginning."

"Yes, I give you my word," I said. "It's why we got into this, after all. You'll be the first to know, once I've confirmed it beyond any shadow of a doubt."

CHAPTER 40

Dotty granted me one last perk before I officially turned everything over to her at the Jackson Place office and walked away from SCT Enterprises for good. She chartered a private jet for me to fly north to the Adirondacks.

Erica Silva had agreed to give me a personal tour of Frontier 2 in the former ghost town known as Tanin on the outskirts of the High Peaks Wilderness. I'd told her that it was important, and that there was more I wished to discuss with her. She hadn't argued much and agreed to meet me there for a personal tour. It gave her yet another excuse to get outside, she'd joked.

The story about the vice president—alongside the House majority leader and the wife of one of the nine Supreme Court justices—and his deep connections with Aleksandr Petrovich and Russia's political and financial leadership was working its way through an army of lawyers at the newspaper. It would run that weekend, on Sunday morning. I knew it would change my life, for good or ill. But I was ready.

The White House had provided a statement, denying the scurrilous allegations as yet another attempt by a liberal national newspaper to attack the White House and the more moderate, pro-business vice president. I was sure they were preparing to launch a counterstrike through their own propaganda channels and media sympathetic to their political aims.

Not surprisingly, though, a story citing anonymous sources had just dropped. It speculated that the president was considering replacing her running mate on the re-election ticket. It was the usual sort of inside-baseball piece that always ran just prior to re-election season. But, in this instance, I knew there was more to it than gossip. Symons had already begun the process of distancing his boss from Phelps. It was smart.

I didn't care whether I was attacked by either national political party once the story dropped. My own politics, and the paper's politics, were irrelevant. The story told the truth, or at least as close to the truth as you could conceivably get under the circumstances. People would reach their own conclusions. Those who chose to defend the vice president, or the House majority leader, or the family of the Supreme Court justice who was a hero to some for his staunch views from the bench would scream loudly that I'd been used by the Russians for their own geopolitical purposes. Those who detested any of the political leaders involved would see vindication in the story—confirmation of their worst fears.

Once Admiral Symons carried the news back to the White House, the president herself initially launched a full-scale attack to keep the paper from running the story. Her private lawyers sent sternly worded cease-and-desist letters, threatening instant libel actions should the story run. But our lawyers insisted that the story would run, and that the facts would speak for themselves. After a brief flurry, the insistent White House calls began to subside.

In fact, the senior editors and the publisher made the decision to make the vice president's tax returns public. I was confident this particular action would set a court challenge in motion that would likely be decided by the Supreme Court. While every president and vice president in the modern era had made their tax returns available to the American voting public, they were not required by law to do so. A previous president had set a precedent that others in his wake, like Phelps, now followed.

Making the vice president's tax returns available in this manner was unprecedented. I was curious to see how it would all settle out in court. But I also knew that, once they were available to the public, there was no pulling them back, no matter what even the highest court in the land said about it. The Pentagon Papers had long ago shown that, once the Fourth Estate puts something in the public sphere, it's difficult to make the clock run backwards.

I'd heard from several senators from the president's own party, imploring me to pull the story back. They all used some version of a single talking point that I assume the senior White House staff had coalesced around—that by doing what Russia's military and intelligence community wanted, I would harm the national security interests of the United States.

I disagreed quite vehemently with that notion. I believed with every fiber of my being that there's no such thing as casual or incidental corruption, and that exposing it is always the right thing to do. Vice President Phelps had decided to go into business with the Russians, who clearly had malicious intent toward the United States. That was his decision, and now he would have to live with the disclosure.

I really had only one thing on my mind today. The story would run on Sunday. The recriminations and hand-wringing would begin. The fallout would take its course. But, right now, on this day, I had another story I wanted to run to ground. It was time.

When the plane touched down at the Adirondack Regional Airport, a car was waiting for me. I took my seat in the back and thanked the driver. We set off on a winding road through the High Peaks wilderness area toward Tanin. The forest canopy grew denser the deeper we drove into the wilderness area.

When we pulled into the parking lot, I could see a great deal of new construction surrounding the massive building that housed Frontier 2. Tanin had clearly come back to life, thanks to Frontier 2 and the Money Exchange.

Dr. Silva waited for me to join her at the entrance to a large, flat building situated at the foot of a small mountain peak. "You ready for your tour?" she asked.

"I am. Let's see it."

The interior of the building wasn't all that impressive, but I hadn't really expected it to be. There were just rows of servers—each with their own massive core processors—all in a straight line as far as the eye could see.

But, I knew, looks were especially deceiving here. There were thousands of servers all linked together, forming one very large computer system that added up to an unreal amount of supercomputer processing speed. The place radiated a quiet power I'd wanted to see for myself.

"So this is the great Frontier system," I said, slightly in awe.

She nodded. "This is it. It may not look all that impressive, but I can assure you there isn't anything this system can't handle. There's no other supercomputer system like it, anywhere. We've added components that extend beyond the Frontier system at Oak Ridge, though we don't advertise those capabilities publicly. We're way out in front of everyone else on AI."

We both stood there for a long time, gazing at the seemingly endless rows of servers. All of them hummed silently, doing whatever task had been assigned them at that moment.

"May I ask...what's it working on at this particular moment?"

"A complicated AI assignment. It's studying millions and millions of pictures and film clips to learn how to be empathetic."

I was stunned. "Empathy? Really? How's it trying to learn that?"

"By reading emotion in gestures and expressions. It's studying movies and photos. It's trying to understand what's actually meaningful to us, to humans, as opposed to simply what's inherently meaningful on its own in the natural world."

"Yikes. So can it learn that? Can it learn how to be empathetic?"

"I guess we'll find out." Dr. Silva turned to face me. "So now you've seen Frontier. Is this really why you dragged me all the way up here, deep in the wilderness of the Adirondacks? To see this? Or is there more? I'm happy to give you an in-depth guided tour. But it's likely to consist of staring at a bank of terminals with knobs and switches."

"This is exactly what I came here to see," I told her. "But you're right. I had a much different reason for wanting to meet you here as well. I'm sorry I made you come all this way, but I felt it was genuinely important to see this place for myself. It clearly means something to you. And I wanted to talk this through here, in a place that matters."

"So what did you want to discuss?" She folded her arms and waited.

"As I said, I wanted to see this place for myself...the ghost town you brought back to life. And I wanted to talk to you about what this place and the Money Exchange mean to you and your mother, Margaret Sullivan. I wanted to ask this question here, in this place—the town that your family once built out of the creation of superhero myths."

Erica Silva Sullivan didn't respond immediately. But she clearly wasn't surprised at what I'd just told her. After taking a few seconds to gather her thoughts, she suddenly broke into a broad smile.

"Well, I knew it was only a matter of time before someone finally solved the equation and added up all of the silly clues my mother always insisted on leaving out in the open," she said. "I told her that someone might figure it out one day. But she insisted on dropping the clues. She said it was her own little test. It paid homage to her grandfather and the origin story of the family business. And, she said, if someone ever figured it out, well, then, they deserved to find us."

"So Margaret Sullivan *is* your mother?" I asked quietly. "And she inherited her fortune from her grandfather, Mathias Sullivan, who credited everything in his life to the three superheroes who'd so inspired him?"

"I'll answer that question shortly," she answered. "But let's take a walk. I'd like to show you something first."

"Of course."

She turned and left the building, moving at a brisk pace. I followed. Once we were outside, she made a hard turn around the building and began to scale a series of steps off to one side. We ascended them quickly until we arrived at the top of a small peak that rose above the building that housed the Frontier supercomputer.

A small wood platform looked out over a valley. From our vantage point, I could see that the small town of Tanin had once thrived there. Some of the homes were being rebuilt now. Directly across the valley, on the opposite side, a very large house towered over the small town. With all its porticoes and porches, it almost certainly had been rebuilt as well.

Dr. Silva pointed at the large home that overlooked what had once been a ghost town. "That's one of my mother's favorite places anywhere. She has homes all over the world, but this is her favorite. She spends as much time here as she possibly can. I try to join her here, but I'm not able to come as often as I'd like. My work at the Money Exchange takes up a great deal of my time."

I looked across the valley at the home. "So I'm assuming that it's all true, then?"

"What, exactly, do you believe to be true, Mr. Thomas?"

"I believe that Margaret Sullivan acquired a considerable fortune from her beloved grandfather, who sold his very first company to DC Comics and then built a fortune from there in places just like Tanin," I said, still scanning the small town. "I believe that she learned how to grow that fortune a great deal more, and that she is now one of the wealthiest people in the world. I believe that there's a very good chance, in fact, that she's the wealthiest woman on earth now, but has never said anything about it publicly. How am I doing?"

"Go on," Dr. Silva said quietly.

"I also believe that she adopted you after your parents were killed tragically in Mexico, and that you share her passion for an interesting life's work. You're carrying on her work now, though almost certainly in a slightly different way. The Money Exchange, which she owns solely and which you run, is an obvious example of that. It's utilizing 21st century technology to control, organize, and manage a great deal of data and information in a rapidly expanding technological world—a world you're quite comfortable in.

"The Money Exchange is also, I believe, now fully capable of highly successful quant and high-frequency trading, thanks to Frontier 2. You both operate in different realms, yet you both have the same aims. Your life's work is cut from the same cloth."

Dr. Silva turned toward me. "And what might that life's work be?"

"You find extraordinary people and offer them an opportunity to explore an uncharted path with no evident rules. John Andrews. Michelle Searle. Sandra Oakes. Me, of course. I'm sure there are others. You give them access to your family fortune, within limits, and encourage them to change the world in ways unique to their individual talents.

"Prominent philanthropists have tried something at a much smaller scale—providing endowments or one-time gifts to incredibly talented people with unique skill sets. The MacArthur Foundation is known worldwide for giving $625,000 apiece to 25 geniuses every year in a wide range of fields. But you've moved that concept up several levels, to a place no one has ever considered before in philanthropy. Yet you're quite serious about this. It isn't a game."

"You're right. It isn't a game," she said. "We're serious about all of this—about everyone invited to take part."

"Finally, what I also believe is that you're especially interested in finding young women like Sandra Oakes and Michelle Searle who can mix it up with the best of them in the upper reaches of the Billionaires' Club. Because, as we both know, nearly all of the members of that exclusive billionaires' club are men."

"We would very much like to change that. And we *will* change that, one person at a time, if need be," she said firmly.

"I can see that." I smiled. "Dr. Oakes is amazing. So is Michelle Searle. I assume there are others, across any number of fields where risk-taking can lead to uncommonly large rewards in society, industries, and communities."

"There are. More than you might expect," she answered. "But I have to say, out of all of the candidates she and I have selected, we've never encountered anyone quite like you. You were a pleasant surprise."

"Why? Because I've decided not to accept the money we've made from your investments?"

"Ha!" she said, laughing. "I wasn't aware you'd made that decision. My mother predicted you'd go in that direction. She said you'd choose the story over the money—because that's who you truly are—and that you'd turn the business over to your assistant, Dotty. I wasn't so sure. I thought you might take the money after all…"

"Your mother was right. I gave the money, and the opportunity, to Dotty. I had no choice, not if I wanted to tell the story I'd discovered about Russia and the vice president."

"Things are in good hands, then. Dotty seems extraordinary in every way," she said. "But, no, what surprised us was how unbelievably relentless you were. You were determined to get to the bottom of things. You were fearless. You never stopped until you found all the answers you needed to tell your story."

"True. I am relentless. Which reminds me, there were two pieces I couldn't quite sort out. The first is easy. You leaked the Panama Papers, using Frontier to sort through the thousands of offshore accounts?"

"What do you think?" she asked with an easy smile.

"I thought so. It makes sense now. It explains why Ivan Fedorisky and his bosses in Moscow were absolutely desperate to find out who contacted me, and some of the others you recruited."

"And your second question?"

"Satoshi Nakamoto. Who is he, really?"

Dr. Silva glanced over her shoulder, at the path we'd taken up to the platform. "The truth? It's a combination of me, and an early prototype of Frontier. I kept feeding the algorithms in, and the machine did the hard work. But the physical manifestation of that person? It's my mother's butler from this house in Tanin, the person whom Michelle Searle met once as Alfred Pennyworth. It's a bit of an inside joke, between my mother and me."

"Ah, that's funny," I said.

"I've always thought so. I've enjoyed watching everyone tie themselves up in knots about his true identity."

"You know, I'm sure you realize this, but I actually found *two* stories," I said. "The first one, the one I'm sure you'd hoped I would unearth about Russia's financial involvement with leaders from our two national political parties, will run in the paper on Sunday. The second story is about you... and your mother. I haven't decided what to do with that story."

"So will you tell that second story, Mr. Thomas?"

"Time will tell," I answered. "So your mother...is she here?"

Erica Silva Sullivan looked out over the small town of Tanin and pointed to someone kneeling on the ground, tending to a garden of the large home on the other side of the valley. She was wearing a wide-brimmed hat. Just then she happened to look up, removed her hat, dabbed away the sweat on her brow, and waved in our direction.

I waved back.

ABOUT THE AUTHOR

JEFF NESBIT has held four highly significant jobs with four different U.S. presidents. Currently the Deputy Commissioner for Communications at the Social Security Administration, he was the National Science Foundation's director of legislative and public affairs in the Bush and Obama administrations, former Vice President Dan Quayle's communications director at the White House, and the Food and Drug Administration's public affairs chief under FDA Commissioner Dr. David Kessler, who was later President Biden's chief scientific officer for COVID-19 response.

Once profiled in *The Wall Street Journal* as one of the seven people who ended the Tobacco Wars, Nesbit—a former national journalist with Knight Ridder and others—was also the founder and executive director (2011-2022) of Climate Nexus, the New York-based non-profit environmental media organization he launched after leaving the NSF in 2011. Climate Nexus is funded entirely by foundations, with a staff that includes former national journalists from the Associated Press, CBS News, and other national media organizations and senior communications professionals from leading environmental groups.

Nesbit also managed a successful strategic communications company for more than a decade with national clients and projects that included the Discovery Channel networks, Yale University, the American Heart Association, the Robert Wood Johnson Foundation, and the American Red Cross. This company helped create and launch three unique television networks for Discovery Communications, Encyclopedia Britannica, and Lockheed Martin. It developed programming and a new cable TV network concept for The Britannica Channel; global programming partnerships for the successful launch of the Discovery Health Channel, including a novel CME programming initiative and the Medical Honors live broadcast from Constitution Hall; and programming strategies for the creation of the first-ever IPTV network developed by Lockheed Martin.

While at the NSF, Nesbit was the co-creator of the *Science of the Olympic Winter Games* and the *Science of NFL Football* video series with NBC Learn and NBC Sports, which won the 2010 Sports Emmy for best original sports programming, as well as *The Science of Speed,* a novel video series partnership with the NASCAR Media Group.

Nesbit wrote a popular weekly science column, "At the Edge," for *U.S News & World Report* from 2012-2018. He also contributed regularly to *The New York Times, Time* magazine, and *Axios*. He is the author of the critically acclaimed *Poison Tea* (St. Martin's Press/Macmillan, 2016) and *This Is the Way the World Ends* (St. Martin's Press/Macmillan, 2018).

Nesbit has written more than 30 commercially successful novels for a wide range of publishing houses, including the blockbusters *Peace, Oil,* and *Jude.*